CATCHING Raven

VOLUME I

CB TUCKER

Copyright © 2020 by CB Tucker

All rights reserved. This book or any portion thereof may not be reproduced or transmitted in any form or manner, electronic or mechanical, including photocopying, recording, or by any information storage or retrieval system, without the express written permission of the copyright owner except for the use of brief quotations in a book review or other noncommercial uses permitted by copyright law.

Printed in the United States of America

Library of Congress Control Number:		2019916228
ISBN:	Softcover	978-1-64376-479-5
	eBook	978-1-64376-478-8
	Hardback	978-1-64376-591-4

Republished by: PageTurner Press and Media LLC
Publication Date: 06/03/2020

To order copies of this book, contact:

PageTurner Press and Media
Phone: 1-888-447-9651
order@pageturner.us
www.pageturner.us

Table of Contents

Preface vii
Chapter 1 The Presentation 1
Chapter 2 Selling Larry on the future 7
Chapter 3 Samantha Raven at Wake Forest 14
Chapter 4 Business is our business 21
Chapter 5 The power of a woman 30
Chapter 6 Meet the Union 39
Chapter 7 Elizabeth Raven 44
Chapter 8 Liz begins looking for Jimmy Dittle 51
Chapter 9 The Story of Jimmy Dittle 56
Chapter 10 The Paterson Corp. 63
Chapter 11 Yes, No, Maybe - - - OH God 69
Chapter 12 The Transformation 74
Chapter 13 Meeting Trevor 81
Chapter 14 The first meeting 87
Chapter 15 A new customer 94
Chapter 16 A mother and daughter conversation 100
Chapter 17 The Hunter becomes the Hunted 106
Chapter 18 The Plantation 110
Chapter 19 The fight 115
Chapter 20 Sam's first day a work 120

Chapter 21   Liz the Hacker 126

Chapter 22   Jimmy's Secrets Stolen.. 131

Chapter 23   Day two at the House 136

Chapter 24   The hunter is exposed 143

Chapter 25   The Kiss... 149

Chapter 26   The first move, a confession, a favor 154

Chapter 27   A departure, a surprise visit 160

Chapter 28   Sam is trapped 170

Chapter 29   Roger Dawson 179

Chapter 30   Things get ugly 186

Chapter 31   Sam is rapped again 193

Chapter 32   The uninvited guest 199

Chapter 33   Liz is kidnapped 204

Chapter 34   Coming to terms with reality 210

Chapter 35   The rules to abide by 217

Chapter 36   Violation of Rule # 1 224

Chapter 37   Taking the bait 232

Chapter 38   Making a deal with the devil 237

Chapter 39   Liz is found and it's Girls night out 243

Chapter 40   Athens police gets involved 253

Chapter 41   Liz goes to the Plantation 261

Chapter 42   Sam tries to regain control 268

Chapter 43   The Show down 274

Chapter 44   Trevor finally confesses 282

Chapter 45   Setting boundaries 290

Chapter 46   Vice and Paris 296

Epilogue 305

CATCHING Raven

Preface

Samantha Raven was a young woman who came from a blue-collar family in Winder Georgia. She worked hard on her grades in High School in order to earn a scholarship to Wake Forest. Her parents helped when they could, but money was tight.

She just began her second year. While attending a fraternity party with her roommate she garnered the attention of a young man with long black hair and beard. She didn't know who he was but did find him good looking and felt embarrassed by his attention.

Later she began to feel confused and the man she was with began taking her out of the party when she passed out. She didn't know it at the time but someone slipped her a Mickey. She awoke in a strange apartment and didn't know where she was.

She was naked and afraid because she didn't know what had happened to her the previous night. This was when she met, the long dark haired young man, who then proceeded to sweep her off her feet. From the first time, since she saw him at the party, he made her feel different. She didn't understand why, but he just brought out a different side in her.

They began to date and Samantha couldn't understand why this man was so enamored with her. She thought it was the thrill of the chase for she refused to give into his carnal desires despite the fact he made her feel all gooey inside.

Her finances were so tight she couldn't afford birth control and the last thing she wanted to do was get pregnant. Despite her longing to have him and give into him, she kept telling herself that he was just a one-year fling and as soon as she gave in, he would be gone. She enjoyed his company, his banter, his personality, the way he made her laugh. Every time they were together, her female body parts screamed for his attention, but she worked hard to resist him until Thanksgiving.

She made the mistake of going to his apartment thanksgiving weekend, because she couldn't afford to go home, and cooked him a Thanksgiving dinner. With the dinner came the banter, the attention, the wine, and soon she was surrendering to him in ways she never thought she would to any man. But he was so exciting, so gentle, and just so sexy, she found herself waiting for him to come to her and again defile her in every way she wanted him to. She was madly and totally in love with him.

For some reason they never talked about families, but she continued to see him the rest of the year until that last week. She stayed at his apartment as he helped her study. She received all A's on her tests before she was to go home. She knew this was it; he would leave her and find another woman. He was the type to fly in private planes, negotiate million dollar deals all over the world, with super models hanging off his arm, which wasn't her.

He would leave and she would never see him again. Then as he was putting her onto the bus to go home, he received a call that rocked his world, and he had to leave. She never saw him again. Then when she got home another surprise came, she was pregnant with his baby.

Samantha tried desperately but in vain to find him, he only went by the name of TIP, and no one knew anything about him, she couldn't find him. Did he really exist? She had a picture of him, that she kept in the drawer of her bedside table. She kept the robe she wore while in his apartment. But he was gone, like a ghost or a ship passing in the night never to meet again.

Her father was heartbroken but her parents supported her anyway. She refused to abort the child and decided that if TIP gave her this child, then she was going to raise it as best she could. After the birth of the child, Samantha attended Community College and received an accounting degree.

She worked for several companies until she found herself at Hutchinson Accounting. She began working in the strict accounting department doing the books for their clients and helping them when she could.

She was promoted to the Acquisition and Merger department. This increased her pay, but she wasn't getting rich. She became one of the best Forensic Accountants in the state. Proving her worth on several occasions by helping several companies to put their resources together to build better and larger firms.

But over the next fifteen years, Samantha's primary concern was her daughter Elizabeth. Elizabeth looked just like Samantha and they were even referred to as sisters when they were together. Elizabeth's security and well-being, was Samantha's biggest worry and she guarded her with the ferocity of a mother bear.

When Samantha's parents died in a car accident, she inherited their house and moved in next door to Mathew Chambers. He was one year older than Elizabeth was, and he fell for her the day he saw her.

Samantha continued to expand her record of successful mergers, when one day she was offered the chance to work with Trevor Paterson. Trevor Paterson was a billionaire, who had a merger problem, and needed help. She had no idea what he was or who he was. She agreed to study his situation and try to devise a plan. Samantha and her partner, Jennifer Wills, developed a plan, and were prepared to deliver it. But life happens, and it never happens as planned.

On the day of the meeting with the officers of Paterson Corporation, Jennifer was a no show. Jennifer was the front man of the team. Jennifer Wills was a 5' 8" beautiful blond that when she entered the room, everyone shut up. The men watched her, the women hated her, when she spoke she was as intelligent as she was beautiful. Her job was to get the attention of the men and then hold until the message was delivered.

When it comes to money, looks are important, but substance wins out. If you can't get the men to realize what is being presented, then the deal can't be closed. That was Jennifer's job. To get the men to shut up long enough, for the brilliance of Samantha, to be delivered.

But on this day Jennifer was missing, there was only an hour before the presentation and the only other person who knew the material was Samantha. She never liked being the center of attention, she never liked standing before a crowd, and speaking, she was the wallflower and brains behind the show, never the show. But if she didn't step up, everything would be lost.

Sam tried to hide in the bathroom but the Receptionist came, and found her. Mary helped her to change her appearance from a School Marm to the presenter of the deal.

Samantha had studied Trevor Paterson and knew his history but when she stepped in front of him she was surprised to see a young good looking man, clean cut, clean shaven, and for some reason calming.

She gave the presentation, but Mr. Paterson was more intent on trading notes with the man beside him, than listening to her. This worried her, and she thought she had blown the deal, because she wasn't the beauty that Jennifer Wills was.

But she was wrong, and as this man entered her life, everything began to change. She didn't know why, she couldn't figure out what was going on until finally she learned who he really was, and why her world was crashing down around her.

Can Samantha weather the onslaught of the changes coming into her life? Can she handle the invasion of Roger Dawson and Jimmy Dittle? Only time will tell.

Chapter 1

The Presentation

The Hutchinson accounting firm conference room was an elegant room with a long, dark, mahogany table and matching chairs. The exterior glass wall gave a beautiful view of the Atlanta skyline from the 15th floor. The interior wall was all glass from floor to ceiling. At one end, the wall was sheetrock with a large mirror hanging on it. The wall at the opposite end of the room was glass from ceiling to floor. A double door was in the center leading to another smaller conference room.

Mr. Hutchinson arrived. He was a tall, thin man dressed in a three-piece, dark blue, pin stripe, silk suit. He entered and walked to the far end of the table before taking his seat in front of the oversized mirror. Today, he had two groups appearing. The Fletcher group, which had arrived earlier, included a father and his two sons. Morgenstern International followed soon afterwards. The five guests were ready. The Fletchers were unaware of what was going on, but the Morgenstern clan had been thoroughly briefed on the meeting's purpose.

Mr. Hutchinson looked to the far end of the table, and Jennifer gave him a nod. He stood up, attracting the attention of both parties that had been talking quietly amongst themselves. He addressed the group. "Gentlemen, I know you are wondering why I have asked you here. The purpose is simple: Fletcher Industries is in trouble and on their last legs. They will be bankrupt in 2 years or maybe 3 years if they are lucky. I have asked Morgenstern International to come in so we can talk about saving the company."

The Fletcher group consisted of three men: Jeff Fletcher, the father; Tom, the eldest son; and Larry, the youngest son. The father sat in the center, and the sons flanked him on both sides. Upon hearing this news, Tom immediately stood up and yelled. "What?!" He glanced at his farther and continued. "Bankruptcy? You're out of your mind! First, we are NOT bankrupt, and we don't need saving. If I had known that this was your angle, I wouldn't have wasted my time coming." The father and the youngest son just sat there in silence. The father, not giving anything away, cast a slight glance towards his youngest son, who remained sitting but looked surprised.

The two men from Morgenstern began firing back at Tom.

The first yelled. "Have you even looked at your P&L? Do you know what is happening?"

"No, I haven't." Tom retorted. "But we are making money and have always made money---to say we are bankrupt is a lie!"

Samantha and Jennifer were sitting at the far end of the table away from Mr. Hutchinson. Both were quiet until Sam looked up at Jennifer. Jennifer nodded and then smiled. She stood up and nodded at Mr. Hutchinson at the opposite end of the table. Mr. Hutchinson then rose and cleared his throat.

The three men ceased their clamor to hear Mr. Hutchinson's insight.

"Gentlemen, I ask that you at least listen to what Ms. Jennifer Wills, ESQ, has to say." He extended his palm to point to the far end of the table. All three men, who were still standing, diverted their gazes to the end of the table. There stood Jennifer Wills.

At 5 ft 6 inches, Jennifer was a tall, strikingly beautiful woman. With her long blonde hair and perfectly proportioned body. Her natural intelligence bolstered her efficiency as a lawyer. Jennifer was wearing an SBD (simple black dress) hemmed just above the knees. The garment wasn't skintight, but it was tailored to accent her curves and provide her with just enough wiggle room to naturally, maneuver within it. Its deep V neckline featured more-than-adequate cleavage. She was magnificent, with a single strain of white pearls circling her neck paired with earrings as her only adornments.

She needed no additional accessories. When she entered a room, the men would go silent just to watch her walk past; she was "that" type of woman. Jennifer was aware of the effect that she had on the male species; however, she not only enjoyed it, she reveled in it. It was her second-best asset with her intelligence being the obvious first.

Jennifer smiled and began to speak. Her soft, southern voice dripped with the metaphorical molasses of a sexy yet commanding southern drawl, and her natural charm instantly transformed the mood of the room. The three men sat down unhurriedly, as if transfixed by the visage. It was difficult to decipher if the men were listening or dreaming, but the effect would have been the same. At least they were not yelling at each other.

She cooed assertively. "Gentlemen, please sit down. We are here today to accomplish good deeds not bad ones. I wholeheartedly assure you that it is our desire for Fletcher Industries to survive and flourish, but we must address the issues at hand". The Fletcher men eyed each other as Jennifer sauntered towards the Morgenstern men, who were studying her every move.

This scene was initially orchestrated to silence the men and gain insight on their proposal. Jennifer paused abruptly between the two Morgenstern men. She rested her hands gently on their shoulders and then explained that the portfolios before them represented the current financial situations of the firm.

This stop was planned with her standing facing the Fletcher men, with the light from the windows behind them bathing her in light. The visage she presented eased the fact that the firm was financially bereft. It needed an infusion of cash and re-organization if the company was to survive. This meeting was to ensure that this goal would come to fruition. Jennifer withheld this news until she arrived at this moment. It was tantamount to swallowing bitter medicine with sugar.

Jennifer slowly continued to complete the loop behind Mr. Hutchinson. She gently dragged her hand from one shoulder to the next. She never stopped talking as she walked slowly, accentuating her movements. She approached the Fletcher group while drawing the attention of the oldest boy, whom she reached first. She made eye contact with and held it as she approached him. She seductively straightened his tie and gently forced his mouth shut.

Had she strangled him with his tie, he wouldn't have noticed. She continued behind the Fletcher men, again with her hand lingering across each shoulder to warrant a response. A slight smile appeared on the father's face as she passed.

She continued back to the end of the table and stood beside Samantha. Without looking at Sam, she announced. "Gentlemen, this is Samantha Raven---possibly one of the best forensic accountants in Atlanta and possibly the country. Samantha understands the needs of Fletcher Industries. If we can all just look at the portfolios that we have prepared, we may be able to explain your current situation. With our help, we can salvage the company and achieve good things today."

When she finished, Tom Fletcher tried to stand but decided to remain seated. He remained angry despite his current affliction. He leered menacingly at the Morgenstern men and pointed at the portfolio. "First off, I don't know this woman or her credentials, so I'm not going to accept anything she might say." Sam looked at Jennifer, and Jennifer leaned over to whisper a response. Sam nodded and picked up her briefcase. She exited into the next room, a smaller conference room, but left one door open.

One of the Morgenstern men stood up and yelled. "Well, if you would shut up and listen, you would know Ms. Wills is a lawyer, and Ms. Raven is an accountant, dumbass!" Tom looked back angrily and scoffed. "So what do I care?" They continued to argue.

Jennifer circled back to the Fletcher group. She leaned in between the father and his youngest son and whispered to them before moving to the far side of Tom, in the direction of Mr. Hutchinson. This power move drew Tom's attention to her sitting beside him, as the other two Fletcher men were now leaving. Although Tom glanced at his father and brother as they left, he wanted to look at Jennifer, so he stayed.

Samantha took her briefcase into the spare boardroom and lain it on the table. She motioned for Larry to sit next to her. His father took the seat on the other side of Larry, away from Sam. She secured the doors.

Positioning was integral to this plan. She had to make Larry feel important while undermining his father's presence. She removed a folder from her briefcase and placed it on the table.

Samantha Raven was the opposite of Jennifer Wills in how she presented herself. She enjoyed working in the background and behind the scenes. She wasn't as tall as Jennifer, only being 5 ft 4 in while wearing 4-inch stilettos. She dressed conservatively, with her long, black hair pulled back into a modest bun, with large owl-like glasses and a simple business suit. At only 120 pounds, she was a stunning woman in her own right, but the last thing she wanted was for anyone to notice.

Sam began. "Mr. Fletcher, you have done a magnificent job in growing this company, but at 72, it is time for you to retire."

The father glared at her and angrily replied. "You can call me Jeff, but you think I can't run this company anymore?"

"No, I'm just saying that after 52 years of building and running this company, it is time for you to reap the fruits of your labor. Let your sons take the company over while you're still around to advise them."

The old man regarded his son with a nod. "What if my sons don't want to take it over?"

Sam addressed Larry. "That would be a shame. Because for the company to survive, it will take a lot of hard work plus several years---years you should be spending enjoying your retirement with your wife and advising your sons."

Larry and Sam locked eyes. He was sizing her up, and she was doing likewise. The only problem was that he had run out of ammunition, while Sam came fully loaded. Larry Fletcher had to be convinced. He put up a valiant fight, but it wasn't long before he realized Samantha's brilliance. She had to show him the trees standing before him when he insisted on merely seeing the forest.

During the several weeks prior to this moment, Sam analyzed each son and discovered that Tom was a commanding presence. Many assumed he would take over the business. He was already running several of the off shoots of the Fletcher industries. He skillfully played the role of the alpha male.

Samantha didn't agree; she had a different view.

Chapter 2

Selling Larry on the future

Larry Fletcher was sitting beside his father, looking at the folder; he had not picked it up as if it might be the harbinger of an infectious disease. Sam touched his arm and asked. "Is what your father saying true?" Larry suddenly looked at Sam and had a sudden epiphany---his father's words actually pertained to him! Was he willing to seize from his father, and could he?

Larry shook his head and replied. "I'm not sure."

Sam did not care for this answer. It was too ambiguous, but it was better than an outright denial. She and Larry eyed at each other for several seconds before Sam inquired and made the first inquisitive move.

"May I call you Larry?" He nodded yes, and Sam continued.

"Larry, have you read the report?"

Larry glanced at his father. "My father gave me a copy last night and asked me to read it."

Sam nodded. "And what did you think?" Larry glanced back at his father

"I refused to believe it at first, so I re-read it. What it said makes sense, but I'm unsure of the solution or what this has to do with me." Sam gave him a smile; this is what she wanted to hear. He understood the situation but didn't understand his role.

Larry was now listening, so Sam began to lay out her case. "Larry, the biggest part of your family business is Fletcher industries. It makes light bulbs, incandescent light bulbs."

Larry nodded once more, keeping intermittent eye contact with his father. "I understand that, but we will always need them. And the last time our bulbs were tested, they were some of the best on the market."

Sam nodded in a respectful yet mimicking fashion. "That is true, but the future of light bulbs is not incandescent. You will be unable to sell Incandescent bulbs in a few years."

Larry retorted. "I'm not sure that is true. Have you seen the price of LED bulbs?"

Sam smiled and replied. "LED bulbs emanate as much light as the incandescent ones with minimal heat. For that matter, they utilize one-tenth of the power and last five times longer. Soon, their price will plummet, and even though they will always be more expensive, they will remain economically superior."

Larry pleaded. "But there will still be a market for our bulbs?"

Sam sat back and probed his disposition briefly. "Larry, when we evolved from horses to cars, what happened to those businesses that supported horses?"

"Most died out."

Sam nodded again then continued. "Fisher Bodies started out as the maker of bodies for horse-drawn buggies. They were renowned as the best body makers. They realized that the death of horse-drawn buggies would signify the death of their business. Their reputation for crafting fine bodies allowed them to fashion bodies for GM cars for another hundred years. That is what I'm offering you now, but we need for someone to rise and propel this company into the future, or it will die."

There it was---the blow. When it struck Larry, he couldn't deny the truth. The funny thing about the truth is that when presented, it can always stand-alone. It requires no support because it is evident. On the contrary, a lie can mask itself as the truth, but it cannot stand alone without support. The fact that the Fletcher industry was a dying company hit home in that one statement, and Larry knew it. However, it also sustained the realization that they were asking him to step forward and take charge.

Larry Fletcher was always the younger son and never the alpha male like his older brother. Tom Fletcher was bigger, bolder, brash, and confident. He was accustomed to the role of a leader. As his filial inferior, Larry avoided challenging his older brother; instead, he took a different path that led him to other pursuits, e.g. science, literature, and philosophy. He lacked the natural talent of authority that came so easily to his brother. Larry had always enjoyed the riches of his father's business but lived a life of leisure. He married his high school sweetheart and pursued the life of a professor, not an industrialist.

Larry looked at Sam intently; he knew what they were asking, but needed to hear it and asked. "Are you saying that you want me to take over the company?" Sam glanced at his father, and this caused Larry to regard his father. Jeff Fletcher pierced him with steel blue eyes that never wavered and nodded his head. Larry looked back at Sam in disbelief, exclaiming. "Me? Why me? Tom has been running the other companies since college while doing a fine job--- why me? You can't be serious!"

Sam's hand grazed Larry's arm as she gazed into his face. He recognized the raw sincerity in her eyes. Larry knew that she was intelligent, and he suddenly realized how beautiful she was. Her intelligence oozed from her like expensive perfume. "Larry, your brother is a fine man, and he is doing exactly what he is supposed to do. The sister companies function as a concrete manufacturer, a construction firm, an electrical/plumbing company, and a restaurant. Those companies are doing fine and require a man like him to deal with the kind of people who work in those industries."

Sam took a breath. "But the light bulb factory was the most profitable, and it requires a different type of leader. You will be dealing with motivated people, and what inspires them is a gentle touch. They need a man who promotes synergy, with a philosophical attitude. These people are highly intelligent. Tom won't prosper as you will, but I believe you are the man for this job. We need Tom to continue what he is doing and help you when you need it. You are the man for this job, because it will take a man like you to accomplish it."

Sam's words lingered in the air like perfume and permeated every pore in his body because they were true. His father's leadership skills were always gentle and unassuming. People wanted to work for him, and he inspired them. The light bulb factory needed this type of leader. Now Larry realized Sam's intentions of him taking over the company.

Larry also knew that this would signal the end of his peaceful, pleasant life. Larry was scared--- what if he failed? Could he do it? What did she mean about "different type of people?" He barked. "Look, Tom is a good businessman, and business is business. There is no difference."

Sam shook her head and scoffed. "No, you're wrong. Tom has to deal with men doing construction. They differ from the type of people who develop technology. Tom deals with people who are impetuous and intimidating, but you're going to deal with people who are scholarly, while you are more philosophical and cultured."

Larry realized she was making valid points, and it was difficult to counter her arguments. But he wasn't sure it would work; so after failing to refute her argument that he was the man for the job, he decided to learn where his support would come from. "So if I do this and I don't know anything about light bulbs, much less LED bulbs, how will I learn?"

Sam gave a small smile that indicated she was winning. She knew the toughest part would be convincing him to accept the fact that it had to be him. So now, with him asking where his support would come from, he was contemplating the concept of him realistically taking control of the company. Sam was prepared for this and was now ready to deliver the coup-de-grace.

Sam turned to face Larry. "There is a company in California by the name of Cree. They pioneered the development of LED lighting and have need of a factory on the east coast. I have talked to them, and they are interested in employing you as their east coast distributors."

Larry sat back as if he had just been punched. He was running out of excuses for denying the position, and this woman was thwarting every argument. The prospect of taking a job in which so many would be dependent upon every decision he made scared the hell out of him. The pitfalls were abundant, and downside was potentially catastrophic. He regarded his father, who appeared to be doing nothing. He wasn't offering any assistance to refute Samantha's argument, as if he shared her opinion.

Jeff Fletcher knew what was running through his son's mind. He had experienced those very same thoughts years ago when he made the decision to create Fletcher industries and manufacture light bulbs. It was his wife, who convinced him to make the leap of faith. Jeff looked at Larry. "Look, son, you won't be alone. You have Tom and me to help you."

Larry stared down at the folder and then at Samantha. "It appears that you have everything figured out." Sam smirked again because he had just surrendered. She had him, and now they could lay out the path to save this company. Sam pulled another folder from her brief case and began crafting the path they needed to take.

Fletcher Industries had been bled dry by the high taxes and a union that refused to compromise. So, in order to correct the situation, they had to stop the bleeding. Fletcher industries needed to declare Chapter 13 in order to reorganize. This power move would allow for a new deal with the local government to stop the high taxes they were demanding. This would terminate the Union that was pilfering large sums of money from the company.

This also allowed the factory to be shut down, because what was needed to make an incandescent light bulb was futile for an LED bulb. Larry would go to California with Jennifer to negotiate the deal and become Cree's east coast manufacturer. This saved Cree the cost of securing the land and building the facilities required to build a factory. Time was important, because they didn't have years to seize the market. Fletcher's conversion would only take months.

While Larry was in California, Sam and Jeff Fletcher would shut the plant down. At the beginning of the renovation of the plant, unnecessary equipment would be removed and sold. New equipment would be purchased and installed. When Larry returned, they would begin hiring a new set of employees and train them with a new company union.

This required capital, which was where Morgenstern International came in. After all, it was a financial investment firm based in Israel, that specialized, in investing in new companies, or old companies trying to reorganize.

Larry, after hearing the plan, stood up and walked to the window to stare out over the Atlanta skyline. This was a big decision, and he was scared…but the decision had to be his in the end. He weighed all of the pros and cons of the options before analyzing everything Samantha had told him.

After a minute, he turned to his father. "Dad, you will be there if I need you?" Jeff Fletcher wanted to jump up and yell hallelujah. Instead, he restrained himself and looked at Samantha. Sam looked up at him at the same time and gave him a smile. She had rendered the impossible possible and convinced his son to tackle a monster that he never even knew he wanted to confront.

Samantha Raven's ability to negotiate prevailed. Jeff knew this because when she first appeared in his office and presented him with the newly found information, he also didn't want to believe it. But like his son, once she began presenting her argument, he couldn't deny her claims.

Jeff Fletcher was happy to know that the company he had spent over 50 years building now had a fighting chance of survival after his inevitable demise.

Chapter 3

Samantha Raven at Wake Forest

Seventeen years ago, Samantha Raven was attending Wake Forest University. She had just returned to her dorm room after finishing the first week of her sophomore year. As she settled into her bed, her roommate came in. This was their second year of cohabitation. Cyndi was a 5-foot 10-inch blonde from a well-to-do family. She was smart, jovial, and she carefully walked the line between slutty and promiscuous.

After watching Sam put her books away, Cyndi turned to Samantha and asked. "Look, the Alpha Beta Fraternity is having a welcome-back-to-college party tonight. You want to go?" Samantha's blue-collar family had skimped and saved just to get her into college. Samantha matriculated into Wake Forest by receiving several scholarships and student loans. She also worked for the Dean of Students and waited tables at a local restaurant to make ends meet.

Samantha perceived her opportunity to attend college as a gift that should not be squandered flippantly. Attending parties and frolicking with boys was not part of her schedule. Furthermore, the finances allocated to Samantha did not include doctors or birth control. Obviously, having sex was out of the question, but this restriction was of no concern to Samantha. She had not spotted a boy that remotely piqued her interest.

Cyndi looked at Sam and begged. "Look, I don't want to go alone, and I promise they won't separate us. Please come with me?" Sam sat down on her bed to leer at her roommate and intermittent friend. They had just attended another fraternity soiree at Duke the weekend before.

Sam had finished her homework, and the previous excursion had gone smoothly. Plus, it was Friday. She had two days to recover. She shook her head and reluctantly sighed. "I have the feeling that I will regret this, but okay, I will go with you tonight. Just give me your word that we won't get separated."

Cyndi squealed and bounced on her bed with glee. "Great, let's get ready!"

Sam asked. "What are you wearing?"

Cyndi giggled and cooed. "I'm wearing skin-tight jeans and a snug-fitting T-shirt."

"Don't be too obvious now." They both snickered. Sam continued. "I will wear my form-fitting jeans with my print blouse and try not to be noticed."

Cyndi grinned and retorted. "Oh, Samantha! Guys do notice you." HEREHERE

That afternoon, they walked several blocks to Fraternity Row to the find the house. As they approached, they realized that the party was well underway, and several of the participants had already consumed their fair share of intoxicants. They no longer felt pain. As they meandered among the partygoers, Sam noticed a man following her with his eyes as he sipped from a plastic cup, watching her.

His long, dark hair framed his chestnut eyes and beard while staring intently at her. She glared at him for a moment before breaking the trance and averting his menacing gaze. Sam couldn't shake the ominous feeling that overwhelmed her when she looked at him. And the questions--- Who was he? Why was he looking at me? He was nice looking, but should I be worried?

Soon, Cyndi approached with two young men. One was tall with short hair. He had a clean-shaven, alluring look. He carried his fit physique with confidence. He approached Sam and smiled. "Hi! I'm Jerry. What's your name?"

Sam was taken aback by his stunningly good looks. She shyly replied. "Samantha." Jerry grinned.

Drinks finally arrived, and Samantha shook her head no. She didn't drink and wasn't sure about this situation. "Look! I don't drink alcohol."

Jerry took offense and scoffed. "What are you--- a buzz kill?"

Cyndi reached over and took the drink, telling Jerry. "Just bring her something without alcohol." Jerry shot Cyndi a disturbed look and returned after a few minutes with another drink. Sam tried it and suspected that it had some alcohol in it but not much. Jerry kept encouraging her to drink, and when she finished it, he brought her another one. What Sam didn't know was that he kept increasing the alcohol with every drink, and as she become more inebriated, the taste of the alcohol slowly faded away.

Samantha began feeling the drinks and wanted to get something to eat or slow down---something. She searched for the snack table, but again, she spied the dark-haired man observing her. She looked away and back to see if he was still looking at her, and he was. Sam didn't know to be flattered or worried. The drinks were taking their toll.

The music was blaring, and everyone was dancing. Suddenly, Jerry pulled Samantha to her feet for a dance. Sam was now officially inebriated. She reluctantly danced with Jerry. It wasn't long before the rhythm entranced her. Before she knew it, she was swaying her hips and dancing provocatively. To say the least, this was not her normal behavior.

She spun around and saw the same, dark-haired man leaning against a small tree watching her. She locked the stare in return, and she could not take her eyes off him. He wasn't a large man---maybe 6 ft or 2 meters tall. His flowing hair and neat beard rendered him a good-looking man. Visions of pirates sweeping her away invaded her mind. She continued to move, swayed, twirled seductively, and then looked back at the dark-haired man, who appeared to be transfixed by her.

She continued to move as she waved her arms above her head. Suddenly, Jerry picked her up and spun her around. She was now drunk, and when he planted her back on the floor, she didn't realize what she was doing. She was in full motion and enjoying the feeling of euphoria that had consumed her.

Jerry brought her another drink and helped her drink it. She continued to dance. Another drink appeared, and soon Samantha was struggling to keep things in focus. Jerry grabbed her around her shoulders and then bid everyone goodnight as he exited with her.

Samantha was barely able to comprehend the events that followed. She couldn't resist the stunning specimen who was now guiding her out of the party. Her feet were barely touching the ground. Soon, they were in the parking lot. Jerry had to pick her up because she was unable to walk.

As Jerry absconded with Sam through the parking lot, he heard a voice from behind him and turned. The dark-haired man with the beard ordered. "Jerry, put her down now, and I won't call the police."

Jerry laughed. "Tip, I told you before to stay out of my way." Tip continued to walk toward him. He held up his cell phone and took a picture of him with Samantha in his arms.

"Not tonight, Jerry. I have a picture of you and her, and if she is found like the others, then the police will know who is responsible."

Jerry released Sam's legs and allowed her slide out of his arms until he released her to the ground at his feet. Samantha crumpled to the pavement, unable to stand on her own. She was barely conscious and unaware of what was happening. Jerry took a step toward Tip and said. "What if just kick your ass and take that phone away?"

"Jerry you have tried that before, and what happed then would be nothing in comparison to what you could potentially face now. Now walk away and leave, and I will take her."

Jerry looked cautiously at Tip and asked. "So what are you going to do, take her home and fuck her?"

"Even that would be better than what you have planned. Leaving her in the bushes naked is not what I consider a great way to start the day." Jerry took another step toward Tip and then heard a noise from Sam.

Sam had pushed herself up and started to vomit. She hurriedly threw up on her pants before passing out on the ground. Her hair was caked with vomit as well as her clothes. Tip looked at her then at Jerry and asked. "So . . . you still want her?" Jerry look with disgust at Samantha lying on the ground, covered in her own vomit and shook his head in dismay. "Forget that bitch! You can have her." He walked off.

Tip shook his head as he walked over to Samantha as she lay on the ground. He gently brushed the hair from her face. She was out cold. He picked her up and carried her to a black Jeep Wrangler Rubicon with the top removed. With one hand, he opened the door and placed Samantha onto the passenger seat. After buckling her in, he closed the door carefully then pulled out of the parking lot.

Saturday morning, Samantha awoke in a strange bed in dark room. She was flat on her stomach, but oddly, this position that would normally be alarming felt different. She reached for the light beside her bed only to realize it wasn't there. She slowly raised her head and glanced groggily over at the table; it should have been, several inches below the level of the mattress--- it wasn't there. She moved the tangled strings of hair from her face and spied an unfamiliar, bedside end table. It was made of dark wood, unlike her furniture. As her eyes regained focus, she realized that this was not her table.

Sam pushed herself up on to her elbows and surveyed her surroundings. She realized that instead of the single bed in her dorm, she was laying in what appeared to be a much larger bed. She pulled herself closer to the edge of the bed and looked around until she discovered a yellow sticky note with an arrow. It read. "Push me." She looked curiously at it then cautiously reached over and pushed the button.

Suddenly, she heard a motor, and the curtains along the far wall to the left of the bed started to pull back. She looked up as the dark room became bathed in light. As the curtains retreated to each side, a large, floor-to-ceiling window appeared. Her suspicions were now confirmed---this was not her room.

She pushed herself up further and noticed another note on a glass with an arrow. "Take this and drink me." She followed the arrow on the sticky note to a pill and a glass of what looked like orange juice. As she slid up in the bed, she realized that she was also naked. She had no memory of what happened to her. Sam's initial thought was. "Oh! My God, what have I done?"

Making sure that she kept herself covered, she decided to take the pill and drink the orange juice. She then returned the glass to the saucer before turning over to sit up in the bed. She was alone. The room was an off white with dark brown carpet and white walls. The bed was made of the same dark wood as the bedside end table with a beige duvet and sheets. The highboy on the other side of the room matched the motif of the bed and end tables.

She perused the room again and couldn't see her clothes anywhere. Reluctantly, she reclined against the large soft pillows and took the room in. She pushed her hair out of her face once more and struggled to recall the events of the past evening. With her hands clasped over her face, and she cursed her so-called "friend" Cyndi, who apparently deserted her. Sam was frustrated, scared, and worried about last night's events as she continued to search for clues in the strange room. She spied three doors.

All three doors were closed, but she spotted another post-it note on the center door. She slipped out of bed to see what it said and read. "Put me on." Another arrow pointed to a nice, terrycloth robe hanging below just beneath the post-it.

She surmised that the robe was better than what she was currently wearing, which was nothing, so she lifted it off the hook and slid into it. It was soft and plush, and it felt nice against her skin. She peered into the door on the left and found a closet filled with men's clothes. The door on the right led to a bathroom, and she could hear a dryer running.

She slowly opened the center door and listened, but there was only silence. She gingerly tip toed in her bare feet down the wide hall and saw another note on the doorjamb; "Kitchen, coffee." Her spirits perked up at the thought of coffee. She peeked into the narrow kitchen, and at the far end, she located the coffee pot. She crept in, and above the coffee maker was another note that simply read. "Coffee." Sam looked at the coffee and couldn't help but think. "No Shit."

Sam was desperately trying to decipher what the hell was going on when she saw the coffee mug with a note next to it on the counter. This arrow indicated. "Sugar, milk in the fridge." She poured herself a cup of coffee; she looked for a spoon for the sugar, and spied another note that read. "Here" It was pointing to the silverware drawer. Sam shook her head in amazement.

After making her coffee, she began to exit the small kitchen. There was a bar along one side, which opened into the dining/living room. The door straight in front of her on the other side of the hallway opened abruptly, and the dark-haired man with the long hair entered.

Sam jumped and screamed, spilling some of the coffee out of the mug and onto the floor. She instinctually recoiled and backed into the refrigerator. She was trapped, and the man blocked the only exit from the kitchen. He was holding a hanger with plastic on it and a paper bag. He grinned. "Boy you're on a roll." Sam was speechless yet relieved; because all she knew was that, he was not Jerry.

Chapter 4

Business is our business

Tom Fletcher was livid! He had been invited back to the Hutchinson Accounting firm to meet with Jennifer and Samantha. Upon his arrival, he was escorted to Jennifer's office. She sat behind her desk with her blond hair cascading to her shoulders, and she wore a red dress that looked expensive. The neckline cut just below her neck, but the back plummeted all the way down to her waist. It hugged her upper body and flared out right from her waist. Elegantly sporting a white diamond necklace and earrings, Jennifer had clearly mastered the fine art of understating her appearance. She was fully aware that her beauty required few frills, so she did not go overboard to accentuate it.

Sam wore a cream-colored pants suit that she had made with a dark blue blouse and her customary, owl-like glasses that reinforced her superior intelligence. They knew that Tom had always haughtily assumed that he would be taking control of Fletcher Industries. They simply needed to convince him to take the subsidiaries, leaving his brother to deal with Fletcher Industries and the malaise that lay hidden within it.

Tom glared at Samantha and barked. "That was a dirty trick taking my father and brother into another room like that. I should have been present. Why didn't you consult with me?" Jennifer rose and motioned for him to sit on the couch in her office. She faced him and perched beside him on the leading edge of the cushion.

Jennifer revealed her thousand-watt smile and replied. "Look, Tom, we understand that you wanted to run it, but let's consider the situation. Learning how to make LED bulbs and retooling the factory is going to take time and a lot of attention. Do you think you can take that much time away from the other companies to accomplish that feat?"

Tom glanced over at Sam. "I would have at least tried."

Samantha was sitting in front of Jennifer's desk with a demure expression. She didn't want to infuriate him, and cautiously uttered. "I understand you would try, but that is a formula for failure."

Tom indignantly replied. "I would have appreciated at least being considered."

Jennifer glanced over at Samantha and said. "We did consider you, Tom." Tom faced both women as Sam studied him. Sam captured the subtle nuances of his body language for his "tell." The Tell---that's what the real problem was. When he switched his focus to Jennifer, she saw what the real problem was. Tom relished being the alpha male---always the strongest and most reliable, only to be cast aside for his weaker, younger brother. This abrupt spark of insight was a colossal blow to his ego.

Sam awaited the opportunity for her opening, and while Tom was looking at Jennifer, she seized the moment. "Look, Tom, you are an outstanding manager of the peripheral businesses, and your father and brother will need your liaisons with those companies. They are essential to the success of this venture."

Tom looked back at Sam abruptly. "I don't see how?"

Jennifer and Samantha had discussed this scenario at length, and now it was time to finally seal the deal. Jennifer took the lead. "Tom, the subsidiaries are all doing well, but three of them require dealing with contractors. You know as well as I do that Larry doesn't have what it takes to survive in that environment. You do. Who is more qualified to take them over and separate them from Fletcher Industries than you? You both have jobs to do. Your brother needs to know that you have his back and will support him. A seemingly insurmountable job lies ahead of him, and if he is to be successful, it will depend on some variables that look grim. For this plan to work, we need you to ensure that they are taken care of. Can we count on you?"

Tom sat. He looked at Jennifer and then at Samantha for a minute. The argument was convincing, and he knew it. Slowly, he nodded his head in agreement. He leaned over and signed the paperwork before him. Jennifer then stood and proceeded to escort him out as Sam gathered the paperwork. A lot of work needed to be performed over the next few months.

This was Jennifer and Samantha's third merger, and each one bore fruit. Their first was a car dealership in Barrow County. The duo engineered the merger with another dealership in Gwinnett County. Both had been devastated by GMC's withdrawal of its support, but both dealerships were in prime locations for their flourishing business markets.

Both had resources that the other needed, but it was the simple case of not being able to see the forest for the trees. Once Jennifer and Sam were able to get the board of directors to listen, they convinced them of the value of the merger. However, the initial merger was just the beginning. Jennifer originally discovered Morgenstern International, an investment company based in Israel. They were willing to invest into the companies, and with that investment, they were able to purchase a third dealership, which also occupied a lucrative location. As every businessperson knows, one of the keys to a successful business is its location.

With three lots under their umbrella, Jennifer was able to introduce them to Volkswagen. VW had pulled out of Northern Georgia in order to resolve some financial issues. With these issues resolved, they were now ready to step back in. The time was right, and the business offer was exactly what both sides wanted. Within 6 months, the dealership was able to purchase a fourth lot in an equally lucrative location.

It took over a year of hard work and research, but the team of Jennifer and Samantha had succeeded beyond what everyone at Hutchinson had expected. However, their second customer appeared at the opening of the fourth dealership lot.

Steve Bushier was the CEO of Country Town Bank. He was a local boy who had gained recognition as a running back on his high school football team. This accomplishment earned him full scholarship offers at several colleges. He could have attended a football powerhouse but decided to attend Vanderbilt University. This was shocking news, since Vanderbilt was not known as a football powerhouse, but it was a notorious business and financial school. After 4 years as their starting running back, he finally had the chance to go into professional football; instead, he chose to try his hand at the Wall Street scene in New York for several years.

After 10 years on Wall Street, he cashed out, returned to Georgia, and purchased Country Town bank. He now wanted to expand his business, but the ability to run a business effectively doesn't always mean that one can spot profitable expansion deals. In this light, Samantha and Jennifer shined.

Mr. Bushier was a childhood friend of Jim Beckman, the CEO of the auto dealership. Mr. Beckman previously boasted to Mr. Bushier of what these two women had accomplished. He focused in particular on Samantha Raven as a Forensic Account and her ability to trace the lucrative deals. Mr. Bushier decided to create a subtly diagnostic test.

Mr. Bushier originally observed Samantha as she wandered around the lot at the opening of their new dealership. Sam spied a white 2005 VW convertible bug and fell in love. Mr. Beckman was a born salesman who could read body language from fifty yards away. He alerted Mr. Bushier, and they hatched a plan.

Samantha wasn't ready to replace her aging 1987 GM Prism. Mr. Beckman offered to service Sam's car while she waited. When they escorted her to the work area where her car was sitting, they found it in the middle of the garage with smoke billowing out from underneath the hood. Sam almost cried seeing her car burn like that, but Mr. Beckman promised he would take care of it. He convinced her to take the VW home for the weekend. Sam departed hesitantly, but not before noticing one of the mechanics tossing a smoking can out behind the garage. She knew something was up.

She spent the weekend contemplating the smoking can and the sudden demise of her precious prism. When they took her back to her car on Monday, she was shocked at what she found.

While the companies were rebuilding, every mechanic had come to know and respect Samantha for her honesty and integrity. When she walked into the garage, she found her car sitting in the middle of the floor. All the mechanics were standing in front of her vehicle, and when they stepped away, she saw they had repainted the vehicle in the same color and reapplied the pin stripping that had peeled off. They found factory mags and installed them as well.

Sam was well aware that this was a group effort and stunned by the determination they had all put into restoring her car. Their work was worth more than what the car's value, but it was the thought that touched her heart. Mr. Beckman stepped forward with the keys. "Samantha Raven, I'm sorry for tricking you like this, but we wanted to do something nice for you after what you have done for us. And I know a new car isn't in your finances, so we decided to make you old car look new."

Sam couldn't hold the tears in any longer---this was the nicest thing they could have done. As they looked collectively at her car, Mr.

Beckman asked her to come to his office. He answered from behind the safety of his desk. "Another thing we discovered when we were looking for the paint for your car---it turns out this car is more valuable than we thought."

Sam was a little shocked by this statement and asked. "Oh! How can that be?"

Mr. Beckman's office was like any auto sales office, with a small cubical and a big window as the wall to the sales floor. As Mr. Beckman leaned forward to explain, Mr. Bushier opened the door and uttered. "When I was 17, I wanted to go to college, but I was short on money. So, my father sold his 1987 prism to give me the money. He had saved for five years for that car, which was brand new, and he sacrificed his car for me. I never forgot that, and now that I can afford to buy him a new one, all he really wants is that car he sold twenty years ago. I had the VIN number, and it turns out the car you are driving was my father's car. I want to buy it from you for $15,000. Here is my card."

Mr. Beckman gave a big smile and replied. "As it happens, that would be what the cost of the VW you like so much.

Sam was shocked at this revelation and didn't know what to say at first. She gathered herself to answer the question that hung in the air like an untouched piñata. But was the piñata full of candy or rancid meat. Sam collected herself and looked up at Mr. Bushier. "I'm impressed by your desire to pay your father back. This is only an 87 Prism and isn't worth the money you're offering."

Mr. Bushier smiled and nodded simultaneously. "Actually, Ms. Raven, the value of an item is what someone is willing to pay for it, and I want that car for my father. I'm willing to pay whatever you want to demand for it. I will go to $20,000." Sam was shocked, but something was wrong here---he was working the deal all wrong. You never set the desire of the car before the price, or the seller will just jump the price.

Sam wasn't convinced." Not admitting that I buy your claim, but why don't you just purchase another one that looks like it and tell him it was his?"

Mr. Bushier smiled and sat down beside Sam." Ms. Raven, I have never lied to my father, and I don't want start now; besides, he still has the original title and would know."

Sam still wasn't convinced, and eyed the two men. She demanded," Look, this feels like a ruse, and I know it is a ruse. If the two of you don't come clean, I'm walking!" She then looked at Mr. Beckman," And you can forget ever seeing me again."

Mr. Beckman looked at Mr. Bushier. "Steve! I love ya like a brother, but she has done too much for me and this company."

Mr. Bushier regarded Mr. Beckman. He diverted his eyes to Sam and chuckled," I didn't believe you, Jim. I apologize, because she is everything you said and more. Yes, Ms. Raven, this was a ruse. I have been led astray by too many so-called financial analysts and forensic accountants to accept these accolades without proof, even when they are verified by a dear friend. I wanted to meet you and see how you handle yourself, and I'm impressed."

Sam kept her stone face. She was now angry that Mr. Beckman would attempt to play her but apparently, the entire façade was perpetrated by Mr. Bushier. So, she needed to redirect her anger towards him. Without looking at Mr. Beckman, she asserted," Jim, can you leave Mr. Bushier and me alone for a minute…Please?"

Mr. Beckman looked intently at Mr. Bushier as if to say," Don't blow this, friend." He exited the office. Meanwhile, he paced back and forth outside the office watching them through the glass wall that separated them.

Sam asked Mr. Bushier," Okay, you have two minutes to explain why I shouldn't walk out of here and never speak to you or Jim again."

Mr. Bushier gave her a small grin." Ms. Raven please don't punish Jim. This was all my idea, honestly. I want to expand my business, and I just couldn't believe all that you and Ms. Wills have accomplished. I had to see if you were as intelligent as Jim has been saying."

Sam kept her expression." So, you don't believe a woman can accomplish everything we did?"

Mr. Bushier shook his head." No! I'm not saying that, but I have never met a team as talented and the two of you. I have met several Forensic Accounts and most don't even measure up to your hemline as to what you two have put together. After what I have seen today, I would like to hire you and Ms. Wills to expand my business."

Sam rested her chin on her fingers and studied him for a second before saying, "Mr. Bushier, I don't like to play games, but if you want to meet Jennifer and me, here is my card; call our office; make an appointment. Ms. Wills and I will pull the public records on Country Town Bank and see if we can develop a plan. If not, we will tell you that as well."

Mr. Bushier studied the card." What about the VW, you still want it?"

Sam replied. "Accepting it would appear to be a bribe, and neither of us needs that. So, if you purchase the VW, at the end of our meeting and with Jennifer's approval, we can trade titles."

After doing their research, they did meet with Mr. Bushier. Jennifer and Sam came up with a financial plan that would expand his bank. At the end of the meeting and after he signed the contracts, he signed the title to the VW bug then slid it to Sam. Sam signed the title to her Prism and slid it to Mr. Bushier.

Over the next two years, they first had Country Town Bank designated as the preferred auto loan facility for Beckman Volkswagen.

They then used Morgenstern's investment capital to assist in purchasing two smaller banks, which extended Country Town Bank's presences into new areas. One year later, they purchased an insurance company. Jennifer and Sam had effectively doubled the financial empire of Mr. Bushier.

Chapter 5

The power of a woman

A few days later, Jeff Fletcher and his wife had just finished lunch in The Magnolia Place Restaurant in Winder. This upscale dining establishment requires reservations, no walk-ins. Fletcher asked for the check and reached over to take his wife's hand. As a loving gesture, he cooed. "This was a lovely idea, honey. Thank you for in inviting me." Mrs. Fletcher gave him a confused smile and replied. "Excuse me dear, but I thought this was your idea?" They both gazed adoringly at each other when Sam approached and said. "Actually, it was my idea. I sent the cards to both of you."

Mrs. Fletcher withdrew her hand quickly and shot Sam a harsh look that she shared with her husband. "Jeff! Care to explain yourself?" Sam was adorned in her gray business suit with a burgundy blouse buttoned to her throat and her hair in a bun. She countered. "Mr. Fletcher didn't know anything about this. I felt it was time you and I talked." Mrs. Fletcher gave Samantha another chilling look and retorted. "Oh really?!"

Sam turned to Jeff. "Mr. Fletcher, would you mind leaving? This is a woman-to-woman conversation." Jeff looked at his wife, who nodded and begged. "Go on Jeff. I can take care of myself." Jeff scrutinized both women and pleaded. "No bloodshed, please." Mary smiled as she looked at Sam and responded. "Sorry honey, but I can't promise that."

Jeff slowly rose and followed both women with his eyes before paying the bill and leaving the restaurant. Sam turned to Mrs. Fletcher and asked. "May I sit?" Mrs. Fletcher leaned forward, placing her elbows on the table. She softly replied. "Please do. It will make it easier to gouge your eye balls out if you think I will allow you to steal my husband." Sam chuckled. "Mrs. Fletcher, I first want to apologize for not coming to meet you earlier, but the logistics were not in our favor." Mrs. Fletcher raised an eyebrow. "Oh really?" The waiter stepped up and asked both women if he could bring them anything else. Sam smiled, ordered a sweet tea, and offered to replenish her reluctant dining partner's beverage. Mrs. Fletcher waved him off in a dismissive fashion while keeping her eyes locked onto Sam.

Sam continued. "Mary---can I call you Mary?" Mary smiled and replied. "Sure, it will make killing you more pleasant." Sam smiled again, because she knew why Mary was so upset. Mary knew that her husband was an attractive and vibrant man; even though he was seventy-two years young. She thwarted numerous females wanting to get their hooks into her husband over the years. Now, the rumor mills pinpointed her as the latest temptress attempting to steal her husband.

Sam rested her arms onto the table, looked Mary in the eyes, and said. "Mary, having met your husband, I can see that even at seventy-two, he is still a fine catch---but the rumor mills have gotten it wrong again. I have no intention of breaking up your lovely marriage." Mary gave Sam a distrusting look. "So how much do you want to go away?" Sam smiled again and replied. "Nothing." Mary sat back and crossed her arms. "What kind of scam are you running here?" Sam grinned and asked. "Are you proud of Larry taking over the business?"

Mary gave Sam a quizzical stare. "Don't you dare break up this marriage?" Sam chuckled again and replied. "Mary, I'm afraid you have the wrong idea. I have no intention of breaking up any marriage. My goal was to save Fletcher Corporation, and I hope I have done that; but to ensure its survival, I will need your help." Mary again leaned forward as if Sam enticed her. "It was you, wasn't it? You convinced Larry to rise to the occasion and take over the company!"

Sam slyly replied. "I had help, but now I need you to help his wife---to fend off any attacks and call me when you need help." Mary crossed her arms as she glared fixedly at Sam. The rumor mill had cautioned her that a dark-haired woman was putting the moves on her husband. Apparently, that was a mess of false claims.

Mary asked. "You clearly didn't arrange this meeting to ask that. What is your true reason for meeting me?" Sam reached down, pulled several brochures from her briefcase, handed them to Mary, and asked. "In the near future, Jeff will have to leave to allow Larry to settle into his new job. The best way to encourage that is to take your husband on a vacation." Mary perused the brochures, and when she reconsidered Sam, her eyes began to spill over with tears. She covered her face with her hands, as she had been trying to get him to go on a vacation for years. This was a dream come true! You never know how relationships well develop.

Sam's mind drifted back to Tip---a man she didn't trust. But she soon found a friend in him. After he entered the apartment, scared the life out of her, and caused her to spill her coffee, he just chuckled. He hung the hanger with plastic on the back of the door, reached over to the counter for the roll of paper towels, and tossed it to her. She caught it haphazardly while trying not to spill any more coffee. He strode into the dining room area. She put the cup down and quickly used some paper towels to clean up her mess. When she stood up, he was leaning over the counter, watching her so intently that it caused her to jump again.

Samantha was getting angry and threw the dirty paper towels at him. But she reconsidered her actions and decided to confront the elephant in the room. "Who are you, and why am I here?" The dark-haired man just chuckled, smiled, and replied. "My name is Tip, and you're cleaning up the mess you made." Samantha stepped back but was impeded by the opposing counter. She set the roll of paper towels on the counter and crossed her arms in anger.

Samantha defiantly pulled her borrowed robe wearing tighter around her naked body. She still wasn't sure what had happened to her. Tip continued. "Look, why don't you come and sit at the table, and I will answer all of your questions." Sam maintained her glare of distrust.

Finally, Samantha took a gulp and insisted. "Before I do anything, I need the answers to a couple of questions."

Tip nodded yes and sat on one of the bar stools while supporting his head with his left hand. "Fire away," he replied. She equally loved and hated his grin.

Samantha demanded. "First off, where are my clothes?" Tip smiled and pointed to the hanger with plastic on the back of the door. Samantha turned, and she could see her blouse through the plastic. "Please tell me your mother undressed me?"

Tip smiled and replied. "Okay, my mother undressed you."

Sam didn't believe him. "So, where is your mother?"

With raised eyebrows, Tip asked. "Right now?"

Sam stood up, stomped her foot, and demanded again. "Yes! Right now, where is she?" Tip averted his eyes upwards and checked his watch. "France, I think."

Sam demanded with eyes of fury. "If she is in France, how did she undress me?"

"Well she didn't, but you asked that I tell you she did."

Sam gave him a desperate yet disgusted look. "Okay, who undressed me?"

Tip coyly held up a finger. "I did." Sam could feel the blood rushing to her face.

She cupped her head into her hands. "Where is my underwear?" As if on cue, they both heard a buzzer.

Tip grimaced. "I think they're ready."

Sam started to ask another question, but Tip interrupted her thoughts.

"Look, you said a couple of questions, and I have allowed more than a couple, but to easy your mind, yes! I did undress you. Yes! I did put you into the shower. Yes! I did put you into my bed, and No! Nothing happened, nothing, so can you please bring your coffee and sit at the table so we can talk?"

Samantha's major fear had just been quelled, but she still had some worries, and yes, they needed to talk. She was leaving with one man, woke up in the bed of another man, whom she had never met, and just now learned his name. Sam picked up her coffee cup and padded in her bare feet out of the kitchen. Tip pulled a chair out, and as she sat, he pushed it in so she could sit at the table. It was hard to hate him.

Tip then fixed a cup of coffee and sat in a chair to her right, but within arm's length. He opened the paper bag and dumped several items onto the table. Apparently, he had stopped at a few fast food places in search of their most popular breakfast items. Sam was sitting with her hands over her mouth; she was embarrassed after he had admitted to undressing her. Finally, she took one of the packages, opened it, and began picking at the breakfast sandwich. She hadn't decided if she was hungry yet.

She glanced at Tip. "When you undressed me, please tell me you didn't look at me?"

"Okay, I didn't look at you," he jested.

"You're a liar." Sam knew the punch wasn't punishment for what he had done, but she needed some retribution for her embarrassment.

"No, I didn't, you asked me to tell you I didn't' look, so I did." Sam gave him a frustrated look.

"You did look--- I hate you."

"No, you don't, and you're just embarrassed that I got to see you naked without your permission." Sam stuck her chin up in disgust.

"Well, how would you feel if you had passed out and someone disrobed you."

"Well, if it was you disrobing me, I wouldn't mind at all." Sam looked at him and knew he was right. Men don't care if you see them naked.

"Why didn't you just say you looked?"

"Samantha, if you want the truth, don't tell me what you want to hear." She gave him a side-glance and looked down at her coffee cup.

"Fair enough. What happened last night?"

"Look, I know this Jerry guy." Tip moved his perfectly styled hair from his face. "He is handsome and charismatic, but he likes to drug women, have sex with them, and leave them naked and vulnerable in the bushes. I didn't want that happening to you, so I confronted him and made him give you to me."

"So, I'm something to be handed around?" Sam attempted to penetrate Tip's debonair façade as she questioned him.

"No! Not true! He really didn't want to give you up—well, not until you threw up all over yourself, your hair, and your clothes. He said if I wanted you, I could have you."

"I did what?"

"Yea, you were a real mess. Vomit was in your hair, and all over your clothes---, you even pissed on yourself. They gave you way too much alcohol."

Embarrassed, Sam wanted to crawl into a box, but she instead tried to hide behind her hands. She pulled some of her hair to her nose and smelled it. "I'm almost afraid to ask, but I don't smell anything in my hair?"

Tip gave an affirmative nod. "Yea, once we got back here, I had to undress you, then I put you in the shower. I washed your hair and I put you to bed. I soaked your clothes in the washer overnight and had them dry cleaned this morning."

"If we didn't do anything last night . . . where did you sleep?"

"Well, I did crawl into bed with you, but I couldn't sleep. I slept on the couch."

Sam looked over at the couch and saw the blanket that was still there, but she could not bring herself to make eye contact. "Why couldn't you sleep?"

"I think having a drop-dead gorgeous woman in my bed had something to do with it. But then I thought about what you would do when you woke up next to me, so I decided to play it safe and come out here." Tip's face had a grave expression.

Sam was studying him hard, but she didn't quite believe him. "I'm not gorgeous, so why would that be a problem?"

"You have to ask, and I have an idea. The washer and dryer are in the bathroom. Why don't you go and get dressed? You will feel better, and since you seem to detest what I bought, I will take you to lunch or your dorm."

Sam nervously studied her coffee, thinking about what he could have possibly done. A chilling shiver radiated down her spine. She nodded, grabbed the hanger from the door, and headed to the bedroom. Tip tidied up the dining table and loaded the dishwasher before turning off the coffee pot. Samantha met him at the door.

"You put the dryer on high and shrunk my bra and panties."

Tip chortled. "What? They can't take the heat?"

Samantha wanted to laugh, but he was too cute, and she still didn't trust him. Her frustration was overwhelming. "That's not funny. I don't have any underclothes to wear."

A broad grin spread across Tip's face. Sam embodied a dichotomy of emotions and thoughts, but she couldn't resist that smile that lit up his face. However, she still didn't know him. He had brought her home unconscious undressed her, bathed her, and washed her hair---and seen her naked! Also, what did he think of her naked? Why didn't he seize the opportunity to sleep with her? Was he lying about not having sex with her, and what would sex be like with him? Now he had her pinned against the door.

Tip eyed her semi-seductively. "So, you're not wearing any underclothes right now?"

Sam gave a gentle punch on his chest. "What do you think?"

Tip placed one hand on the door over her head and leaned in close. "Well, I find you quite alluring. Should I take you to purchase new under garments? I could pick some out for you." Tip leaned closer, and Sam was pinned against the door with him just inches away.

She blushed. "No, I . . . I can buy my own under garments, thank you." Sam's head was looking down slightly avoiding Tip's irresistible eyes. He was breathtakingly close! That smile, those lips--- Oh Jesus! I don't know this man yet, so I can't kiss him. And what if I like that kiss? I'm stuck in his apartment, wherever that is, and he has already seen me naked.

Tip chuckled again. "Yea, I have seen your underwear, so I have a few ideas from some Victoria's Secret that would look outstanding on you."

Sam gave him a playful look of shock and punched him again. "What makes you think I would let you see me wearing them?" Tip gave her a huge smile then raised his eyebrows at her, twice. Wow, she thought. She could see herself parading around in this apartment in nothing but a Victoria's Secret thong and bra. For some reason, this image excited and appalled her, even though she was sure that could never happen.

Sam finally squeezed out more appropriate thoughts. "You promised me brunch." She had to divert the topic from her underwear, especially with Tip just inches away. His lips were dangerously close to her lips, which she was trying not to bite. She yearned to be kissed. Tip smiled and unlocked the door. Sam let out a sigh that was pregnant with a mixture of relief and frustration. He was the first man to appeal to her since she came to Wake Forest, but he scared her. He sparked feelings that she couldn't afford to indulge, like sexual empowerment.

This encounter haunted her with memories that would never fade. In a sense, he began as an adversary, but their rapport quickly blossomed into something special, not unlike her new relationship with Mrs. Fletcher.

Chapter 6

Meet the Union

On Tuesday of the second week in April, Larry Fletcher and Sam met with the Union. The boardroom was a well-lit room 20 by 15 ft room with an oversized, mahogany table in the center. Ten matching chairs were placed strategically around the table and two cadenzas at opposite ends of the room. The Union members patiently awaited their arrival.

The past meetings with the union bosses never went well. As Sam walked into the boardroom with Larry Fletcher and his lawyer, the five Union men confronted them. The rage from the union side of the room was tantamount to the sweltering heat from a kitchen stove. The union boss and another sat with three large men standing behind them.

The Boss, Jimmy Dittle, shook his finger at Larry. "If you think you're going to break the Union, forget it! You still owe 3 years of dues, as stated in our contract." Larry, with his lawyer on his right and Sam on his left, paused momentarily at the door before taking a seat at the table.

The Union arrived with their lawyer and several, unfamiliar, large men who clearly weren't handpicked for their *beauty* or intelligence.

After looking over the papers from his lawyers, Larry addressed the Union Boss. "Jimmy Dittle, you were a bully in high school, and you're still one now. This meeting was supposed to be between the management of Fletcher Industries and the Union; may I ask whom these gentlemen are?" He raised his hand to indicate the three large men standing protectively behind the boss.

Jimmy Dittle had never been fond of Larry Fletcher; he thought he was a spoiled rich boy and loved to torment him back in high school. But they weren't in school anymore, and Jimmy was now the Union Boss while Larry was the CEO of Fletcher Industries. During the Union meetings, Jimmy enjoyed making snide remarks at Larry's expense, knowing that Larry couldn't reciprocate. But today, it was different.

Jimmy didn't bother to turn around. He made this power move to intimidate Larry. Jimmy gave Larry's lawyer a knowing look and then turned his eyes to Sam. "Only if you tell me why you brought your father's whore to this meeting."

Sam had been quietly studying the papers before her when she heard the Union Boss' words. Holding her steel expression, she raised her eyes to look at the man making the disparaging remarks. She knew this was an offer to get tempers flaring and distract them from the objective. That wasn't going to happen. Before her eyes fully focused upon the Union Boss' features, she vowed to remain quiet and allow Larry to control the meeting.

Larry didn't look at Sam. He remained focused on the Union Boss. In a quite tone, he continued. "This is Samantha Raven, a Forensic Accountant. She he is here to assist us in liquidating this firm, now your turn." The Union Boss replied. "They are friends of mine."

Larry perused the Union contract--- he had several areas highlighted. Larry, his lawyer, and Sam had analyzed the contract for several hours the previous day. They discussed what would be the Union's demands and how to appease them. They decided the best way to deal with the Union was to cut them off at the knees. When his father attempted to negotiate with the Union in prior meetings, the Union had always used the same tactic.

Larry pinpointed the clause he wanted to convey. "Okay, as for your first demand that we continue payments to the Union for the next three years, I would like to point to Clause 6, paragraph 6. The Union's dues will come from deductions taken from the workers' paychecks, and then paid to the Union by Fletcher Industries monthly. I would like to point out that under the bankruptcy order there is no payroll; thus, there are no deductions and zero payments to the union."

Jimmy was incensed as he looked down at the paperwork in front of him and silently pleaded for help from his lawyer. Larry spoke up. "If you are having trouble comprehending it, you can ask one of your friends to read it for you." Jimmy stared daggers of pure hatred at Larry.

Jimmy knew there was nothing he could do. After all, his own, lawyer had pointed out that clause earlier. Jimmy knew that before he came, his only hope was to manipulate Larry into surrendering and agreeing to payments. But Larry had already killed that idea with the first salvo. Jimmy resorted to a different plan. He leaned over to his lawyer and for a quick discussion. Jimmy turned to Larry with a smile on his face.

"Okay, so there is no payroll, but have you considered your employees? They depend on those jobs to pay their bills, and you can't desert them like this. They are family."

Larry nodded and smiled back. "No, I don't want to hurt them, but where were they when you were doubling their salaries and bleeding us dry. It is partially because of you that we are declaring bankruptcy. There was more money going out than there was coming in. My father, alerted you to this potential disaster at the last meeting, and what was your reply? Oh, wait---I remember. You insisted that it was not your job to run the company and that if my father fell short, he should resign. Well he did, and now I'm in charge. Things have changed."

Jimmy's smile disappeared as he looked to Larry for solace that was brutally rebuffed. "Careful, Larry boy. We know where you live, and I will fuck you and your whore."

At this Larry's lawyer rested his hand on Larry's arm. "Excuse me, but that sounded like a direct threat. Your lawyer and I are both officers of the court, and a statement like that is admissible in a court of law. If anything happens to Mr. Fletcher or his family, you will be held responsible, and not only you but your union."

Jimmy's lawyer was now pleading with Jimmy to listen, but Jimmy was beyond furious. Jimmy flew off the handle. "Oh yeah?! Consider this: there are 5 of us, and only 3 of you. Who has the upper hand here?"

Larry sat quietly for a moment then let out a sigh. He pointed to the camera on the wall to his left and then to his right, then to the one behind him, and finally to the one behind Jimmy's group. Jimmy looked around then back at Larry. Larry then pointed to the light hanging from the ceiling and stated the obvious. "There are microphones in the lights."

Larry leaned back in his chair. "I convinced my father to start recording all negotiation sessions with you after you threatened him. So, the last two meetings between Fletcher and the Union have been recorded, along with those who were in attendance." He focused his attention on the large man standing behind Jimmy. "Which reminds me, John, John Cutler, isn't it? What would your parole officer say if he knew you were here witnessing these men threatening us?" The man suddenly looked nervous.

At that, Jimmy and his entourage rose from their positions and suddenly circled around the table towards the door. Jimmy stopped at the door and turned, but before he could say anything Larry interjected. "Oh stop it, Jimmy! You have clearly been neutered. Take what is left of your dignity and get out of here. "Jimmy scowled at his lawyer, turned, and left.

Larry convened with Sam once more. "I want to apologize for that whore comment. He was just trying get something started."

Sam smiled amusedly. "I know, but I want to applaud you for how you handled it. You were perfect. I will see you next week."

Larry nodded, and they departed. Sam started back to her car and called the office. It was 4 in the afternoon, and she wondered if she needed to return to the office or go home from here. Jennifer told her to go home.

Sam put the top down on her Volkswagen, undid the bun on the back of her head, and sported a scarf as she headed home. She called the house from her cellular. Elizabeth looked at the phone to see who was calling and answered. "Hi, mom! What ya doing?"

Sam smiled warmly at the sound of her daughter's voice. "I'm on the way home--- be there in 5 minutes. And make sure your boyfriend is gone when I get there."

Liz rolled her eyes. "Okay, but can't I just hide him under the bed?"

Sam laughed at the amusing banter. "No! You had better not have a boy in the house, and you know I will check under the bed."

Liz mockingly entertained the routine yet comical parental repartee. "Okay! Matt, get dressed. You must leave now." Liz sat back with a smug look on her face.

Chapter 7

Elizabeth Raven

Sam squealed with a smile. "Mat … you better tell Mat I will skin him alive if he is there."

Liz chuckled. "No Mom, I know the rules. No one allowed in the house when you're not home, so when will you get here? I can start dinner."

Sam nodded. "I'm in Lawrenceville and will be home in 30 minutes. See you then." Liz hung up.

Elizabeth Raven was 15 y/o. She was a duplicate of her mother in myriad ways. If you didn't know there was a 15-year difference between the two of them, you would think they were sisters. Elizabeth liked to be called Liz. Even though her mother was excellent at her job, she hadn't garnered a large salary. They had money in the bank for emergencies, and Sam was able to minimize her expenses. They had limited money to splurge on luxuries; things were tight. Liz knew if she wanted something, she had to figure out how to come up with the money. Today, Liz was focused on making money.

Liz convinced her mother to let her create an account on E-Bay. Before she died, Liz's grandmother bonded with her by frequenting weekly yard sales. They found personal treasure, such as marbles and various other items to sell on E-Bay. Liz took pictures of the items and embellished descriptive phrases that seduced people to bid. Often, the bidding drove the price up because the buyer wanted to win. But that wasn't where she profited the most.

She made her money from the shipping and handling costs. She bought an item for a low price and listed it for $5. She charged $5 for shipping and sent it through the post office with pick up the Click-N-Ship boxes, which were free. Her Click-N-Ship online account allowed her to calculate and print out the shipping labels before sending off the packages. She typically made 2 to 3 dollars per sale, which added up to a decent profit if she made at least 10 to 15 sales per week. This legal hustle was impressive for an unemployed, 15-year-old girl.

Liz also created accounts at UPS and FedEx. She tailored her method of delivery to customer preferences. Regardless of the shipping method, she was earned at least two dollars for packing it up and mailing it. People enjoyed a deal, but the shipping made Liz's business profitable.

She was making $100 to $200 per month. Her mother never realized the full extent of her daughter's activities and was unaware that she was earning this kind of money. Liz streamlined the money into a PayPal account to avoid the necessity of a credit card for access to her money. Liz also used her mother's birth date to create the credit card account.

As Liz was finishing her last sale, a Microsoft message popped up. "YLHTD." Liz looked at the line and giggled. She typed. "How are you, Matt?" She waited, and a new line appeared.

"How did you know it was me?"

Liz shook her head. "Who else would say I look hot?"

"Okay, you have me. I'm sorry, but I have wanted to tell you that all day."

Liz smiled again. "Thank you, but why didn't you tell me that today when we talked?" Liz waited for a reply.

"I'm sorry, but whenever I get around you, I find it hard to speak. I wanted to say this, but I just couldn't."

Liz nodded and typed. "Boys! I don't know why you have so much trouble talking to me. We have known each other since we were 6 years old."

"But you have changed so much over the last few years. I find it hard to speak to you."

Liz smiled again. "I'm still the same person I have always been, and you know you can talk to me about anything." Matt disconnected, so Liz closed the computer and started dinner.

Sam arrived home 20 minutes later and assisted in the final dinner preparations. As they dined, Liz asked. "So how did the meeting go with Union?"

Sam shook her head in dismay. "I have never met a more despicable person in my life. I can usually find some redeemable qualities in anyone, but in this man, I saw nothing."

"Do you think he will come back to hurt us?"

Sam shook her head. "He is a low-hanging fruit in most categories---ripe and easy for the picking. I doubt that his mediocre intelligence poses any threat to us." Liz was silent.

Liz ordered Sam to take a bath and relax and she would handle the dishes. Sam needed to type up her notes on the meeting and wind down after her day. After a relaxing and replenishing shower, she did some research on the company laptop. Liz washed the dishes then left them in the drainer.

Liz returned to the living room and fired up the home computer. Over the past year, she had flourished as an entrepreneur, transforming garbage into gold with her natural flair for financial alchemy. Acquiring those computer skills required a mastery of the intrinsic inner workings of E-Bay, so she joined the school's computer club. She made friends with a peculiar clique that many had unfairly labeled "geeks". Although the masses disregarded them as outcasts, Liz did not. She studied the information they were willing to teach her and learned some handy tricks.

Liz felt that Jimmy Dittle presented a threat and she believed an ignored threat could only lead to danger. Her first mission was to discover the real name of the Union of Fletcher Industries. She would find the Union leader, Jimmy Dittle, and scrutinize him. Knowledge of one's enemies is crucial to success via fierce competition. It can expose their core weaknesses and pave a path to defeat them. This epiphany signified the birth of her master plan.

Liz was an accomplished entrepreneur, but she really shined through her computer skills. She could find anyone and hack into almost any computer. Liz set her sights on Jimmy Dittle and she would relentlessly invade his space.

Sam exited the shower in an old, worn, terrycloth robe, compliments of Tip. She removed a picture of her and Tip from the top drawer of her bedside table and her mind spun with various worries, such as bringing the wrong man into the house or coming across a man like Jimmy Dittle. After all, she was a single mother with a teenage daughter.

She reminisced about her first encounter with Tip. He treated her to a late breakfast, and they talked---they really talked. He spied a secluded able in the back corner and guided her to it. He merely placed his hand on the small of hers and pointed to the intended destination. She willingly followed his lead.

His seductive mannerisms were gratifyingly innate, as if it was fate. She struggled to understand this new yet intimate connection. The waitress took their order and returned with coffee and orange juice.

Tip sat back and momentarily drank in her essence. "What do you like to be called---Samantha or Sam?"

Sam eyed him with coy reticence. "Let me ask you a question---you know my name?"

"When I first noticed you, I did my homework. I asked numerous people about you. Are you aware of them?"

Sam gave him a sheepish look and quickly scanned her surroundings. "I don't know anybody except for my roommate, whom I'm going to kill when I find her."

Tip chuckled. "Heavens no. The way you handle yourself, treat others, and make insightful inquiries in class makes you alluring to passive observers. Your kind heart, strong will, and intelligence is impossible to ignore."

Sam's jaw almost dropped. "What did you do, have me investigated?"

Tip shook his head in denial. "No, I just asked people about you, that's all. People notice you."

Sam looked around the restaurant and dipped her head. She briefly considered sliding under the table, but she suddenly felt exposed. "So why you? Why me? Why did you.... come to rescue me from Jerry? And why did you do what you did?"

Tip smiled. "To return a favor."

Sam was shocked. "What do you mean by 'a favor'?"

"Okay, you remember that first weekend you were here when attended the fraternity party at Duke?"

Sam vaguely recollected the party and nodded yes. Tip continued. "You and your friend were sitting at one of the tables, when this tall, portly boy approached you."

Sam's eyes suddenly widened. "Yes! The heavy-set young man who pompously proclaimed that he had just downed 6 beers. I remember him."

"Your answer was perfect. You said, 'I'm glad you finally accomplished something worthy of bragging about.' It caught him totally off guard and rendered him speechless." Sam remembered the young man but didn't know what to say, so she simply nodded.

"He is a friend of mine," Tip explained. "and you could have ripped him apart like the women from some of his past encounters. But you didn't---last week, you started tutoring him, befriended him, and made him feel important. You also made him 50 bucks."

Sam's eyes grew large and asked. "Excuse me, 50 bucks? How did I do that?"

"Well, I bet him 50 bucks if he could strike up a conversation with you, and you did talk to him--- unlike your friend and the rest of the girls there. They were looking for potential meal tickets, and you accepted him for what he was, nothing more."

Sam let the information sink in. "What, he is a person with feelings? Just because he isn't as smart as some others, it doesn't mean he lacks potential."

"Exactly. Instead of belittling him, you accepted and helped him."

Sam mused over the influx of new information. "Let me get this straight. You have been following me for over a week because I was nice to a boy?"

"I have friends at both colleges, which makes it difficult during football season, and apparently, my connections collectively agree that you are someone worth knowing."

Sam was taken aback by this revelation. "Why? I haven't declared a major; I don't have any political pull; and I don't have any money. Why do they think I'm the one to watch?"

"Because, Ms. Samantha Raven, you are an exceptional person. You unknowingly exalt everyone around you. Men and women want to be near you, and strangers even look forward to seeing you. You are the type of woman I would like to know."

Sam recalled that statement, but then he disappeared and left her with his child. It hurt that the man she fell madly in love with deserted her after enticing her and shed a small tear. She placed the 8X10 picture of her and the dark-haired man laughing back into drawer and pushed it closed. This was her secret.

Chapter 8

Liz begins looking for Jimmy Dittle

Liz began her search by typing the name into Google. Several hits showed derivations of his name, like James, John, and of course, Jimmy Dittle. She also discovered numerous Facebook pages for people with the same name. She checked out the Facebook pages but needed to know what he looked like. Because she hadn't met him, that was a bust.

She tried People Finder and remembered what her mother had said: he was close to the same age as Larry Fletcher. Her mother did some of her research from home, and Liz was able to retrieve the Fletcher folder from the box of Sam's saved notes.

Liz's remembered her mother saying that Larry and Jimmy went to the same high school. She reasoned that he would be in his late thirties to early forties, which narrowed down the search. After checking the men who attended that same high school, she narrowed it down to one person.

Hutchinson had an account with People Finder because Sam often used it at work. Liz brought up the URL and signed into the app. With this information, she was able to see if he had a police officer record---and he did.

Liz quickly learned that Jimmy Dittle was a scoundrel even in high school. He habitually got into fights, and was expelled several times. Although his juvenile records were sealed, his adult records were public information. She began looking at the crimes he had committed.

She found a few arrests for drunk and disorderly conduct, theft, and prostitution. To date, he had no incarcerations, but Liz surmised that it was only a matter of time before he slipped up. The records also revealed that he had served time in a juvenile detention center.

It was getting late, so Liz decided to start fresh the next day. She arrived home, finished her homework, and checked for orders from eBay. After completing her orders, she went to work again. After drawing him out, she returned to Facebook and found several inconsistencies. None of her searches matched his age group. She thought about it and decided that the ones who had admitted being older were out. For this age group, why say you're older if you're trying to attract a younger person. She checked the younger ones, but none jumped out as the Jimmy Dittle she was looking for.

Liz checked her mother's records that she kept at the house. Sam had told her that Larry Fletcher and Jimmy Dittle had a history in high school. She wanted to see if her mother had called any of their high-school friends if any of them knew Jimmy Dittle.

Liz ransacked the closet until she found the box with the Fletcher research. Liz spent over an hour going through the records. As she composed her list of people to call, the phone rang. The caller ID showed her mother, so Liz picked up the phone and said. "Hi!"

Sam asked. "Hi, Why you so happy? Is Mat there with you?"

Liz chuckled. "No, he has been gone for almost ten minutes now."

Sam asked. "Well, excuse me! Why did he have to leave?"

Liz yawned. "Yea. We wore each other out to the point of exhaustion. Besides, he had homework."

Sam fired back. "I'm talking to Old Lady Bell from across the street and have her to babysit you."

"Ah Mom."

"I'm heading home and will be there in 45 minutes. Start dinner."

"Okay, Mom, see you soon." Sam smiled as she hung up. If someone were actually there, Liz would never have told her mother. The witty banter indicated that she was alone.

As Sam journeyed home, Trevor Paterson was holding court with his inner circle in a boardroom roughly an hour away from Winder. Mr. Paterson had taken over his family business in groceries stores and real estate. He began by investing in business overseas and eventually built a billion-dollar empire. He was famous for his ability to negotiate and organize business matters, and he developed a franchise with himself as the key organizer and guru of company development.

To his right was Jamie Mathers, his first recruit. Her 5 ft 6-inch, athletic build, and blonde hair the embodiment of beauty and danger. She was one of the few women who had almost finished Delta training. Despite qualifying as a sniper with top scores, she had just been released from the Army. A Master in Wing Chun Kung fu as well as several other types of martial arts fighting forms, she was Trevor's personal bodyguard. Her weapons of choice were knives and swords.

Susan Walker sat next to Jamie. With dirty blonde hair, she towered over Jamie by a good four inches---her figure was svelte and shapely. However, she was not to be rivaled in toughness. Ms. Walker, who started as a police officer in Atlanta, was Trevor's second hire. Because of her criminal justice major in community college, she was only 20 when she began her 10-year career as a homicide detective. At one point in time, she ranked #3 in the Women's MMA until Rhonda Rousey defeated her and broke her arm. No one dared to utter Rhonda's name in Susan's presence. An expert in small weapons, Susan held multiple black belts in Judo, Hapkido, and kickboxing.

Gary Hastings was one of the integral members of Trevor's team. After hacking into the CIA and FBI databases, he was on his way to a 10-year stint in prison. Luckily, Trevor had CIA connections and convinced them to allow Gary to serve his sentence on his plantation. Trevor wanted to take advantage of his gifts and Gary was more than happy to be sequestered on the plantation rather than prison. His pudgy, 5-foot 10- inch frame resembled that of most hackers---more stout than physical. His only problem with plantation life was the requirement of spending time in the gym. Regardless, it was a menial price to pay to avoid turning into Guido's bitch.

On the other side of the table sat Jeff Daniels, a 6- ft 2-inch black man of 220 lbs. who oversaw security on the Plantation. A retired Navy SEAL, he had survived an excess of one hundred missions in Iraq, Afghanistan, and various other countries.

The last suspect was Trevor's lawyer, Horatio Elbert Robert Barthelme or H.E.R.B Van Dorn. At 5-foot 6-inches and 150 lbs, he was small for a man but a metaphorical giant in the legal arena. He resembled a black male model, but as a lawyer, he had few peers. In ten years, he had never lost a case.

Jamie stared at the picture of the dark-haired woman on the table. "You think it's her?"

Trevor shook his head. "It has been a long time, and she looks much like I remember. I suppose it's a possibility."

Herb asked. "We have to be careful with the legal aspects here. You haven't seen her in a very long time, and she might not want you back in her life."

Trevor regarded Herb momentarily. "She has my child. I need to know one way or another if it's her, but we can't blow our covers until the time is right."

Susan asked. "Why not just confront her? In my experience, beating around the bush just muddles and complicates situations."

Herb spoke up. "That is fine in small and incoherent situations, but this one is unique. A number of legal ramifications must be considered before we make any moves. I suggest taking it slow---one step at a time and let's see what we find."

Trevor looked down the table at Gary Hastings. "You've been quiet, Gary"

Gary was perusing some of the paperwork on the table. "Look, I can dismantle and rebuild a computer with a toothpick, but when it comes to women and matters of the heart, I'm as ignorant as toddler."

The women laughed mockingly. "When was the last time you got laid, Gary?"

Gary turned beet red and turned his gaze to Jamie. "I have checked into her background." Everyone chuckled. Gary looked back up and plaintively protested. "Look, just because all of you are attractive, it doesn't mean that others enjoy the same social perks that you enjoy so freely. Some of us are more comfortable in the shadows without all the drama."

Jeff agreed. "Here, here, my friend! The biggest mistakes I have ever made were because of women."

Trevor spoke up in support. "Gary, please continue."

Gary nodded. "I have traced her back a number of years. She has been cautious. She gave up on dating after giving birth, and she guards her daughter like a lioness. No one threatens the daughter without dealing with the mother. I have a feeling that Herb is right about taking it slow, and learning who she is now, because people do change."

Trevor asserted. "I agree, Herb. Please send the documents and request an analysis with a meeting. Also, make sure it is them and that they don't extend the offer to another team." Herb nodded, and they left the boardroom.

Chapter 9

The Story of Jimmy Dittle

Liz found Jimmy Dittle on Facebook and she sent a poke. She was taken aback when he promptly responded the next day. She had to be careful.

Liz didn't want to respond to quickly. She needed more background information. Calling Larry Fletcher's friends to gain information was her first move, but she paused for a moment to contemplate the most effective approach. She considered the fact that her mother had contacted them to discuss the Fletcher deal. Of course, she would reveal the aspects of the merger. Instead, she would probably say she needed background information was for an investigation concerning new investment strategies.

Liz decided to use the same ruse, but now she was working as her mother's assistant, and they had some investment concerns with Jimmy Dittle. She opened a word document and titled it "Jimmy Dittle." Sam mother also had listed the occupation of each man and noted that she did identify herself as an accountant for Hutchinson was the purpose for the call.

She did this for two reasons. First, if she needed to call them back, she would already be familiar with the story. Second, she would embellish on the story line on the second call. If a court case did arise, these notes would be important evidence of what was discussed.

One was a night watchman; one sold insurance; and the last was un-employed. Liz decided to introduce herself as "Samantha's Assistant." This guise would allow her to pose follow-up questions about another person they were considering. She double-checked the numbers before calling.

Her mother usually purchased a set of cordless phones with headsets when she did this kind of interview. She did them in house and away from any prying ears in the office. Liz plugged in the phone's headset to free both hands for typing.

She called James Thomas. He was currently unemployed, so she figured that he might be home. Unfortunately, reached his answering machine and hung up without leaving a voice message. Concentrating on her voice was key---she needed to sound like an adult, not a teenager.

She moved down the page and typed in Fred Simpson. He was currently working as a night watchman, so he might be up and getting ready to head to work. A masculine voice answered the phone, and Liz began her introduction.

"Hi, may I speak to Mr. Simpson, a Fred Simpson?"

Fred was slow to respond. "This is him. Who is this?"

"Hi! My name is Jessica, and I'm Samantha's assistant. I was hoping to get some background information of one of your high school classmates if I may?"

Fred was quiet for a half a minute. "Look, if you want more information about Larry Fletcher, I'm afraid you will have to go to him. I can't tell you any more than what I already have."

Liz smiled. "No, no, that information was priceless, and we really thank you for your help. But we have another person we would like to know about, if you don't mind. It will only take a few minutes, please?"

He sighed reluctantly. "Okay but make it quick. I'm getting ready to head to work."

Liz smiled again. "We need to know about Jimmy Dittle. Do you remember him?" Liz could feel the pressure through the phone. Apparently, there was something here.

"Jimmy Dittle, Dittle---that scum bag! If you do business with that son of a bitch, take out life insurance. Excuse me for being frank, young lady, but he will fuck you like a cheap whore. That bastard can rot in hell! "The phone suddenly went dead. Fred slammed down the phone with no further words.

Liz sat back and thought. Apparently, Fred was not fond of Jimmy Dittle. His response was harsh and immediate. She tried her luck with the next person on the list. She thought to herself, "I don't want to talk to the insurance man yet. Let's try calling James Thomas again."

Liz heard the ring, and a woman suddenly answered the line. Liz delivered her introduction. "Hello! My name is Jessica, and I'm Samantha's assistant. I was hoping I could speak with Mr. Thomas?"

"This is his wife. May I ask why you are calling?"

"Yes! My boss spoke with your husband about Larry Fletcher for an investment venture, and his responses were helpful. We are now seeking background information on another classmate of his."

"Whom are you talking about now? You are well aware that Larry Fletcher took over the factory. It immediately went under and put my husband out of a job. So, who are you going to screw now?"

Liz had to think quickly. "Yes ma'am. We are corresponding with Jimmy Dittle. Do you know him?"

The woman laughed. "Do I?! That son of a bitch---I hope you intend to put him out of business as well. The only thing he deserves is a bullet between the eyes."

Liz was taken aback. Two calls with no sign of this person wasn't even on the list, and the feelings were far from positive. She asked, "I'm sorry you feel that way. May I ask who you are and how you know him?"

" As I said earlier, I'm James' wife, Cindy. We went to school together. Who else have you called about that bastard?"

"I called Mr. Fred Simpson, but he hung up on me."

Cindy laughed. "You're lucky he didn't come through the phone. Jimmy Dittle raped his girlfriend; and was never prosecuted. He harassed her all through high school, and she committed suicide. No, I don't think you will find anyone who will say anything nice about that bastard. So, what kind of investment are you looking at?"

Liz responded. "I'm getting not much from the feedback. Do you know anyone else I can call?"

Cindy sighed. "Have you called Dave Thrasher? He can give you a lot of information about him."

Liz asked, "Why would he know so much?"

Cindy laughed. "One of Jimmy's friends, if you want to call him a friend, was Roger Dawson. Roger was a real player in high school. He had a reputation for deflowering young girls. He seduced Dave's girlfriend and turned her into a prostitute. Dave and Jimmy squared off a number of times because Roger wasn't man enough to face him."

"It sounds like Roger and Jimmy had some sort of prostitution business going. Did they have a number of girls?"

"Ha! They had a couple of girls until Jimmy got busted. He was Roger's muscle, so that ended it for a while. I heard that when Jimmy got out of jail, they picked it back up again."

Liz thanked Cindy for the information and disconnected.

Now she needed to call Dave Thrasher. So far, the picture was grim. She finished typing her notes and decided to call Dave Thrasher.

It was still early in the afternoon, so Liz decided to call him at his office. The receptionist immediately put her through to his phone. When he came on the line, Liz said, "Hello, my name is Jessica. I work for Samantha, and I appreciate you taking my call. May I ask you some questions about a former classmate, if you have time?"

Dave cleared his throat nervously. "Look, I don't have the time to be answering questions about every one of my classmates. I'm a little busy but make this quick and ask one question."

Liz took a deep breath. "We need to know who Jimmy Dittle is and what can we expect from him."

Dave was quiet for a moment. "Whom have you spoken with?"

"I called Fred Simpson, and he hung up on me. I also talked to Cindy Thomas, James's wife. Is there any information that you can share? By the way this is off the record, and nothing you tell me will be made public"

He uttered nervously, "If you talked to Cindy, you know about my girlfriend."

"Yes, she did mention her. Is that a problem?"

Dave's voice was full of sadness, but at least he was cooperating. "Janice. Janice Nash was her name. We dated since our freshmen year of high school. We had a fight one day, and purely out of spite, she got onto Roger's motorcycle and took off. She let him take her virginity that night. Before I knew it, Roger was pimping her out with Jimmy Dittle as his muscle. After Jimmy got busted and sent to jail, she stopped. Everything seemed to be back to normal until he was released. That's when she committed suicide rather than going back to him."

Liz was floored. "I'm sorry. I didn't know. Do you know what happened to Roger Dawson?"

Dave's reply was hesitant. "Yea. He was a lot smarter than Jimmy, which is why he didn't get pinched in the sting that got Jimmy arrested.

He was able to get into college, and from what I heard, continued to get his way. He seduced some college girls and pimped them out to some professors whom he blackmailed into giving him passing grades while he skipped classes. He even did a young female teacher and used her too. He is a real manipulator, that one."

Liz asked, "Do you know where Roger Dawson is today?"

"No, but if you plan to do any business with this Jimmy Dittle, be careful. He seems to lack whatever part of the human brain that is responsible for morals or a conscience. He will lie, cheat, and even murder to get what he wants. I can't prove anything, but to this day, I don't think Janice committed suicide--- it was just made to look like that."

Liz shuddered; this news made her nervous. Jimmy Dittle was dangerous, and apparently, he was still getting his way. She had to be careful. She thanked Dave for the information and promised that everything he said would be kept confidential. But this information was useful.

Liz completed her notes and allowed this influx of information to settle in. Suddenly, the phone rang. She jumped, having been totally engrossed in her notes. The caller ID showed that it was her mom, and she answered on the second ring.

"Hi Mom," Liz announced.

Sam smiled at the voice of her daughter. "Okay, who were you calling?"

Liz smiled and lied, "I just hung up with Bobby. You remember Bobby from the computer club at school?"

"Yes, I know him. All your homework done?"

"Yes mom. All done."

Sam joked, "Okay, kick Mathew out of the house and start dinner. I will be home in 15 minutes."

Liz giggled. "First off Mom, Mathew is not here, and yes, I will start dinner."

"Thank you, honey. Love you." She hung up and continued towards home.

Chapter 10

The Paterson Corp.

Sam went back into her office the second Monday in April and updated the online database on the latest developments of the meeting. Jennifer was impressed with Larry's progress. He was gaining confidence in his decision-making and the potential direction of the company. There was still a lot of work to do, but the commissions would be bountiful when everything came to fruition.

As Sam typed her notes, Jennifer stopped by and laid a folder on the desk. Sam looked puzzled. Jennifer smiled, "A new client just contacted us. They were recommended by Country Town bank and Mr. Beckman."

Sam's eyes widened. "Okay, what's the story?"

"We first have to find out about the company before we do anything. According to Mr. Beckman, the party in question is having a problem with some recent acquisitions and needs help merging them and streamlining his company."

"So, we first find out as much as possible about this company and the owners to see if they are worth our time." Jennifer nodded and walked away. Sam felt invigorated by this new puzzle to solve, new ground to explore, and new commission source. She could use the money.

Sam first opened her outlook account to see if she had overlooked anything. As she weeded out which ones needed to be deleted immediately, read later, and read now, she noticed one from the Director of Security, Roger Dawson. He was reinstating penalties for the removal of sensitive information from the office. Sam deleted the email thinking, "I never take sensitive files out of the office."

After she finished her notes on the meetings with the Union Bosses, namely Jimmy Dittle, she dove into the file. This didn't look very interesting. The new company was Paterson Corporation, who's CEO was Trevor Paterson. Sam thought to herself, "Nice name. Probably in his 70s and looking for a girl toy in his old age."

The files consisted of all fluff and no meat, namely the owner's name and the PNL of the company. She needed to find definitive details about Trevor Paterson and his corporation. Before she can determine what they can do for Paterson, she must determine what Paterson needs to have done. She had to crank up the investigation and start peeling back the layers of the Paterson Corporation.

Sam started by typing the company into Google and then following the leads. Much to her pleasant surprise, she quickly found a great deal of information about the company, including its history. Much of it was accessible on the corporate website. This route of investigation is normally superfluous and full of dead ends, but she found some useful information. It was enough to jumpstart the research and learn who and what they were.

Paterson Corporation was started by Trenton Paterson in his own namesake. He began with a grocery store in the 20's in the tiny town of Greenville, Georgia. He did well and was able to expand to a second store. However, the depression of the 30's had done a number on the business. But Trenton and his sons were able to turn misfortune into profits.

The history of the company told a story of a family that had weathered hard times by facing them head on, and treated people with respect. Instead of running and hiding, they confronted the situation and made the best of it. During those hard financial times, many companies just cashed out and ran off with the profits leaving their creditor behind. Paterson Corp owned Grocery stores and rental property and carried a large debit for their customers for several years until the economy began to turn back around.

Because of this, many of those customers were loyal to Paterson and stayed with them. The company now owned several apartment complexes and numerous grocery stores. As the grandson, Trevor Paterson had taken over years ago the company continued to grow.

Trevor had just acquired two more companies; and was baffled as what to do with them. Sam thought the poor little rich kid had taken over the company and skated along for a few years, but now he was lost in the harsh reality of self-sufficiency. He had mastered purchasing, but he lacked the savvy to turn it into a profitable venture.

Sam dug up numerous pictures of him attending public events with a beautiful blonde on his arm. She assumed that this was his wife or girlfriend, but the tabloids failed to divulge those intimate details. However, it was always the same girl, which indicated that he was in a steady relationship. Interestingly, he was always behind her. She was the focal point of the picture, not him. There were only 1 or 2 photographs where he could be clearly seen. All she could determine was that he wasn't fat, but he was average looking.

Step one: what were the acquired companies acquired, and what did they offer to the original company?

She needed to make the merger appear viable to Paterson Corp and present a plan to complete the merger---but she had to find out about the new companies. The first company was a moving company, and the second was a furniture supplier. Sam first thought, "What was his motive in pairing a moving company and a furniture supplier?" Sam realized that she needed to gather three crucial pieces of information about his apartment complexes: where they were located, what demographic of people were moving, and why. This feat seemed impossible.

Step two: more research on Paterson Corporation and its holdings.

Her discoveries titillated her. Paterson owned Oakwood Apartments, which had complexes all over the world. The corporation offered long and short-term leases apartments, depending on the tenant's specific needs. Apparently, there was a need for this type of rental.

Companies sent teams and crews worldwide to work on projects. This setup required them to remain in an area for long periods that spanned from one week to a year. A year was too short for a property purchase and too long for a hotel. With Oakwood membership, they could rent efficiencies cheaper than a hotel, but they avoided shelling out the money for a real estate purchase, especially if their stay turned out to be less than one year.

Due to the fragile economy, companies were moving their corporate headquarters to new areas of the country to take advantage of cheaper costs. The expense of doing business was key. The cost of doing business in Detroit, Michigan drove the auto manufacturing industry from Detroit to other national and international areas. If Paterson Corp. could reduce the cost of moving, they would reap the benefits of relocation.

Sam's goal was now clear and simple. Why didn't he see it? He purchased the companies for a reason but seemed blind to the prize that his eyes should be focused on. This was the proposal---now she simply had to put it together.

Sam typed up her report and sent it to Jennifer so that she could research the legal aspects of the idea. She knew what needed to be done, and now she needed to skillfully and covertly put her plan into action. Sam sent an email to Jennifer requesting a meeting.

Sam beamed when she entered Jennifer's office. "When do you think we can get them in here so I can start putting the proposal together?"

Jennifer scanned her calendar. It was Tuesday, and it would take several days to tweak the proposal; realistically, it wouldn't happen until next week. She looked back at Sam. "Let's shoot for next Wednesday. I will call them put things in motion."

Meanwhile, in an office about two hours north, Trevor Paterson sat in his boardroom office table with his people. Jamie Mathers and Susan Walker, his personal bodyguards/investigators, sat strategically to his right. Gary Hastings, a computer geek who was infamous for ability hacking websites, sat next to them. Last but not least were CEO John Doughty and Herb Van Dorn, his lawyer.

Trevor scrutinized a picture of Samantha Raven intently. The CEO ended his call and announced to his entourage, "We have a meeting with them on Wednesday at 10am."

Jamie diverted her eyes to Trevor. "Do you still think it's her?"

Trevor let the picture drop from his hands onto the table. "Very close---she had longer hair and never wore glasses. She rarely dressed in a provocative manner, but she was definitely not this conservative. It could be her, but I don't want to get my hopes up."

Trevor turned to Susan. "What are the results of the background check?"

Susan bowed her head in accord. "She drives an '05 VW that she got from Steve Bushier. She then moved into her parents' home after they passed. No bills, but since she and this Jennifer Wills teamed up, their work has been extraordinary, particularly with Fletcher industries. She reorganized them and shut down the Union. The one concern here is the Union Boss' direct threats."

Trevor's stare was purposeful. "Should we be concerned?"

Jamie glanced uncertainly at Susan. "We are not sure, but based on our interviews, he has few moral impediments-- he might be a matter of concern."

Trevor nodded as he walked toward his large desk, leaned against it, and began issuing orders. "Alright. Here is the game plan. Jamie and Susan keep nosing around and see what else you can find while Gary keeps digging. I would like to know more about this Union Boss. John, generate a background report on the Hutchinson Corp. Herb gather the necessary documents. Hopefully, she is who I hope she is. Most importantly, I want to thank everyone for all the work you have done." He sat down at his desk. All rose and left the room.

Chapter 11

Yes, No, Maybe - - - OH God

Sam had been dating Tip now for 3 months, but the strength underlying her futile attempts at resisting the pull of carnal desire weakened by the day. Thanksgiving snuck up on her, and she had no funds to go home---and the idea of leaving him was a moot point. She decided to prepare a feast for him that would turn the original settlers of the Mayflower green with envy. She became excitedly aware that there would no safety net or chaperone---no reason to say no. And what frightened her most was that she didn't want to say no.

Just for fun, she indulged in being alone with him. He was so handsome, intelligent, and dangerously invigorating. She coaxed him into taking her grocery shopping, and when they returned, she cooked dinner and playfully ordered him to help. He possessed the culinary skills of a shade tree mechanic---but he was willing. He did exactly as she instructed him and cracked jokes the entire time. She reveled in it.

They feasted on turkey with sweet potatoes, cranberry sauce, and baked beans, and she supervised his creation of a salad. His only culinary aptitude consisted of choosing the wine. Afterwards, they talked and settled onto his couch overlooking the city of Durham. The 10 floor and had a beautiful view that was loftier than the surrounding structures. As the lights shone from the streets, they spied on the people walking below.

Tip placed his glass of wine onto the end table and cradled hers. She shuddered at the thought of what he would do next. Normally, their make-out sessions were outside and in public. Regardless of her burgeoning carnal desires, she always had the safety net of a public venue--- Tip would only go so far in front of an audience. Now they were secluded in his apartment.

He gently raised her face to his and kissed her tenderly on the lips. That kiss was so right, sweet, and tender; as if he was afraid, he would break her like a porcelain doll. He crept towards her, and she slowly surrendered to the soft confines of his beige couch. She wasn't trying to stop him---she wanted him to kiss her. She had wanted it all afternoon but was afraid to tell him.

He nuzzled her neck and kissed her ear lobe. His hands started to explore her physique, and she liked it. She yearned to feel his strong hands on her tender skin. When her natural response of fear kicked it, she ignored it. She didn't want him to stop. She wanted to relinquish all control and beg for more of his attention, but now she was afraid of giving in again.

With all of the strength she could muster, she pushed him away. Tears filled her eyes as she pleaded. "Please stop!"

Tip's expression was overflowing with carnal longing, but it quickly softened as he spied the conflict in her face. " What's wrong?" Sam had tears running down her cheeks due to a cornucopia of emotions. She wanted him but was afraid to say yes---yet she was powerless to say no. She feared that she would regret her next decision.

Tip pulled her close and kissed her forehead. "Why are you scared?" Sam looked up into those irresistible, dark brown eyes. She wanted him. She wanted him to possess her, to take her---but no, she knew she would get pregnant.

She cupped his face with her hands and pleaded. "This is not fair. It is two against one, and I can't afford to get pregnant."

Tip looked at her quizzically. "Two against one?"

Sam gently caressed the side of his face and replied, "You and me against me." Tip smiled and stirred.

Sam got scared again. Was he mad? Their physical and emotional relationship was symbiotic---she expanded when he contracted, and he contracted when she expanded. She didn't want him to move away; she wanted him with her. He gently pulled her off the couch and took her by the hand, guiding her towards the bedroom. Sam was worried again, that he was going to take advantage of the way she felt about him. "Tip…no. I can't!"

Tip glanced over his shoulder with an alluring grin. "Don't worry. I just want to show you something." He led her to one of the bedside tables and pulled the drawer open. Stepping back, he pointed at the contents---the drawer was full of condoms.

Sam eyed Tip and the drawer back and forth with suspicion. "How many are there, and why do you…?" She lost herself in his beautiful visage as he pulled her to him. His lips grazed her forehead. "There are 500, and they're all for you."

Sam raised her eyes to Tip. "But I don't…. they can't be for me…. I don't?"

"Are you sure?"

Sam shook her head with uncertainty. "No, I can't . . . not 500… you don't mean…you can't be serious?"

Tip placed his hands on the side of her face and lowered her to the bed as he pressed his lips against hers. He wrapped his arm around her waist, and with one knee on the bed, he swept her entire body beneath him.

Sam was again torn between conflicting desires: to have Tip or finish college. As he continued to kiss her, she basked in his attention. She could not get enough of his touch, but it made her shudder. Catching her breath, she finally asked. "But Tip, you don't intend to use all of them...do you?"

Tip smiled that million-dollar smile that made her heart skip a beat. "Not tonight, but maybe this weekend." Sam trembled with the sudden realization that all of her excuses where fading, and she was running out of reasons to say no. Tip continued to caress her body, and soon she was drowning in his touch, his smell, his presence. She belonged to him. She gave herself to him willingly for the rest of the weekend until it was time to go back to school, i.e. reality.

When she arrived at her dorm, her roommate gave her a once over. "I would ask what you did this weekend, but I think I already know." Sam's face turned red as she turned away. The thought that her roommate knew what Tip had done to her that weekend with her absolute consent was too much to bear. The only thought that she wanted to linger in her mind was the burning desire to please him, and she didn't care what he wanted her to do.

She shyly looked back at her roommate." Is it that obvious?"

" It wasn't until you turned red; then I was sure.

" Sam put her hands to her mouth." I don't know what to say."

Her roommate chortled. "With that good-looking man, I'm shocked you resisted for so long."

Sam looked down and up again. "So am I."

" So how was it? Do you feel any different?"

" Incredible, to both questions." They both doubled over in laughter.

Samantha and Tip continued their affair, but they took all of the necessary precautions for the rest of the year. Sam was entranced; in being with such a dynamic person. She would find herself counting the moments prior to his arrival. She resisted the offers to move in with him as well as the ones of him paying for her birth control. This relationship seemed too good to be true.

At the end of the year, he would go his way and she hers, and they would never see each other again. She would look back on this liaison as a wonderful memory, but nothing more. He was too perfect, too good, and too dynamic to allow himself to be tied down to a simple woman such as herself.

And that is how she viewed herself---a simple, blue-collar woman. Samantha Raven didn't view herself as some worldly, dynamic, earthmover who affected people's lives on a grand scale. She was a humble woman who enjoyed the simple life.

She pictured her future self-residing in a quaint community with a husband who matched her work ethic. Possibly one or two children? Church on Sundays, PTA meetings, and community socials.

As for her future projections of Tip, he would be a dynamic person with connections around the world, traveling with super models, and jet setting globally in private jets. He would form strong business liaisons and frequently correspond with foreign companies and governments about million-dollar investments. There was no place for her in this lifestyle. She was an unpretentious girl who enjoyed simple pleasures based on humble desires.

For example, she took great pleasure in the little things, like sitting at home with a glass of wine and a good book after a nice meal she had prepared---or merely hanging out with her friends in hopes of someday finding a forever man. Two different worlds had briefly merged like two ships passing in the night only to disappear in the ocean of their lives and onto their chosen paths. Paths that were as inevitably divergent as they were. But she would always remember him and reminisce about this affair with blissful nostalgia of the time when she had a relationship with such a man.

Chapter 12

The Transformation

Sam finished the rough draft and emailed it to Jennifer. Jennifer responded that she had set up a meeting in their office at 10 am for the third Wednesday in April. They only had one week, plus a weekend. The initial proposal needed to be completed by Friday with work on the props to finish it by Monday or Tuesday. This plan of attack would allow the ladies two days to iron out the presentation. When Jennifer delivered the presentation, she had to look stunning; more importantly, she had to sound intelligent.

A stunning appearance would capture the attention of the audience, but it was not the only requirement. Superficial showboating might work for the Kardashian sisters, but discussing money required a specific type of finesse. In this particular situation, substance took priority over pageantry. For the rest of the week, Sam and Jennifer worked steadfastly to iron out the proposal. Sam even worked from home that weekend searching for any new information that might appear. She googled and yahooed, querying about his name as well as the company's name in numerous searches--- yet she found nothing.

Wednesday arrived---Sam and Jennifer were going out on a limb. Corporate foresaw no long-term profits from this venture. Still, the dynamic duo was confident that they had a solid proposal. The only caveat was that there were financial questions about the company that were not revealed in the IRS or SCC reports or even the PNL.

Obtaining that information meant making Paterson Corp. a client. On Wednesday, Sam arrived on time and double-checked the presentation. All ducks were in a row, so to speak. Jennifer's office was empty. It wasn't like Jennifer to be late on a big day. Sam wore her black pencil skirt with a matching jacket and a white, silk, frilled blouse that buttoned to the neck. Her customary bun remained in place with one perfectly- placed hairpin.

Sam surveyed the layout of the refreshments in the conference room. Coffee, soft drinks, and tea were ready. She then fiddled with the overhead projector and various displays showing cost and profit ratios, tax liabilities, and various other slides. Everything was in place.

At 9am, Jennifer still wasn't there. Sam called from Jennifer's office so no one could eavesdrop on their conversation. Home---no answer. Cell phone---an unfamiliar voice answered. Sam's heart stopped.

Sam asked, "Jennifer?"

The voice answered, "No? This is Dr. Montrose. Who is this?"

"I'm Samantha Raven. I work with Jennifer. Is she okay?"

"Yea, she is now."

Sam's heart leapt into in her throat. "What do you mean 'now?"

"Without going into detail, I can tell you that she was brought in by ambulance last night, but she is fine now."

"Do you think she will come to work today? We have a major presentation that only she can deliver."

The Dr. laughed. Sam detested that laugh. "What are you laughing about? This is serious."

"Ma'am, I wouldn't count on it. I have already breached the code of medical ethics for divulging this much personal information, but we are waiting for her family to arrive. I can confirm that she will recover and be fine. As for today, forget it."

Sam thanked him and slowly hung up the phone. She then dropped her head down onto the desk and fought back tears. They had put two weeks of work into this, and their reputations hung delicately in limbo. The board had always been doubtful that they could pull it off---their jobs were officially in jeopardy. The big show was scheduled in less than an hour, and the star was in the hospital. Dear God, what was she going to do? As if on cue, the epiphany hit like a ton of bricks. She wasn't Jennifer, but she was the only one who knew the material well enough to act as her understudy. It had to be her.

Sam stood up on shaky legs and walked briskly to the bathroom. She knew that she had to make some changes. She could not impersonate the nuances of Jennifer, but she had to do something. As she stood before the mirror analyzing her reflection, the receptionist walked in.

Mary stopped in mid step and recognized the expression of utter despair on Samantha's face. She knew something was wrong. "Sam, you okay?"

Sam kept her back to Mary. "No! Jennifer is in the hospital, and we have a presentation in less than an hour. What am I going to do, Mary? I hate standing in front of a room full of people, much less being the center of attention! Look at me! I could never grab their attention as Jennifer does. If I tried to fill her shoes for even a minute, they would leave."

Mary took a slow, calculated step forward and looked at the Sam's reflection. "Oh, I don't think men mind looking at you. They are just too scared to do anything else."

Sam cut her eyes to Mary's reflection. "Excuse me?"

Mary took another step forward, seeing the look of terror on Sam's face. Mary knew instantly what needed to be done. "Okay, with a couple of changes, we can make you a little more approachable. Let me help." Mary reached around and unbuttoned Sam's suit jacket. "Okay, let's start here. Take off the jacket for now, and let's see what we are working with."

Sam's looked shocked. "What do you mean by 'I don't look approachable?" And why are they scared to approach me? I'm not... dangerous."

Mary guffawed. "Right! You don't dress as if you want to be approached, and with that expression, you look like you could castrate a bull. Come now, let's see what we have."

Sam was perplexed. "Castrate a bull--- that sounds horrible, and what do you know about bull castration or fashion?"

Mary's expression softened. "Ms. Raven, I don't have your smarts, but I grew up on a farm, and I do know what it takes to get and keep a job. How do you think I can afford these outfits on my menial salary? Now you sit tight, and I'll be right back." With that, she turned and trotted out of the bathroom.

As Mary exited the bathroom, she spotted one of the secretaries walking by and grabbed her by the arm. "Cynthia, I need for you to watch the front desk. When the Paterson people arrive, get them settled in the conference room. Tell them that Sam, no, Samantha Raven will be right there. Okay?"

Cynthia looked shocked, and started to say something when Mary barked, "Don't ask. I will explain later, okay?" Cynthia nodded and hurried off. Mary followed her to the front desk, grabbed a bag from under the desk, and headed back to the bathroom. As she neared the bathroom, she saw Mr. Hutchinson approaching--- his expression said everything. Mary put up one hand. "Everything is okay. Just go to the conference room and keep them there until Sam is ready."

Mr. Hutchinson took a gulp. "Sam?"

Mary had no time to explain. "Go, go! We need you there." Mr. Hutchinson started slowly while glancing over his shoulder before rushing to the conference room. This was ether going to be a home run or a complete disaster.

When Mary entered the bathroom, Sam was still looking at herself in the mirror. Sam was almost in tears when Mary placed the bag onto the counter. Mary's voice was firm but kind. "Look, we don't need you breaking down. You're too good for that. Now we need to sex you up, so take that hideous blouse off."

Sam was baffled. "Sex me up? I'm not sexy?"

Mary laid Sam's jacket aside. "Sam you don't know how sexy you are. The men stop after you pass just to catch a glimpse of you walking down the hall. God, I wish I had half of your sex appeal. Now hurry! Give me the blouse and that skirt. Take them both off."

Sam started to unbutton the blouse and paused. "Great idea. I walk in there wearing nothing but my bra and panties. That will make an impression."

Mary chuckled and examined the ruffles on the front of the blouse. She grabbed her scissors from her bag and cut them off. "The skirt---quick, we don't have much time."

Sam unzipped her skirt and stepped out of it. Mary handed her the blouse. When Sam saw Mary's destruction of the ruffles, she said. "I liked those."

Mary smiled warmly. "That's nice. Now put it back on while I do something with this."

Sam did as she was told while Mary knelt down to pin and hem the skirt. She spread the skirt onto the bathroom counter and turned it inside out. She then overlapped the skirt and shortened it to the desire length. Out came a needle and thread. The thread was almost a perfect match to the black skirt. Using broad strokes, she quickly hemmed the skirt. Sam had just finished buttoning up the blouse all the way to her chin. She handed Sam the skirt. "Put this on."

Sam complied, and Mary helped her pull the skirt up. After smoothing out the skirt to the hem, she then reached up under the skirt and pulled the blouse down. It fit perfectly. Mary then faced Sam and unbuttoned her blouse to slightly expose her bra line.

Sam started to protest, but Mary interrupted. "Look, Sam, you are a beautiful woman. You're smarter than most men, which is not surprising, but the problem is that you look smarter. You must distract them from your intelligence by reminding them that you are also a woman---a beautiful woman."

Sam was thrown off by the comment. "You think I can do that? Should I let my hair down?"

Mary looked her over and pulled the hairpin out. Sam's hair cascaded across her shoulders. Mary grabbed a brush out of her bag and ran it through Sam's long mane of hair. "You first have to believe, and then you can be anything you want. Now, nobody knows the material better than you do. I have watched you working late and on weekends putting this together. When you look whoever is at the far end of the table in the eye for 5 seconds, they will have time to study you. Start slowly and do just as I have watched you and Jennifer do for the last two days. You can do this--- you are beautiful; you are intelligent; and you are woman. Now go."

Sam turned to look at the woman in the mirror. It was still her, sans ruffles removed and with much more cleavage. It was not a Jennifer Will Cleavage, but it was there. Her skirt was hemmed well above her knees, but her hair flowed down her back. Without her glasses, she no longer resembled a sexy schoolteacher. Her eyes remained locked on her reflection, and she asked Mary. "You think I can pull it off?"

"No! I don't think--- I know you can do it. You are Samantha Raven, the woman who spotted deals and turned them into huge successes, when nobody thought you could. You can do anything. Now go show them what you are capable of."

Sam gave Mary a shy smile. "Wish me luck."

Mary gave her a knowing wink. "You don't need luck; you make your own luck. Make us all proud."

Chapter 13

Meeting Trevor

Sam steadied herself, exited the bathroom, and walked intently down the hall toward the conference room. Several men and women stopped in their tracks and stepped aside as she strode confidently past them with a powerful gait. The air picked up her hair as it soared like a cape from her head. Her blouse was open, and her skirt was short with a slit up the side. She exuded confidence and purpose.

As Sam approached the conference room, she saw that 4 men accompanied Mr. Paterson. They were all seated at the table with cups and drinks before them, discussing football and whatnot. As she slowly approached the door, she noticed that Mr. Hutchinson was not at his usual seat at the far end of the table. Instead, he stood at the other end talking to another man when he spotted Sam. A stunned expression washed over his face.

Before Sam could reach for the door, Mr. Hutchinson sprung up uncharacteristically to open it for her. This was not what she expected. As she sauntered in and made her way to the head of the table, the room fell silent. Mr. Hutchinson announced. "Gentlemen, I would like to present to you Samantha Raven, one of the best forensic accountants in the country. I implore you to please listen to her carefully." With that, he stepped back and gestured to the end of the conference room table with an open palm. It was the exact spot, that Jennifer should be taking, but now it was hers for the taking.

Sam advanced to the end of the table, standing erect with clasped hands as she regarded the man seated at the other end of table. It was Trevor Paterson, and he was far more attractive in person---his pictures did him little justice. He was about to take a sip of coffee but froze midway and gently returned the cup to the saucer. His eyes were fixed on her. He wasn't looking her up and down; he was staring directly into her eyes. Maintaining the locked gaze, he wrote something quickly on a pad and slid it the man to his right.

As Sam studied him, a sudden calm came over her. The fear she possessed of standing before a crowd diminished as her eyes met his. Inexplicably, she suddenly felt that she was exactly where she was supposed to be, yet time was slipping by.

Sam had to break the connection and to start the show. She smiled for the first time and said. "Gentlemen, thank you for coming. I was asked to look at your recent acquisitions and ascertain how to make use of them. At first, I was a little confused as to why you purchased the Moving and Furniture Company, but after studying it, I see a brilliant move here."

Sam noticed the man on the right scribble something on the pad and slide it back. Mr. Paterson glanced at it and smiled. Sam was certain that the notes where about her, but she ignored it and continued. "What I realized was that regarding the Oakwood Corporate Apartments, the moving and transportation of furniture and family goods from one site to another can be a very lucrative business. However, by bringing these two businesses under the same umbrella, the parent company will have extensive savings. A word of caution: I would not make them part of Paterson. I would allow them to remain as separate entities."

The man on Paterson's left spoke up. "So, what you are saying is that you think they should remain separate but also part of us? That doesn't make any sense."

Sam smiled reassuringly. "At first, I thought the same thing, but then I realized that remaining separate allows for certain concessions that are not permissible if the company functions as a single entity." She noticed Mr. Paterson write something on the pad and pass it to his right.

The man on the right chimed in. "Like what?"

Sam was not ready for the question but fired back with a response. "For starters, if you can convince the moving company to transport the goods at cost, Oakwood could reduce its operating costs."

Before she could finish, the man on Paterson's left interjected, "But if we own them it doesn't matter?"

Sam stopped and stared him down. "Please allow me to finish. There is a difference between operating costs and the cost of material. The cost of doing business is deducted immediately. Of course, that affects the bottom line, but the cost of goods and materials will depreciate over time. Therefore, you need to treat them differently."

The man leaned forward to ask another question, but Sam made a power move and held one finger up. He took the queue, and she continued, "What we can do is you pay more for the furniture and use the additional costs as repeated tax deductions over 5 years. You apply the reduced cost of moving to the bottom line now, and the furniture company pays the moving company a bonus depending on the amount of furniture moved. This will in turn more than make up for the initial loss of revenue in the beginning. Essentially, the entire company gains a major reduction in your tax liability." With that, Mr. Paterson hit the man on his left in the arm. The man sat back and looked rejected, but Mr. Paterson beamed with satisfied delight.

Sam picked up the remote and displayed graphs, pie charts, and fancy artwork that they and spent so much time on, when she noticed Mr. Paterson scribble something on the pad and slide it to his right again. Sam stopped and looked directly at Mr. Paterson. "Does Mr. Paterson have a question?" The man on his right looked at the pad and then at Mr. Paterson.

Mr. Paterson leaned back in his chair and looked intently at Sam. "How long did it take you to put this together?"

Sam was taken aback by this unexpected question. "We spent a week putting the proposal together."

Mr. Paterson stood up, picked up the proposal, and handed it to his left-hand man. As he straightened out his Brooks Brothers suit, he leisurely walked around the table towards Sam. Sam did her best to stand as tall as possible. He was over 6 ft tall and towered a good 8 inches over her. She had the sudden sinking feeling she had blown the proposal, but as she gazed at this beautiful man approaching her, a wave of calm washed over her.

Mr. Paterson asserted, "No. Not the proposal. How long did it take for you to arrive at your conclusions on this merger and develop a strategy?"

Sam studied his eyes. Oh---those beautiful brown eyes! The closer he came, the more she liked what she saw. He was gorgeous but that was not going to affect her. She had to regain her composure and finish the proposal." It took me a week to complete my research and calculate the value here. At first, I didn't know why you made the purchase, but once I did, the advantages became clear."

Mr. Paterson smirked and looked at the man on his left. "It only took her one week…one week!" He extended his hand to shake hers, and she slowly lifted her hand to place it in his. His handshake it was firm but gentle, and his musky smell reminded her of Thanksgiving dinner---the turkey, the beans, the wine, the sweat on her tongue.

The calmness that she recently felt returned and swathed her in his presence. She felt an uneasy around most men, but not Trevor. He was like the calm eye in the center of a storm. This overwhelming feeling caught her off guard, and she didn't understand why.

Mr. Paterson started towards the door. "We'll be in touch." Mr. Hutchinson jumped up and almost ran over a chair following him out of the conference room. The rest of the men quickly rose and filed out of the conference room. The entire proposal was over. She had blown it--- taken her shot and made a total mockery of it all.

Sam dragged a chair over to sit down, ready to cry. She knew she would be fired. Although she stepped up and tried to pull it off, she failed. Her career was over. She sat there for several minutes in solitude when Mary suddenly pushed her way in the doorway. Her face lit up." How do you feel?"

Sam's eyes practically overflowed with tears. "They got up and walked out. I never even got to present the full proposal. I blew it, and I'm going to be fired. What made me think I could pull this off?"

Mary pulled a chair over in front of Sam and looked into her face. Sam looked back at her. "Why are you smiling? I blew it."

Mary shook her head no. "No, you didn't. Mr. Hutchinson told him this was your first presentation, and that it was just lack of experience that made you blow it. He urged him to come back for Jennifer Wills, and do you know what Mr. Paterson said?"

Sam held back tears and shook her head no. Mary continued, "Mr. Paterson told him if he fired you, he would have his balls. He preferred to look over the presentation and contract in private, and if he likes it, he will be back next week. You did it! You sold it, and you landed the contract."

Sam was dumbfounded. "But they didn't let me finish, and what is this with men's balls?"

Mary smiled and retorted, "That or their stomachs--- it's the only way to get their attention."

Sam nodded in agreement and started to clean up, but Mary stopped her. "No. You have work to do; I'll take care of this."

The men exited to their vehicles. As Mr. Paterson loosened his tie, he turned to the man on his right." Find out what you can about Samantha Raven. I want phone numbers, address, financial statements…everything." He traded nods with the man, who walked off. He then turned to the man on his left." So, what do you think?"

The two men headed to the parking garage, and the other man said, "She is brilliant! She figured that out in one week; it took me a month to get on board with your version of the plan. So… you are going to bring them on board?"

The two men gave their tickets to the parking garage attendant to retrieve their vehicles. As they stood there, Mr. Paterson rolled up his sleeves. "I don't know yet, but that is her; I know it. I will look over the proposal and contract and let you know next week. First, I want to know more about her."

Mr. Paterson's colleague replied, "Fair enough. I will see you at the house." At that, the attendants pulled up in a 1936 green Ford pickup truck and 2010 corvette. Mr. Paterson walked over to the truck and checked the odometer before handing the attendant a $50. He got in and drove off, followed by the corvette.

The next Saturday morning, a green Ford Truck pulled up in front of Samantha Raven's house. Elizabeth was mowing the front yard when she saw the truck stop at the curb. She was decked out in her her favorite daisy dukes, t-Shirt, and sneakers with her hair in pigtails. She watched as a man exited the truck and headed up the driveway.

Liz stopped the lawn mower and stepped towards him. "Can I help you?"

Chapter 14

The first meeting

The man stopped in the driveway and looked at Liz. He was tall, 6 ft at least, maybe 200 lbs. He wasn't fat by any means but nice looking. He wore a white, short-sleeved, Guayabera shirt, jeans, a cowboy hat, and boots. He tipped his cowboy hat and smiled at Liz. "You must be Elizabeth. You look exactly like your mother."

Liz looked at him with utter distrust. "How do you know my mother?"

"Please allow me to introduce myself. I'm Trevor Paterson. I know your mother, well, we met this week at a business meeting. I wanted to ask her a few more questions, and I hope it is okay. I know she is a private person and don't want to intrude. If this is a bad time, I will leave."

Liz nodded slowly. "Wait right here. Let me get her." Liz bounded towards the house and glanced over her shoulder to make sure he was still there. She charged through the front screen door and found her mother vacuuming the living room. Sam was wearing her favorite jeans with a tank top with the same hairstyle as Liz.

Liz asked, "So when did you start dating?"

Sam shut off the vacuum. "What are you talking about, I'm not dating anyone."

Liz smiled knowingly. "Why is there a totally hot guy at the front door asking to see you?"

Sam stopped mid motion and turned to her daughter with a shocked look on her face. "What are you talking about, what man at our front door?"

She dropped the vacuum abruptly stormed to the front of the house. She pushed through the screen door and walked out onto the front porch. There wasn't anyone in sight, but the antique green ford truck was still parked on the street. Sam asked. "Liz. who are you talking about......?" As she turned around, she found him standing behind the screen door with his hat in his hand and a strange smile on his face. She didn't recognize him at first in his casual attire.

Sam was in a complete state of shock. How on earth did this man find her? Her first thought was," God, I look horrible!" After she regained her composure, she realized how invasive this stunt was. "How did you find my address, and what are you doing here? This is my home!" Anger flashed across her reddening face. "Who do you think you are coming to my house scaring my daughter half to death? You think I'm some kind of floozy that needs a man, so you checked me out? Is that your M.O.?"

Trevor's smile grew larger as he pushed away from the wall. He moved sideways towards the steps. "Sorry, Ms. Raven, but I like to know the people I'm going to do business with. So . . . yes! I checked you out. But I didn't mean to intrude, and I know you don't date men, no . . . no I mean . . . I know you don't bring clients home. I know I'm being a total jerk for coming over here unannounced, but I'm sorry. I just couldn't . . . I couldn't help myself. I had to come here. I just had to. I hope you can forgive me. Please?"

Sam scrutinized him as he was tried to charm his way out of trouble. Although her arms were securely crossed in front of her as she feigned anger, she wasn't angry. He was defiantly nervous, but he pushed the envelope, and that didn't sit well with Sam. Sam wasn't going to let him get off that easy. She put on a stone face and came at him, placing her hands on her hips. With a good foot of distance between them, she stared up at him and as coolly as possible. "This is unacceptable. My private life is my own, and you are not allowed to invade it for any reason. Are we clear?"

Trevor admired her face---he was familiar with that look and had seen it before. He longed to see it again. But now was not the time. He had gathered all of the information that he had been seeking. He took a step down from the stoop and nodded. "Ms. Raven, my humble apologies. I hope that in time you will find it in your heart to forgive me for this intrusion. I . . . I will leave now."

Infuriated, Sam backed away towards the door. Liz was standing just inside the door and asked. "You want to stay for lunch?" Sam turned sharply to look inside at her precocious daughter.

Trevor turned before Sam could say anything and offered, "Why don't I treat the two of you to lunch?"

Sam turned back to Trevor when she heard Liz reply, "How about Pizza?"

Sam looked back at her daughter when Trevor immediately offered, "Okay, I can have it delivered."

Sam shot a dirty look at Trevor. "Now wait a minute! I haven't agreed to anything!"

Liz quipped, "Ah mom, he doesn't look that dangerous; in fact, I think he's kind of cute."

Trevor now realized who was talking. Sam looked back sharply to face the door when Trevor stepped up behind her and remarked, "It looks like there is dissention in the ranks."

Sam turned quickly to face Trevor who was now directly behind her in two-inch heels boots that made him almost fourteen inches taller than her. She was eye-level with his chest, so she had to raise her eyes up to his. "I am the boss, and what I say goes!"

Trevor winked at her. "So, you're saying that we order the meat lover's?"

Sam tried her best to look as stern as possible and not give in. It wasn't that Trevor made her nervous. For some reason, she felt that familiar calmness from in the boardroom. His essence made her feel equally secure and anxious.

Sam couldn't put her finger on why this man was different, but she liked the sense of safety and serenity that warmed her in his presence. Women typically have a sixth sense that tells them about men. The innate ability to cultivate it and learn how to trust it reveals: if a man is lying, if he can be trusted, and if he is a cheater. Some women nurture this gift, and some choose to blindly ignore it at their own expense.

Sam's sense of cautious self-preservation allowed her to trust him, but her strict rule of not allowing any man into her house never been broken. She had not dated for quite some time and purposely avoided men for the sake of her daughter. Now her daughter was 15. Liz was starting to come into her own. This was not the time to change her parenting model.

She was worried about what letting him penetrate her world would signify. Liz crept out of the house and hugged her mother. "We normally get a supreme."

With that, Trevor made an executive decision. "Supreme it is . . . if your mother agrees. The last thing I want is to break any rules, so why don't you call it in while I finish mowing the lawn?"

Sam looked at Liz hesitantly. "Fine then. Call it in." She pointed authoritatively at Trevor. "You mow the lawn, and when it gets here, we can eat on the front porch."

Liz squeezed her mother and scampered off into the house. Trevor held back a shit-eating grin as he eyed Samantha momentarily. The small smile and eyes took in her face as she returned his penetrating gaze with curious wonderment, slightly perplexed at what was happening.

Trevor tossed his hat over to the bench on the front porch and trotted over to the lawn mower. With two sharp pulls, he started it and began mowing the lawn. Sam stood for a minute on the front porch and watched Trevor. It was so natural--- a man and a woman working together to comprise a family unit, much like the life she had imagined for herself when she was younger. The dream of the man as the supplier of the resources and the woman as the gifted homemaker came to life in this moment.

Sam retreated into the house. For some unknown reason, she felt tranquil around Trevor. She pulled the card table from the closet and noticed Liz who standing in the living room gawking at Trevor mowing the lawn. Sam lovingly embraced her daughter. They were almost the same height, and it wouldn't be long before Elizabeth would grow to the same height or taller. Sam sought her daughter's approval. "You like him?"

"What's not to like? He has manners, and the way he is attacking that front lawn shows that he doesn't mind hard work. And let's be honest---he is easy on the eyes."

Sam smiled. "But good looks are not everything. I'm not ready to bring a man into this house, especially not one I just met." She patted Liz on the shoulder. "Have you called the Pizza place to confirm their E.T.A.? Go get some dishes and set them up on the front porch."

"Yes. We have 20 minutes, and can't we eat at the table like civilized people?" Sam gave her daughter one of those impregnated looks that said everything---but most importantly, NO!

Sam excused herself to wash up for lunch and examined herself in the bathroom mirror. Oh God, this was not a good look, but if she changed, he might get the wrong impression. She let her hair down and brushed it back. "That's fine," she thought to herself. By the time pizza arrived, Trevor had finished the lawn. He gave the pizza delivery boy a fifty, thanked him, and told him to keep the change.

Sam placed the card table on the front porch while Liz grabbed some cups and soda. The trio settled in comfortably to the front-porch setting and dug in to the delicious, piping-hot pizza. After devouring her first slice, Liz looked at Trevor inquisitively. "So, tell me, how do you know my mom?"

Still chewing on his piece, Trevor held up one finger so he could swallow before answering. "She gave a presentation and proved how a woman could figure something out that it took a month for one of my best men to decipher---only she did it in one week. She gave an outstanding presentation, which is why I'm here. I want to know more about her."

Liz looked at Sam with one of those knowing smiles that says nothing but communicates volumes. Sam looked coolly at her daughter. "Don't get your hopes up. He is not staying."

Trevor laughed. "I guess she doesn't want fancy me as her boy toy."

Sam looked sharply at Trevor. "That is not true."

Liz retorted, "Oh! You want him as a boy toy?"

Sam gave Liz a look that could kill. "This is not a proper conversation between manager and employee."

Trevor sighed and agreed. He turned to Liz. "I understand you're quite the computer geek?"

Liz glanced back at her mother. "I don't know, not really."

Sam was staring daggers at Trevor. "Exactly how do you know what she likes?"

Trevor smiled again. He recognized a mother's instinct to detect any perceived threat against her child. He took gulp of his soft drink.

"I do my homework too. You did a whole lot of research on me; in fact, you went back to my great grandfather to find how my company started. I have it on good authority that you have a list of medals my grandfather won in WWII, and you know I went to Duke but only stayed one year. If I'm going to allow someone into my inner sanctum, I also want to know who they are, what they are, and what they want. And to answer your question, "I had a long talk with Jennifer in the hospital."

Chapter 15

A new customer

Sam was incensed. "You called Jennifer in the hospital?"

Trevor held up his hand as a form of surrender. "No! She called me, and we had a long talk. She apologized for having appendicitis on that day. I told her that I was looking forward to meeting her, but you covered for her brilliantly. She told me how gifted you are in your research skills and that your daughter was a computer geek---which begs my next question. Liz, what kind of computer do you have?"

Sam approved of his directness and the compliments that he so willing dished out, but she felt that he invaded her privacy. He knew something about her that she didn't know about him. As she chomped down on another bite of her pizza, she pondered her situation. *Here was a man who took the time to research her. What else did he find out? What was his take on her?* This juxtaposition of enthusiasm and apprehension toyed with her *mentally*.

Liz finally responded to his question." It's not anything special. It's an old computer with a standard processor and hard drive. I would love to get one of those <u>Solid-State Drives</u> and see how fast they are."

Trevor gave Liz some insight. "Yea, I had one put into my old laptop, and it's speed is unbelievable. It's better than my other laptop with a faster processor. Those SSDs are good if you can afford them. You are welcome to come see it some time."

Sam interrupted. "We don't need to upgrade our computer. It's working just fine."

Liz was frustrated. "But mom, it could be so much faster."

Sam gave that look again, but Trevor sided with her this time. "Now listen to your mother. Her track record of making good decisions has been outstanding. Anyway Liz, when you do your research, do you use a VPN service?"

Liz shrugged her shoulders. "We can't afford one. Mom says they are too expensive."

When Sam couldn't speak with her mouthful of pizza, Trevor faced her. "Look, both of you research from home, and I think it is unsafe to do that without a VPN. Can I supply you with one?" Sam almost choked on her food, which caused Trevor to chuckle.

Liz replied, "That would be great. What do you think, mom?"

Sam swallowed her food and turned to Trevor. "This is too much too fast. I don't even work for you and . . ."

Trevor held up a finger to shush her. "Hold that thought! Wait here." Trevor retrieved a folder and a GPS from his truck and placed them on the table. He leaned over to whisper something into Liz's ear, and she immediately darted into the house.

Sam eyed Trevor suspiciously and asked, "What are you doing?" Liz came bounding out of the house with a pen and handed it to Trevor. He took the pen and continued to thumb through the pages. Sam recognized the papers as the contract.

Trevor gave Sam a reassuring look. "I've resolved the issue of you working for me." He found the page he was looking for, signed it, and dated it. "Okay, I have just hired your firm; I will not allow access to anyone else except you at my house."

Sam sat back with a confused look on her face. "Me? Your house? What does your house have to do with it?" The prospect of going to his house was daunting. She wasn't expecting this, and she still didn't understand the way he made her feel. Being alone in his house made her feel somewhat unnerved.

Trevor was pleased that Liz who was smiling from ear to ear and turned his attention to Sam. "I have a little house about an hour from here; it's not much, but I call it home. The information you requested is there." He picked up the folder and GPS and placed them in front of Sam. "Plug the GPS in and hit home. It will take you there."

Sam stared at the items on the table. "Who will be there?"

Trevor looked pleased. "I'm leaving tomorrow for San Francisco, but I will return on Tuesday. Can you come on Wednesday?"

Sam was still looking at the GPS, mulling over the auspice of going to this man's house alone. She was about to say no, but Trevor could see the war that was waging within her. "But before you get any ideas, please understand we won't be alone. I have a staff, and we work very hard there."

Liz giggled. "So, you going mom?"

Sam eyes cut sharply to Liz and then to Trevor. She wasn't having ideas, but she was worried about him having ideas. Knowing they won't be alone put some of her fears to bed, but she was still a bit uneasy. She sat back in her chair, fixated on him. Briefly, she dared to fantasize about being alone with him, about the two of them getting dangerously close---closer than she had allowed a man to come in years. With her eyes closed, she was able to bring the thought to a halt, and nod in affirmation. "Okay, because this is for business, I will come out Wednesday; I can be there by 9."

The smile on Trevor's face delighted and frightened her. She enjoyed his smile, but he was a little too happy at the news of having her at his house. Of course, he said they wouldn't be alone, but she couldn't be sure until she arrived. Trevor confirmed," That will be fine. I look forward to seeing you." Sam thought to herself, *I'm sure you will be.*

Trevor stood up. "I hate to eat and run, but I need to get ready. Can I help you with all of this?"

Sam refused, and Trevor grabbed his hat and started towards his truck. He stopped halfway, turned around, and looked for several seconds at the two women still sitting on the porch. They heard the low rumble as the engine started and drove off. Sam and Liz sat there looking at each other.

Liz broke the silence. "He likes you."

"What makes you say that?"

"Mom, I'm 15, not blind. You like him."

Sam tried to deny it but knew her daughter was right. "Yes, I like him, but that doesn't mean anything. I have met a lot of men I liked, but none of them worked out. Now grab the plates."

"So…you gonna let him buy us a subscription to VPN?"

Sam was picking up the trash and putting it into the pizza box. "We'll see." With that, they walked into the house.

Sam folded up the table when she thought back to the last time she allowed a man to get close---she naturally thought of and how he used his charm to break down her barriers until she reluctantly gave in and began seeing him. He had escorted her to the library and told her stories of John Locke, a philosopher whose writings captivated her. He explained how John Locke's sense of politics was lousy, and he tended to pick the wrong politicians. It wasn't long before she was doubled over laughing, despite her efforts to ignore him.

After their stint in the library, they were finally kicked out because she couldn't contain her laughter. He provided her with ample information for her report, but the price was that now she was totally smitten. They started hanging out together on weekends. It took a while before she agreed to go to his place---she knew what would happen if she entered his personal space. And she was right.

Sam peered through the screen door at the freshly mowed lawn and thought about that Thanksgiving weekend when Tip made love to her for the first time. She previously had a brief fling as a senior in high school and gave into a seductive young man. Unfortunately, it was a wham bam thank you ma'am one-night stand, and he shamed her by bragging about it to all of his friends.

Sam was traumatized by this indiscretion, but when Tip moved in on her, she was powerless to stop him. Nothing was "wham bam" about his debonair demeanor. He took his time and made her suffer until he finally fulfilled her ultimate fantasy of having an orgasm that almost caused her to pass out. She thought that was it, but he toyed with, her enticed her, and made her feel wanted. Tip slowly and carefully brought her to fulfillment two more times---the last time leaving her in a sexually induced coma that finished her off for the night.

The next morning when she woke, she found him lying next to her watching her sleep, with a smile. He was still hungry for her and tried to start it up again. Sam squirmed as he began teasing her and let out a plaintive cry. "What are you doing? . . . Oh, God! . . . Tip . . . Tip . . . AHHHHHH!"

Tip allowed her to catch her breath before asking, "Ready to do it again?"

Sam looked up into his face and pleaded joyfully. "Again?"

The only time they left the bedroom that weekend was to eat and use the restroom. They spent most of Saturday and Sunday in carnal bliss. By Monday, she was sore in all the right places, and her mind was mush. Samantha was in seventh heaven.

Suddenly, Liz walked back in from washing the dishes and broke Sam's nostalgic trance. "Mom, are you okay?"

Sam snapped out of it. "Oh! Yes! Why?"

Liz gave her a funny look. "Because you have been standing there holding that card table for 10 minutes."

"Oh! Yes, I need to put this away."

" He got you thinking, didn't he?"

"Who, honey? What?"

Liz just laughed and walked away. Sam put her hands to her face, shook her head, and thought, *get a grip, Samantha!*"

Chapter 16

A mother and daughter conversation

That evening after dinner, they settled onto the large sofa in the living room. Sam was reading a book at one end of the sofa, and Liz was reading a book at the other. Sam just settled down with a glass of red wine.

They didn't own a TV. Once Sam's parents' TV died, they didn't see the need for a new one. In order to cut costs, they didn't have cable, only DSL for the computer. During the evenings, they would sit on the couch, read, and talk.

Suddenly, Liz looked up from her book at her mother. A smile slowly crept across her face. "So…you going to see Mr. Trevor at his house on Wednesday?"

Sam looked up from the page she was reading. "Yes, I have cleared it with Jennifer, and I will be going to his house on business."

Liz was still smiling. "Okay, just business…of course. You will be there all alone with one nice hunk of a man, with no one around."

"Get your mind out of the gutter. I'm not going there for that, and you know it."

Liz was highly amused. She knew when her mother got angry it meant that Liz was hitting a soft spot. "I'm not thinking anything, but he is a hunk, and you think so too. I saw the way you watched him. You changed your hair, and he noticed. Come on, be honest."

Sam took a sip of her merlot. "Fine, yes, he is very nice looking, but . . . I have no plans of getting any more involved with him than the business deal we have arranged." She took a sizeable gulp of wine this time.

Liz leaned forward. "Can I have a sip?" Sam gave her glass to Liz for a sip, if Liz wanted to drink wine, she could take some while Sam was at work, but it was better if she knew it was okay as long as they were together. Liz took a sip and handed the glass back.

Sam looked at her daughter with introspection. "How did that taste?"

"It was nice. Can I have some more?" Sam thought about this. In Europe, youths drink wine as early as 12 years old. That way, they learn how to handle intoxicating beverages so that when they grow up, they know how to deal with it. In the US, we normally frown upon that, thinking we are corrupting our youth. For that matter, Europe's rate of alcoholism is significantly lower than that of the U.S.

Sam disappeared into the kitchen and filled a wine glass with 1/4 water, topping it off with wine before handing it to Liz. She knew it was time for one of those mother/daughter talks.

Sam asked, "You obviously want to know something. What is it?"

Liz took a sip of her wine and looked at her mother. "It's better without the water, but yes, I have a question. Who was my daddy?"

"It's better for you to start off light, and he was a man I met in college. We had a torrid affair, and I never saw him again."

"You never tried to find him?"

Sam sighed. "Yes, but no one knew where he was, or how to find him. He just disappeared."

"Do you regret having me?"

"Never! Not for one second. You are everything to me."

Liz had partaken in wine before, but she was not used to drinking from her own glass---it was affecting her. It gave her the liquid courage to ask some hard questions, and she wanted to ask them right now before she lost her nerve. This was probably why her mother was allowing her to drink---to get it out.

Liz stumbled clumsily over her words. "If you could find him, would you?"

Sam nodded yes. "I have tried. The problem is he went by a nickname, "Tip," and no one I talked too knew his real name. The registrar's office refused to help because he was enrolled under an anonymous scholarship. I wasn't family, so they couldn't release any information. "

"So, you just gave up?"

"It wasn't as if I wanted to give up. I tried for several years but I was penniless, and I had to build a life for us. I focused on getting my degree to earn more money, and somehow, finding him just became less and less important over the years. Besides, we are doing just fine without him, aren't we?"

Liz smiled took a more sizeable swig of wine. "We are okay, but it would be nice to have a man around. I go over to Mathew's house, and he has both parents. It would just be nice, that's all.

Sam tried to lighten the mood. "Yea, it would be nice to have someone who could fix the roof, or change the oil in the car, or mow the lawn!"

"Yes! Mow the grass, I was so happy when he said he would mow the grass; I hate mowing the grass."

"But with a man around all the time, you have to put up with man things---like leaving the toilet seat up, smelling up the bathroom, taking up the bed, and stomping all over the place as they walk. And the worst of all is having menial tasks 'mansplained' to you when you clearly don't need it."

Liz gazed bleary-eyed and lovingly at her mother. "I liked the way Trevor smelled and how he stomped around the front porch. I don't know what he would do in the bathroom--- that would be your problem."

Sam's jaw dropped to the floor. "My problem? Why would that be my problem?"

Liz became playfully emboldened as she sipped more wine. "Well, you would be the one sleeping with him, not me."

Sam threw a pillow at her daughter. "What makes you think I will be sleeping with him?"

Liz knew that statement would earn her a pillow and caught it. "Yea, now that you mention it, he doesn't look like the type that would be sleeping that much anyway."

Sam searched for a second pillow to throw as ammunition for the back-and-forth banter. "First off, what do you know about that, and what else would we be doing?"

Liz tossed the pillow back just as Sam put her glass on the coffee table. "I can read, I read the Color of Grey, and I took sex ed. at school, but that was a joke. And besides, there is always porn."

Sam caught the pillow. "I had no choice in the sex ed thing, and as for the Fifty Shades of Grey, that was not a healthy sexual relationship. And where did you get a copy of that? What exactly do you mean by 'porn'?"

Liz guffawed with grape-infused confidence. "Mathew stole a copy from his mother when she began book two. I have seen some porn, and it's everywhere."

Sam tried to contain her amusement. "I'll have to talk to Mathew's mother, and you don't need to be looking at porn."

"Well, how else am I going to learn about sex? I don't have a father around to ask."

Sam snorted. She was feeling the wine having now killed her glass. "Oh, please! A man is the last place you want to go for sexual advice. All they want is to get into your pants and dump you."

Liz was feeling the wine too, and that statement dulled the mood. "Is that what my father did---have sex with you and dump you?"

Sam was suddenly lost in a contemplative recollection. "I thought he was a very nice man. He was easy to be with---gentle, patient, and God was he a great lover! Yes, I was head over heels in love. When he suddenly disappeared, it turned my world upside down. I really didn't think he would do that to me, but he did. I'm sorry honey, but I guess I should have chosen a better man to father my child. I thought I was making a good choice, but I was wrong. "

Liz could feel her mother's pain at having to admit that. The woman gets pregnant and bears the child. It is her job to choose the man to father the child, and if she chooses correctly, she gets a man that will go the distance. If she chooses wrong, it can go wrong---sometimes very wrong. In Sam's case, he just disappeared. He could have stayed around and resented her getting pregnant. Even when men are also to blame, their bitterness often manifests as physical violence, emotional battering, and the eventual demise of the mother and the child. In the case of Samantha and Elizabeth Raven, they were lucky enough to avoid this fate. They were thriving and surviving, impervious to any ill-treatment.

Liz looked at her mother. "But let's say . . . there was no reason for you not to, and when you arrived at Mr. Paterson's house, he was the only one there. Picture the two of you---alone and hidden from the eyes of the public. Would you?"

Suddenly, the sad face that Sam was wearing slowly changed as a wicked smile crept upon her face. "No repercussions; no damage; no one knowing. God, he is handsome! He smelled very nice, and he did respect my boundaries of no man in the house. He didn't question it. He simply accepted my decision and mowed the grass. I don't know. But no, I would have to say no, because every deed done in darkness eventually comes into the light. Someone will find out---no, I refuse to do that to you."

Liz giggled. "But you at least thought about it, didn't you? Don't deny it. I saw that look on your face. You like him, and if he made a move, what would you do?"

"Ha--- to have a man again! That would be nice, but no, it is a recipe for disaster. Trust me, it never works out. Life is not a fantasy. I won't bring a man into your life that I can't trust. I don't know him well enough to trust him, and I'm not giving into some lascivious infatuation for an empty one-night stand."

Liz stood up then bent over and kissed her mother on the forehead. She picked up her book and started toward her bedroom. Sam suddenly sat up. "You going to your room to watch porn?"

Liz laughed. "I don't have a computer in my room, mom, so no, I'm not going to watch porn." Sam relaxed back into the sofa and thought to herself, *I don't need porn. I have memories of Tip.*

Chapter 17

The Hunter becomes the Hunted

On first Sunday in May, in a small-town alley behind a row of buildings, a large man forced himself out of a black Cadillac. He walked over and pounded on the door of the building. It took a minute before the slide opened up. No words were spoken between the man standing there and the person on the inside, but the slide closed, and the door opened. He charged up the stairs.

He was out of breath and sweating by the time he climbed the stairs and stumbled into the office. "Hi, boss." Jimmy Dittle turned around in his chair from the monitors that were on the wall. The room was lit mostly by two skylights that adequately illuminated the room. Filled with cheap furniture, it reeked of cigars and spilled whiskey. Jimmy sat at a large desk to the left of the door. He spun around to the large man and leaned back in his chair.

The room was large with a table to the right and just inside the door; to its left was a rug in front of an old dark brown couch. At the other end of the room was another door that led to the main hallway with the rooms where he kept his whores. The customers would actually enter from a door in the alley on the other side of the building. Jimmy's setup showed that he infrequently dealt with the public.

Jimmy glared at the large rotund man. "What can you tell me about this Samantha Raven bitch?"

The large man shook his head and settled into a large chair in front of the desk. He pulled out a notebook and flipped through the pages. "Not much. I checked with the police department, and she has no warrants, speeding tickets---nothing. According to her DMV records, she drives a white VW beetle convertible. The parking garage attendant pointed out her parking spot in the garage."

Jimmy didn't look happy. He placed his forearms on the desk and gritted his teeth. "What good is a crooked cop on my payroll if I can't get the information I need?! You think I let you fuck my girls for free?"

Jasper responded, "Look, I'm no longer on the force, so I'm not a crooked cop."

Jimmy was irate. "I don't care! I want that bitch under our thumb. The IRS is asking questions about the investment I made with the Union Retirement Fund. If they find out I used it for whorehouses, they won't like it. And if they pinch me, they will anonymously receive the movies of you fucking that 12-year-old. Do we have an understanding here?"

Jasper shifted nervously. "I thought you said if I did that thing for you, you would destroy it."

Jimmy leaned back in his chair. "I lied. Why I would destroy the best weapon I have to fuck your ass? Let me make this crystal clear---I want that bitch. I want to know where she lives and where she goes. I want to fuck that whore like she fucked me. Got it?"

The large man nodded and started to push his way out of the chair. Once he got to his feet, he straightened his coat and started for the door. "I'll find her, boss. You can trust me."

Jimmy turned back to the wall of monitors. "I believe in results---get me that bitch." The large man exited.

That Monday, Liz had finished her homework and sat back down to look at her investigation into Jimmy Dittle. She knew that this man was dangerous, maybe even deadly. But she felt confident in her ability to remain hidden and believed she could dig up something that would help her mother.

She knew he was going to ask for a picture, but she was be careful not to use a picture taken from a cell phone. If GPS is enabled on the phone, which it is on most smart phones, it will embed the GPS coordinates into the properties of the pictures. A simple photo, even a mundane one taken within a room with no marking or pictures, could alert someone to the location via the properties of the jpeg.

She decided to use a GIF instead. Using her digital camera, she took it to her room. Once she made sure there was nothing on the wall behind her she set the camera to movie mode and streamed a small video of herself.

Afterwards, she edited the video down and embedded a Trojan virus into the video stream. She was now ready to infect Jimmy's computer. She figured out which person on Facebook was Jimmy Dittle and sent him a poke. He responded and asked for a picture.

When she was ready to comply with his request for her picture, he was going to be happy with this GIF. Liz signed onto Facebook as "Tweenie" and saw Jimmy's message. He was still keeping up communication and asked again for a picture. *Should she send it now?* She decided to tease him.

She pulled up Jimmy's message and read, "I am here for you whenever you want to talk. Sorry to keep missing you---can you send me a picture?

Liz decided to string him along. "I would love to send a picture. I will take some pictures and send them to you when I can." She sent the message and went back to her other research.

First, she went back to locate to her file from Intelex. She wanted to find what property he might own, but it didn't list any. He must have put his property into some corporation's name so it couldn't be traced back to him. She sat back to think of where she could go now and heard a "ding" that indicated a new message.

The message was from Jimmy. "Okay, I understand, but I have my picture on my site, so you know what I look like. Why can't you send me yours? You can't be that bad looking?" Liz his picture was fake---no surprise there---but she figured he was begging now, let him have it. She attached her GIF and sent the message. It would take a while for the Trojan to take effect, but she would have access to his computer by tomorrow. Liz logged out of Facebook and shut the computer down.

As she was getting up, her mother called and said, she would be home shortly. Liz went into the kitchen to start dinner. After dinner, the two ladies snuggled into the old, overstuffed couch in the living room where they usually spent time talking, reading, or both. These quiet times on the couch meant the most to both women, and this was going to be one of them.

Chapter 18

The Plantation

On Tuesday, Jimmy Dittle stewed in his office. He opened up his Facebook page, and much to his delight, there was a message from Tweenie. Jimmy grinned when he saw the GIF. He immediately downloaded it onto his desktop and clicked on the picture. He clicked it again and watched it again…he clicked it again and again he watched it. He smiled and sent a message to his greenest conquest. "Tweenie; why don't you use my private email address? It is jd17@yahoo.com." It was 3 in the morning, when he opened message, and he was impatient. He figured that it will be that afternoon before he would get a reply.

Jimmy reclined in his desk chair and scanned all the screens on the wall behind his desk. Each monitor was wired to a camera connected to 16 rooms. Inside 12 of those rooms was a teenage girl servicing customers for him…and this wasn't his only elaborate setup. He had three more where could watch each girl having sex. In his twisted mind, the porn industry was paying him while he benefited as a sadistic voyeur.

He scouted his girls at various venues, but he remained hidden as the master. For example, he offered young men a monetary reward for each girl they brought to him. These demonic minions monitored the bus stations for runaways whom they seduced and sold against their will. On nights when the savagery of these minions reached peak performance, they would pick up a young girl of 12 to 14---date her, have sex with her, abscond with her across state lines, and sell her to Jimmy. Jimmy had no qualms about drugging the girls to make induce submission. The problem was that when their unsullied looks and childlike dispositions faded from forced trauma, customers no longer wanted them. Jimmy would have to "dispose" of them for fear of being exposed.

His favorite recruitment venue was through social web sites. He frequented Facebook and Craigslist the most. When he rescued a lost soul, he earned their trust and convinced them to meet him somewhere----somewhere that he could discreetly kidnap them. He raped them into submission and put them to work. Once he had a full house, he contacted an acquaintance in another city or state and sold the girls, who were essentially lost at this point. It was a miracle if any of these girls made it to age 21. This trap was, in fact, a death sentence. He couldn't risk getting busted by disposable vaginas that could implicate him once they realized their rights as mature adults. But that problem is easily solvable for a soulless monster parading as a human.

On Wednesday, Sam didn't go into the office. She did some paperwork from home and emailed the updated files to Jennifer. She left the house at around 8am. It was a nice day, so Samantha put the top down on her car and wrapped a scarf over her head. She pulled the GPS out, plugged it into the power port, and laid it on the console. It would take a minute to connect to the satellites, so she put the car into gear and started to leave. Once she was on the street, it recalculated. Suddenly the voice of a 12-year-old girl announced. "You've really done it now!" It recalculated and instructed. "Turn left onto route 11. Drive straight."

Sam looked at the GPS in disbelief. *This must be some kind* of joke---he has a 12-year-old girl giving him directions! For the next forty-five minutes, she listened as the girl told her to turn left, turn right, and the one she really loved, "Somebody is not listening!" Finally, she was told to turn left, and she passed between two large, concrete pillars. She saw the plaque on the gate "Paterson Corp" as she passed through. She assumed it was the correct place. The narrow road was barely two lanes, and it curved left before leading down a straight away. Then there was a left turn trough some low-hanging limb that suddenly revealed a large, open area in front of a house.

Sam slammed on her breaks; she couldn't believe her eyes! His "little house" was easily over 50,000 sq. ft. It was white with a portico in the center section that rose three stories. There was a two-storied wing on each side that extended out from the center.

The drive continued directly toward the house, curved to the right, and circled in front of the building with a parking area where several cars were already parked. The exit route was convoluted_and seemed to lead back into the abyss of the forest. She couldn't believe her eyes. This is the little house? This must be where he was spending his money.

Sam drove slowly toward the building and parked in one of the numerous open spaces. As she parked, the 12-year-old girl proudly announced, "You've reached your destination, now get out of the car!" Sam shook her head as she turned it off and unplugged it. She grabbed her brief case and exited the vehicle. There were at least six other parked cars of varying makes and models. None would be considered collectables, but the green truck wasn't there.

Sam walked across the small parking lot with her brief case and toward the double front doors. She stopped and turned to absorb the landscape when the door swung open behind her. There stood the blond woman Sam recognized from the photos.

She was beautiful without makeup. She was wearing a light blue workout outfit and tennis shoes, with her hair pulled back into a ponytail. Sam extended her hand. "Hi! I'm Samantha Raven, and I'm here to see Mr. Paterson."

The woman warmly clasped her hand. "You're Sam. Is it okay for me to call you Sam? It's a pleasure to meet you. You're a little early, but come on in."

Sam nodded. "Sam is fine." The woman's knowing smile indicated she knew something that Sam didn't.

Sam entered a foyer that was as large as her house. She suddenly realized that the first two floors of the center section comprised one floor. The floor was white marble with two circular stairways on each side of the foyer. As she took it all in, the blonde approached her. "My name is Jamie, and I work for Mr. Paterson."

Sam nodded. "I have seen you in the pictures of Mr. Paterson's public appearances. I must say that you're very photogenic."

Jamie laughed. "Come on; he's this way."

They walked through the foyer and exited onto a balcony that ran along the back of the house. Sam noticed a pool with two young, bikini-clad girls. One was on her laptop while the other was swimming. Sam figured they were his girl toys and remained silent. Jamie noticed Sam's reaction to this unconventional scene." Those are the daughters of one of the guys working here. They are on break from college and are more comfortable here because boys won't bother them. "Sam's tilted her head and gazed gracefully.

They continued along the balcony until they reached two doors that opened into the gym area. The room was 30 ft by 60 ft with a sizable square ring in the center. The two people fighting, wearing headgear, gloves, and body pads. Several people watched and cheered when a good punch was thrown.

Much to Sam's surprise, one was a man and the other a woman. She watched as they traded punches. The woman deftly stepped to her right, hitting him with her elbow. Before Sam knew it, she spun around and delivered another powerful blow with the back of her other elbow-

--the man flew back against the ropes! She caught him in a headlock on the rebound and tossed him over her hip onto the floor. She almost had him pinned when he twisted out and punched her with a couple of body blows, including one to the head.

Chapter 19

The fight

Sam leaned over and whispered into Jamie's ear, "Where is Mr. Paterson?" Jamie pointed to the ring. Sam was dumbfounded; he was in the ring fighting a woman. But the woman wasn't losing! She wasn't sure about him---the woman was dishing out blows as well as she was receiving them. He wasn't cutting her any slack, and she wasn't asking for any. Oddly, she was not phased in the slightest by his male prowess. Sam was impressed and appalled.

The woman delivered a vicious right hook followed by couple of body shots and an over-the-hip toss. He landed with a resonant thud, and she was still on top throwing punches. As he cowered in fear, she whirled around and captured him in an arm bar. Trevor tapped out immediately because the woman was the obvious victor.

Several men bounded into the ring and removed the protective gear from both fighters. Trevor hugged his opponent with an air of admiration and she hugged him back followed by a kiss on the cheek. When he noticed Sam standing with Jamie, he walked over to the ropes and yelled, "I see you found the place---glad you came! Jamie, kindly show her to my office. I will be there after my shower." Jamie nodded and motioned for Sam to follow her.

They ascended the stairs and entered a large room with a vaulted ceiling that must have been at least 12-feet high. The floor-to-ceiling windows bathed the majestic room in sunlight and made the antique-chic furniture sparkle in the classiest manner possible. Trevor had a cozy setup and the built-in bookshelves that lined the walls indicated that he had deeper and contemplative levels beneath the mask that he wore for those excluded from his inner circle. Sam turned to Jamie. "Excuse me, but that wasn't boxing. What was that?"

Jamie grinned as if she had heard this question before. "Have you ever heard of cage fighting? Sam shook her head no.

Jamie continued. "It has been around for over a thousand years under different names, but the most recent term is ultimate fighting, or the Octagon. You may know it as MMA or Mixed Martial Arts. Fighters can use whatever technique they feel is necessary to win. Judo is a major component as well as boxing and karate. It is as close to street fighting as you can get without sparring illegally in the streets. The female fighter is Susan Walker, and until she retired, she was ranked 3rd in the world in female MMA."

Sam nonverbally agreed. "Let me get this straight---I shouldn't be surprised that she was able to beat Mr. Paterson?"

Jamie chuckled. "Given the fact that he is giving her 10 years plus daily training, I would say that there are very few men who would be able to take her."

Sam surveyed the office. "This is a beautiful room."

Jamie pointed to the books on the shelves. "You see all these books? They are in three different languages and don't even make it to the shelves unless he reads them. Over here, you can see that he has met with different leaders all over the world." Jamie walked deeper into the room. "He worked with the man in Pakistan who made this table and that desk over there. He is fluent in French, Spanish, and Urdu." Jamie paused strategically beside the table. "This is the family's old homestead. It has been in their family for over 200 years, and he owns the 5000 acres that surround it."

Sam interjected, "Speaking of family, I always see you in the pictures with him. Are you his girlfriend or wife? Does he have children?"

Jamie's smile broadened. "No, I'm not... my mate might find that offensive, so the coast is clear---but between us girls, several women have tried, and all have failed."

Sam was slightly embarrassed by her presumptuousness. "No, I'm sorry, No---I just like to know as much as I can about the person I'm working for. That's all. What does your husband think of all of this?"

"You saw my mate---she was the woman he was just fighting."

Sam took a step back and put her hand to her chest. "Excuse me; your mate is that woman?"

Sam felt a duality of relief and confusion. "But I have seen you and her in several photos with him---I don't' understand."

" Well, it is pretty simple. Trevor likes to say when you look at the three of us---Susan, Trevor, and me---just consider us the three lesbians."

Sam's face displayed utter confusion. "Wait, Trevor is a man. He can't be a lesbian . . . can he?"

Jamie found Sam's bewilderment highly amusing. " It is all in what you consider a lesbian. For example, what do lesbians like?"

Sam started to reply with a naivety but stopped herself when she caught Jamie's drift. "But he is such a handsome man. Haven't you ever … considered … maybe?"

Jamie was used to this line of questioning and not at all offended by it. "I have never been attracted to a man, but if I was going to do one, it would be him---and if you tell him, I will deny it. "

Sam twisted the lock on the key to her lips as a friendly gesture. "But as a lesbian "man," what does he do for female companionship? Or is he celibate?"

Jamie guffawed. "Him? Oh! Hell no. He dates occasionally and he has a woman he visits in Atlanta from time to time when he needs… that type of attention."

Sam understood that this arrangement was more of a throuple based on factors that surpassed sexual satisfaction…at least for Trevor. "Oh! Isn't that interesting? So, he does date. By the way, did he know you were a…that…before he hired you?"

" I told him I had just been kicked out of the army for being a lesbian. I was their top marksman, and I held three belts in martial arts. I'm an expert in all kind of weapons and one of only 5 women, who ever gained entrance into the Delta school and passed, but they kicked me out. It was in the papers. I figured you knew."

Sam respectfully pitied Jamie. "What happened?"

"I was deeply depressed, so I found this seedy hotel with a redneck bar where I got drunker than I should have. Several of the men there were not behaving like proper Christian gentlemen, so to say. I got into a fight with two of them, and two more jumped in. I was losing and knew I was going to be raped, when this mystery guy stepped in and fought alongside me. After I broke free, the two of us mopped the floor with about 10 guys.

Together, we defeated them by a landslide. That was the night Trevor penetrated my life and asked me to come work for him. I asked him if he knew I was a lesbian. He confirmed that he was fine with it and simply asked if there any other assists he should know about."

Sam was taken aback. "Did you ask him why?"

" We both were drunk, me especially, and we stumbled out of the bar. I had a room, so we crashed on the king bed together that night---fully dressed! I awoke the next day in his arms."

Sam was unsure if she was following the story correctly. "What did you do?"

Jamie reassured her. "I wanted to see what he would do, and even though he had the universal, male predicament of morning wood, he didn't do anything. I got up and hit him."

"Why?"

"I asked him, 'what kind of man sleeps with a woman and doesn't try to cop a feel? I wasn't interested, but my ego was bruised."

Sam laughed because she understood completely. "What did he say?"

" He said he didn't think it would be appropriate, but he wouldn't mind at all if it made me feel better. We have been thick as thieves since that morning. I think he was drawn to me because he needed a woman to accompany him to these public events. With me as his arm candy, other women would surely keep their distance---and most have. In a sense, he is safe with me. That is what he wanted. Besides, very few people consider me a threat because I don't resemble the stereotypical bodyguard. And if anybody tries to hurt my friend, they will answer to me. Understand?" Sam nodded in compliance.

Suddenly, they heard a door slam. Trevor had finished up at the gym and joined them.

Chapter 20

Sam's first day a work

Trevor stood right inside of the door. His freshly washed hair was still a wet mess and looked like a model for a men's body wash commercial with his towel casually draped around his neck and his t-shirt in hand. His white, ghee-type pants barely clung to his hips, trying desperately not to fall down to his bare feet. His well-defined chest and six pack abs were impossible to ignore. Despite the protective gear, Sam could see the cuts and bruises he sustained from the fight. Sam could not help but think, *God, is he beautiful.*

He tossed the towel onto the chair and strolled into the room. Sam caught her breadth and put her hand to her mouth. Trevor asked, "Jamie, are you giving the secret recipe away already?" Sam pried her eyes off Trevor and turned to face Jamie as her thoughts ran wild. *Why was he affecting me this way, damn it?!* Jamie chuckled quietly at the restrained anguish painted all over Sam's face.

Jamie leaned against the table. "Na, just the keys to the kingdom. I'll leave you two alone." She looked at Sam and delivered a playful punch to Trevor's shoulder as she went on about her business.

Trevor winced. "Ouch!" and continued towards Sam. Sam raised her hand to plead with Jamie to stay, as if to say, *Oh, God! Don't leave . . . me alone . . . in here with him!* But it was too late.

Just before Jamie left, she winked back at no one in particular. Sam wondered what this wink meant…it could have multiple interpretations. She wasn't sure, but she suspected that all he was wearing was those pants, and they were getting ready to fall off. Oh, please don't fall off! ---Oh, please do fall off! Sam took a moment to gain her composure.

Trevor's eyes were steady on Sam as she looked up at him. His Mona Lisa smile just spied a delicious morsel and wanted to devour it. Sam had an undeniable feeling that she was that morsel---and she liked it. Her mind was racing with contradictions. Is he going to take me? Yes, take me--- no, you can't do that! I will definitely let him if he wants to, but I MUST say no, but how can I when I can't speak? Can I speak? Please let me speak.

He was within arm's length now, and she placed her hand on his chest, foolishly thinking she could halt his advance…but when the tips of her fingers made contact, she almost went weak in the knees and clumsily stumbled into the antique table. She steadied herself with the edge of the table as the distance shrank between them.

Sam muttered in thinly veiled ecstasy, "Mr. Paterson can . . . could you . . . would you . . . Please put on your shirt?" Her hand was still on his irresistible chest. It was warm and smooth but also manly. He obviously didn't shave this area of his body, but he wasn't covered in a rug of gorilla-like fur that needed to be manscaped. She struggled to draw her hand back, but the effort was pointless. She yearned to surrender, and her natural instinct of reason was rapidly fading away as desire took the wheel. Trevor tossed the t-shirt onto the table beside her.

Sam suddenly felt weak and tried to back up, but the table wouldn't move. She closed her eyes and turned her head to one side, trying to catch her breath---she was shaking. He was standing just inches away; she could feel his warmth and smell his cologne.

Trevor broke the silence. "In every picture I have seen of you, your hair was in a bun." He reached up and pulled the hairpin that held the bun, and her hair fell down across her shoulders. He gently pushed it back behind her ears, and his touch was like a soft caress that sent shivers down her spine.

Sam was adamant that she wasn't going to let him affect her in this way. She wasn't some innocent schoolgirl with a first-time crush. She had a teenage daughter to protect, and she had to put her maternal responsibilities first.

Her renewed determination vanished the moment she focused upon his eyes. She closed them and melted away. Every time she looked at him, some type of carnal desperation rose from within her. No! This feeling was all too familiar and riddled with red flags. Why is he doing this, and how can he do this? I can't let him do this to me.

Sam's thoughts were a cornucopia of mixed emotions. *If he kisses me, I won't be able to handle it. Dear God, please don't kiss me or touch me---it has been so long, and no, I can't handle this, no.* Trevor whispered, "I definitely like it better this way." It took all of her strength to answer him. "Mr. Paterson . . . I'm here to work . . . not this, please don't, I . . . I can't . . . please!"

She paused because she knew he was going to touch her. If he started to kiss her, she would be lost in sweet oblivion. She snapped out of it when she heard his voice from across the room and noticed him walking towards his desk while putting his shirt on.

Sam was relieved and upset. At least she knew she had the power to say no, but she wouldn't mean it. He respected her wishes, and she appreciated this courtesy. But she hadn't had a man in so long, and he is so . . . he was . . . and he just walked away. *Damn him!*

Sam straightened her jacket, adjusted her glasses, and started to walk toward the desk, albeit a little shaky, but she was able to maintain control. She took a seat in one of the chairs next to her briefcase.

Trevor sat down behind his desk. "Okay, you'll need to first look at the books of the new companies and Oakwood to fine tune the pricing structure. I have assembled the records in an office just down the hall, and you can work there. After we have developed that strategy, you will probably want access to more records. Whatever you need, don't hesitate to ask. We have lunch on the veranda at 12, and I would like for you to join us, if that is acceptable."

Sam sat there watching him. He was so at ease, as if the precursor to a modern romance novel didn't just happen. What was his angle here? He knew he turned her on, and she knew that he felt the same way. A woman can usually detect a man's feelings before he is even aware of what is happening…but he just walked away. He dialed Jamie phone to alert her that they were ready, and she promptly appeared. Sam followed Jamie out, but not before Jamie retrieved something from the table. They exited through the second door and down the hall to another office. It was like Trevor's office but smaller.

The high ceiling hovered over a hand-carved desk equipped with a computer and printer. The desk was strikingly similar to Trevor's. Against one wall, several boxes sat atop a long table, each labeled with the names of the three companies assigned to her. A large window behind the desk exposed a picturesque view of the area behind the house. Sam heard Jamie close the door.

Sam looked at her. "What?"

Jamie took a step forward. "Your hair is down?"

Sam raised her hand to touch it. "He . . . he took it down."

"Is that all he took down?"

Sam looked harshly at Jamie. "Yes! I . . . I told him I was here to work not to do anything else, and he . . . he stopped."

Jamie look at her tell-tale, flushed cheeks. "But you didn't want him to stop, did you?"

Sam tears glistened in her eyes. "I didn't know what to do. I have a 15-year old daughter to worry about. I can't go around screwing my bosses---it's just not right . . . and yes . . . yes . . . thank God."

Jamie gave Sam that knowing smile and handed Sam her missing hairpin. "Thank God is right."

Sam took the pin from Jamie. "What is that supposed to mean?"

"You are the first girl I have seen say no. I'm impressed, but you didn't want to say no, did you? Don't lie. As a woman, I can tell."

Sam fought back tears. "It has been 15 years since I've been with a man, much less one that could affect me this way. I was scared, if he hadn't stopped, I . . . it doesn't matter." Sam suddenly looked scared. "You're not going to tell him, are you?"

Jamie gave her a sly smile. "Do you want me too?"

"No! Of course not."

"I will say this---at least you're honest. Besides, if he could get a devout lesbian to want him, I can only imagine what you're going through."

Sam agreed. "I'm okay. I was just not prepared for him today, but I will do better next time." Sam opened her purse and dabbed her eyes and nose with a Kleenex.

Jamie comforted her. "For a little thing, you're one tough cookie." Jamie's tour of the office was complete, but when she slowly shut the door behind her, she suspiciously leaned against it as she twisted the lock.

Sam couldn't help but think back to her affair with Tip at Wake Forest. She had managed to resist his charms, but by Thanksgiving, she knew she was going to give in. Honestly, who was she kidding? She knew the first time he kissed her.

After Thanksgiving, she lost the power to deny him. Unfortunately, the fear of pregnancy constantly loomed in the recesses of her mind…

but they had always been careful with condoms, the pullout method, and that sort of thing. However, their passion was in direct correlation with their self-preserving customs of adult responsibility. The more he made love to her, the more she wanted him. She wanted to give him everything: her body, her soul, and a child. The thing was that her plan was to graduate college before having children. As the trusted and validated old saying goes, "The best laid plans…"

As the end of the school year crept up on them, she knew that he liked her but also planned to resume his life back at home. She couldn't imagine going three months without seeing him, but he never revealed where he lived or any details about his family. She tried to convince herself that this was a fleeting college fling, but she knew she was in love with him.

At the bus station, she was getting ready to board, when interrupted their lengthy farewell to take an urgent call on his cell. The color drained from his face when he answered, and his eyes grew as big as saucers. She had never seen him so…off kilter. When he hung up, he stepped forward, gave her a kiss, and bid her adieu---and then he was gone. He vanished from her life with no trace whatsoever.

Chapter 21

Liz the Hacker

It was 3 in the afternoon on the first Wednesday of May, when the sounds of heavy steps on the stairs stirred Jimmy from his slumber. He checked the monitors, and most of the rooms were empty of customers. Only the girls remained---they were never allowed to leave. He turned around to wait for the oversized investigator to stumble through the door. It wasn't long before his expectations were satisfied.

Jasper Grebes was a former cop who retired from the force before they could prosecute him. He had a penchant for having sex with the whores and runaways that he abducted. Jimmy and Jasper had a history, and Jimmy needed an investigator. Jasper was not known for his investigative competence, but his rates were dirt-cheap. For a few bucks and an underage whore, he would willingly do Jimmy's bidding. At 300+, lbs. that was more than what Jasper could ever hope for in terms of satisfaction.

Jasper wheezed from walking up the stairs and made his way to the large chair in front of Jimmy's desk. Jimmy looked at him with contempt. "If you lose some weight jackass, you won't die trying to walk up those steps."

Jasper laughed and shook his head. He pulled the notebook from his pocket and started to flip through some pages. Finally, he found the page he was looking for. He looked at Jimmy, smiled, and started to read, "Samantha Raven lives at 2114 East Side Street in Winder, GA. Her phone is 779-555-2152. She has one old 15-year daughter who is a freshman at Winder High School."

Jimmy nodded deviously like some sort of evil mastermind. "Here---watch this." He clicked on the GIF, and the picture suddenly appeared. Jasper struggled out of the chair and so he could see the picture. Liz's GIF suddenly appeared on the screen. Jasper caught his breath; she is dead ringer for that Samantha bitch. Jimmy continued, "I'll bet you 100 bucks that she is Samantha's daughter."

Jasper wiped his mouth with his grubby paw. "I'd like to do that."

Jimmy laughed. "After me, my friend, after me." I want you to go out and watch that house. I want to know about their comings and goings, sleep schedules, when they take a shit, and what color it is. Got it?"

Jasper gave him a clumsy thumb up with his chubby finger. "With pleasure, boss. "He hobbled out like a hobbit whose legs could barely support him. Jimmy turned around to satisfy his voyeuristic urges and spy on the girls sleeping. He spotted the one he wanted and closed in on her.

Liz called her friend, Bobby, from the computer club. He immediately recognized her voice. "Hi, Liz. What's up?"

"I might need to download a bunch of data from a computer. Do you have enough storage to hold a couple Gigs of data?"

Bobby paused before responding. "Um… am I going to get into trouble for this?"

Liz giggled. "Of course not. I'm not doing anything illegal, but I might have a chance to get an SSD. I if I do, I will need to back up my hard drive."

Bobby's mood lightened. "Where did you get the scratch for that?"

"A friend of my mom's said he would get me one."

"It's not the same guy who sold her that VW is it?"

"No, it's another customer who really likes her, but I need someplace to back up my data, can you help me?"

Bobby softened even more. He couldn't say no to Liz. "For you, anything. I'll send you a URL of the site. There's 10 gigs of space that's all yours."

Liz beamed with gratitude. "Thanks, Bobby. You're the best."

Liz hung up the phone and waited for Bobby's email. She keyed in the URL and located the disk storage before accessing the client version of the Trojan server she had sent to Jimmy. She needed to know if it worked. In a few seconds, a window popped up on her screen. She could now access Jimmy's computer as if she were sitting at his desk.

Liz watched the desktop of Jimmy's computer. She waited to see if the curser moved, which would indicate that he was on it. Nothing so far. She checked for a microphone or camera connection, and luck was on her side. The camera was intact, but the microphone didn't work. The camera alerted her to anyone sitting at the computer in a separate window on her desktop. He would be blind to her activities. No one was in the office.

Liz continued to tinker with her findings. She opened "My Documents" on his computer and clicked to copy. When prompted for the destination, she typed in the URL and hit return. She clicked "close when finish" and minimized the copy window. It would take a while for the copy to complete, but hopefully, no one would return before that. She monitored her mission in a separate window.

It would take a few minutes for it to complete. Just as it reached 50%, Jimmy returned, rubbing his crotch and smiling sadistically. The copy was almost finished. Jimmy walked over and put something on the table across the room. He walked over to a bar and poured something into a short glass before relaxing on a couch facing the computer. As he flipped through the pages of a magazine, she simultaneously watched the bar indicating the copy process and the camera. Jimmy suddenly walked to his desk chair and sat down. The cursor moved, but because of the background task, it was slower than usual. His voice was inaudible, but she could read his lips. He was cursing because it didn't respond.

Jimmy eyed something above the monitor. He smiled and moved the mouse again. Finally, the copy finished, and his computer started to work. Liz disconnected from his computer, which shut the camera off as well. Hopefully, the camera didn't have a light to indicate that it was on.

Liz examined the contents of her findings. It was encrypted, so she incorporated her own decryption algorithm and typed in a command---it was no longer encrypted.

The contents of Jimmy's computer, showed 15 picture folders, which were...disturbing, to say the least. Liz saw different people, mostly men, and a couple of women. One particular folder contained a plethora of pictures, each with a man and a young girl. The man was a constant in the pictures, but the girls changed. They were in various stages of undress, and he was performing unspeakable sexual acts on them against their will.

The folders of the women were the same. One woman switched off between liaisons with boys and girls in various stages of undress --- some were even having outright sex. Apparently, Jimmy Dittle satisfied the erotic desires of numerous people, but it always came at a price. Several of the girls looked like they had bruises and cuts that corresponded with forced rips and tears in their clothing. Apparently, Jimmy was the number one fan of his work.

Liz found at least 20 folders in the documents section under different names. At this point, the amount of data was at 3.5 gigs, so she copied the contents onto a DVD. A DVD normally can hold up to 4 gigs easily, so she was certain that it would hold all of the data.

The phone rang, and Sam's name flashed on the caller I.D. "Hi Mom. Where are you?"

"I'm farther out than usual this time, but I will be home in about 45 minutes." Liz said she would wait 20 minutes before starting dinner. *It would take at least 10 minutes to copy one DVD.*

After Liz started dinner, she made a second DVD copy. She slid the original one into a sleeve and hid it on the bookshelf inside of a copy of Jane Austen's, "Pride and Prejudice". She then made a third copy that she left in the drive and put the second DVD into a sleeve that she taped underneath the end table.

Chapter 22

Jimmy's Secrets Stolen

When Liz's mother finally made it home, they sat down at the kitchen table to enjoy their ritual of dining and banter. Sam allowed Liz to pour two glasses of wine for the two of them with dinner. As they started to eat, Liz looked up at her mother and asked about the 800 lb. gorilla in the room. "So how did it go with Trevor in his little house?"

Sam smirked. "You can fit this house and property into the foyer of that little house."

Liz gaped at her mother with an open mouth and a fork full of food. "So, I guess it is not that little. How big is it?"

"It has to be at least 50,000 sq. ft. --- it was huge! I slammed on breaks when I first saw it."

"In other words, it was an easy place to get lost with a gorgeous hunk like Trevor."

Sam narrowed her eyes in amusement. "I only saw a small bit of it: the gym, his office, and my office."

Liz was now intrigued. "You were in his office alone?"

"No! There was that woman there, you know, the blonde in all of those pictures, and several other people--- so no, I was never alone."

Liz sensed that her mother was holding back. "She was with you the whole time?"

Sam put her fork down and looked across the table at her daughter before taking a huge swig from her glass wine. "Okay, let's hear it. You're skirting around the question you want to ask---out with it."

Liz was emboldened and ready for constructive confrontation. "Fine! You spent the entire afternoon in a big house with a drop-dead gorgeous man; now please don't tell me all you did was pore over some dusty old ledgers."

Sam took in a mouthful of grape courage from her nearly empty wine glass. "No! I didn't. When I arrived, Mr. Paterson was sparring in the boxing ring."

"Oh, really? How did he do?"

"He lost."

"Really? What happened?"

Sam took a breath. "Well, they were doing…what it's called … cat fighting, no cage fighting. . . Mixed Martial Arts. Trading blows left and right. Then out of nowhere, the other person punched him silly and got him in this arm bar thingy or something. Then he tapped out."

Liz cackled. "What did the other guy look like?"

Sam tried to suppress her laughter. "Actually, she looked pretty good."

Liz's mouth dropped open. "No way! You're telling me that he was beat by a woman. Please tell me that isn't so?"

Sam let out a tipsy giggle. "Well, to be honest, she was ranked # 3 in the world in female MMA, so she was no slouch--- of course, Trevor put up a great fight, but she was tough."

"Oh, Trevor?"

Sam searched for her maternal composure. "Mr. Paterson is a gentleman and nothing happened."

Liz was unconvinced. "Why do you sound so sad?"

Sam rolled her eyes in disgust. "He is my boss, and I am working for him on occasion. There will be no funny business, so quit fishing."

Liz stuck out her lower lip, and they both started to laugh. "Okay, but if I was stuck in a house that big with a hunk like that, I would want him to find me. "

" Well he did, but nothing happened. Okay?"

Liz smiled with mild disbelief. "Okay."

Since Liz made dinner, it was Sam's turn to clean up. Liz went into the living room, deleted the DVD copy from the URL storage, and started examining the contents of the last DVD that was in the computer. Just in case her mother walked in, she made sure she did not open any of the picture folders. But what she found was overwhelming.

There were three folders under "Site" and in each was a spreadsheet. She didn't understand what the spreadsheet meant because they were separated into months, each one set like a calendar. In the left column, was a list of numbers from 1 to 16? The next column showed a list of names but not all of the numbers corresponded to the names. 30 columns after that had numbers, which were totaled along the bottom and on the far right.

She started to look at the other folders and found one file with three addresses. She also found a second spreadsheet showing more numbers. Liz heard her mother approaching and shut the computer down.

The two sat down on the couch. Sam perused some work documents while Liz read a book. Liz peered over the top of the book. "You going to the little house again tomorrow?"

Sam diverted her eyes momentarily from her paperwork. "I need one more day to finish what I have to do, and I will brief Tre...Mr. Paterson on the proposal on Friday. I will return early Friday afternoon."

"I'm sorry, but what I am hearing is that you get to spend Friday with him, all alone in that big house?"

Elizabeth was like most women when a conversation gave them pleasure---*she wanted to savor it*. And the fun she was having toying with her mother's thinly veiled enticement brought on by this Trevor Paterson was just too much fun to relinquish just yet. Sam liked him, and so did Liz---but for different reasons. Always true to their mother/daughter banter, Sam figured that maybe she could have fun with her daughter about this as well.

Sam smiled and said, "Yea. I will spend about 30 minutes going over the proposal, and then we will obviously do it in every room in the house."

"You wouldn't dare!"

Sam gave a fake pout. "Why wouldn't I? I would be crazy not to. We will be alone in the house, and as you said, he is a fox!"

Liz was laughing so hard that she could barely breathe. "Oh, you hussy!"

Sam admired her daughter's innocent wit. "What do you know about it? You don't even know what a hussy is."

Liz's expression of mock defiance spoke volumes. "Yes, I do---it is a woman who likes sex."

Sam was satisfied with her teasing jab at Liz's naïve candor. "Well, that includes roughly every woman between the ages of 12 and 72."

"Really? How do you know I like sex?"

Sam was ready to playfully fire back. "For starters, you keep asking if Mr. Paterson and I are doing something. Why else would you care if you're not interested? Besides, how much sexual experience could you possibly have?"

Liz knew she could get a sincere reaction out of her mother with this response. "I have a little."

Sam broke the frisky repartee and transformed into mama bear. "Excuse me? With whom do you have a little experience…and what experience?"

Liz knew she had her, but she still wanted to test the waters of her mother's comfort with this new genre of discussion. "Mathew, of course. He comes over in the afternoon, and we have a little sex---all over the house, in fact."

Sam was now angry. "I'm calling his mother, and I'm going to kill him. Where is my gun?"

Liz giggled in satisfaction. "Mom, you don't have a gun, and Mathew and I stay on the front porch. He never actually comes in."

Sam mocked anger for the pure joy of mortifying her daughter. "You do it on the front porch? That's what the kids are calling it these days?"

"No, mom. I'm sure if we were doing it on the front porch, the neighbors would have told you by now."

Sam let out a maternal sigh of reluctant submission. "I still have to talk to Mathew's mother about giving you a copy of Seas of Grey… or Shades of Grey…whatever the kids call it these days."

"Yea, it was probably the same copy you read." They ended the evening in the aftermath of bonding. Liz started towards her bedroom and blew a kiss goodnight to her mother.

Quietly, a dark-colored Cadillac pulled to a silent stop against the curb across the street from the house. The occupant picked up his cell phone and made a call. When the party came on the line, he breathed, "Got 'em, boss."

Chapter 23

Day two at the House

Jasper's black Cadillac was parked across the street in from the house. This vantage point granted him access to the activities of the girls via front windows. He called Jimmy Dittle with an update. "Got 'em Boss. It's them. This is the place."

Jimmy's blood boiled at this interruption based on a minor detail. "Look, you dumb bastard, don't play with me. How do you know?"

"Because I've been sitting down the street for over two hours and watched that little cunt sit on the porch with the boy next door. Then the mother came home. They ate dinner in the kitchen, and now they are talking on the living room couch. So warm and cozy, the two of them …the little whore just went to bed, and the mother is in the living room by herself. You want me to bring her to you?"

Jimmy calculated his response. "No! I want to know their schedules. That little cunt gets home from school probably the same time every day. I want to know the path she walks. Look for a spot where we can snatch her off the street before she gets to the house. And don't fuck up." Jasper agreed and pulled away.

On Thursday morning, Samantha used the GPS to take her to Trevor's little house instead of Atlanta. This drive was much more enjoyable. No traffic --- just a nice easy ride through the country. She wished that Hutchinson Accounting was out this way. It would be a pleasure to take this route to work, but they needed to be in the heart of the city. Not only for the prestige, but also because of the location, and mainly because the majority of their clients resided in the vicinity.

As Sam turned into the sign that read, "Paterson Corporation," the wooded surroundings, filled her with inner peace. When she exited the woods and entered the parking lot in front of the colonial mansion, she felt an ease…as if she was home. She didn't know why, and she didn't expect to feel that way---it was strange but nice. As she parked, she closed the top of the car and put her hair into a bun. Today, Sam was wearing her dark-gray business suite with white a white, silk blouse that buttoned to the neck…and she had not forgotten her glasses.

Sam grabbed her briefcase and made a beeline to the house. She didn't know if she could just walk in, so she rang the doorbell---after all, it was someone's house. It was only a second until the door opened and there stood Trevor. She realized that she was smiling and to stop it---this was business. Sam wasn't going to give him any kind mixed messages. Trevor noticed the smile and sudden retraction with a business mindset and stepped back.

As she entered into the foyer, she nodded to Trevor and headed to her office. When she heard the door close behind her, she realized she wasn't alone. Once again, there stood Trevor. He wore jeans, tennis shoes, and light brown Guayabera shirt. He placed his hands into the front pockets and slowly walked towards her.

Sam backed up against her desk as he approached until he was only a foot away. The smell of his cologne, the warmth of his body---she drank in his essence. *Damn it! Keep it together, Sam!* Trevor smiled. *God, he has a beautiful smile.* She was determined to remain calm, cool, and collected---he couldn't affect her as he had the day before. She took a deep breath and slowly raised her gaze to his face. He almost took her breath away, but she maintained her composure. Losing control was not an option.

Trevor felt the intense connection, but he to go slowly. She was an intelligent, proud woman who didn't need him complicating her well-organized life. She had everything under control, and that was how she liked it. As he looked down into her face, he saw the same expression he had seen the very first time he met her. That was what impressed him then, and that was what impressed him now.

She wasn't a gift or some kind of cheap, collectible trophy that any man would vie to possess. Trevor spoke softly, "When you work here, you are family; you don't need to ring the doorbell. Just come on in, okay?"

When Sam heard that word---family---she knew she was officially invited into his world. *Please don't do this to me. Please! One more day, and I'm gone.*

Sam couldn't detach her eyes from his face. In his presence, she felt safe...at ease...no pressure except for the flames of passion he reignited within her. Sam nodded while locking her eyes those dark brown beautiful ones of his.

Trevor tenderly pulled the hairpin from her bun. It felt like a weight being lifted, but she didn't know why. He pushed her hair back behind her ears and cupped her cheeks. She knew he wanted to lean down and kiss her.

She longed for him, but she was afraid. If he kissed her, she just felt like she couldn't say no. But she couldn't allow that. A familiar war of wills waged within her---one side wanted him, and the other side didn't. *How can he resurrect these feelings? I don't know him that well, and for that matter, he knew exactly what he was doing. Damn him!*

Trevor wanted to kiss her so bad that it physically hurt. He wanted to press his lips against those red lips and inhale her. But he sensed her inner turmoil. He bent down, and just before reaching her lips, he whispered, "I still like it down." With that, he held up the hairpin for the taking. As he left the office, he paused and gripped the handle, "There's coffee and tea in the kitchen." He was gone.

Sam teetered on the edge of relief and anger. Twice he had come that close to kissing her, and twice he didn't. She wanted *him to kiss her, but she didn't. Why is he torturing me like this?* She needed something to perk her up---coffee, tea, or a shot of tequila. It was early, so the coffee and tea were probably the best options.

She was gripping the edge of the desk when suddenly, the door opened again. Jamie walked in with Susan. They smiled as Susan closed the door behind her. Jamie said, "Your hair is down again?"

Sam put her hand to her chest like a Southern belle clutching her pearls. "He...he did it, again. I don't … I don't know why?"

Jamie looked at Susan as if they were sharing a secret and laughed. Susan boldly stated, "You look more jumpable with your hair down."

Susan and Jamie were decked out in workout clothes. Jamie was wearing a dark blue track outfit and Susan sported a tank top with spandex shorts. Sam could see the muscles on Susan and knew she would be more of a match for 90% of the men in this world. She was taller than Jamie at 5' 10" and 140 lbs., but she had a nice figure. Though her breasts weren't large, they were defiantly present. Susan was a beautiful woman in her own right.

Sam looked at Susan. "More jumpable? What does that mean? I'm … jumpable … maybe." Jamie and Susan cracked up laughing. Sam picked up her briefcase and sat down at the desk. In a simulated gesture of defiance, she dared to ask, "He said there was coffee and tea in the kitchen?"

Jamie and Susan pulled the chairs in front of the desk and sat down. Jamie spoke first. "First things first---did he kiss you?"

Sam was slightly irritated. "You and my daughter, what is it? Why is everyone trying to hook us up? I don't do hookups, and he is my boss. That's just not going to happen."

Jamie gave a disgusted look to Susan. "He didn't. He chickened out again."

With that, they stood up and moved the chairs back. Sam looked at them and asked, "What do you mean by 'chickened out?' He didn't chicken out."

Susan looked Sam directly in the eyes. "Tell me something, did he kiss you or not?"

Sam was still getting used to the directness of these new acquaintances. "No, he didn't. He … came … but he didn't. I respect him for that."

Jamie smiled. "Cheese and rice! You two are a trip! I'd be all over you like white on rice, but nooo! We have to maintain a status quo." Jamie and Susan laughed and started to leave.

Sam stood up. "Excuse me, but why would he . . . be on me like…white on rice… he has more important things on his docket than me. "

Jamie and Susan looked at each other, laughed again, and continued to leave. Sam didn't understand what was so funny or what was going on. Jamie sensed her trepidation. "Come on, we'll show you the kitchen. That is where the serious baking is done."

Sam circled the desk in mock indignation. "What do you mean by serious baking? I can bake."

With that, Jamie and Susan burst into wild laughter, which made Sam smile. "You ladies are incorrigible."

Susan looked at Jamie and scoffed teasingly. "I would rather be incorrigible than unscrewable." They were walking down the hall towards the enormous kitchen.

As they walked, Sam corrected Susan. "The word is inscrutable, not unscrewable."

Jamie and Susan turned into the kitchen and Susan replied, "No! The word is Un-screw-able---as in can't have sex with."

Sam was somewhat offended. "Excuse me, but I do have a daughter, so I guess I did ... screw once."

Susan and Jamie laughed again. Jamie took the lead on this topic. "Methinks we are corrupting her; we have her talking dirty now." All three women were now laughing.

Jasper arrived at the house at six in the morning and waited. When Sam left at 7am, he observed a young boy from next-door walk over to Liz's house and ring the doorbell. Soon, Liz came out, locked the door, and walked with the boy around the corner to the bus stop. They waited there with several other kids until she escorted him onto the bus.

Jasper drove back to the house and parked down the street. He watched the street for a while before getting out of the car. He walked down the sidewalk as if he was just out for a stroll and then trotted clumsily down the drive behind the Ravens' house to the back door. He was able to pick the lock in a few seconds with his special tools.

Once inside, he started to look around. On account of Jimmy's instructional "shit" comment he opened the toilet seat just to say that he checked it. He walked back into living room and scanned the bookshelves, but then he spied the computer and turned it on. It required a login, so he wasn't able to do anything there. Just for the hell of it, he pressed the button to the DVD player, and it opened. He pocketed Liz's DVD copy.

Jasper invaded Elizabeth's bedroom and looked around. He opened several drawers until he found the drawer with the panties, which he scavenged through until he found his prize and pressed it to his face---and breathed it in. He repeated the pervy process in

Samantha's bedroom, and with panties in pocket, he walked out the back door and made sure he locked the door on the way out before he drove away.

He returned at 02:30 pm to case the neighborhood. Finally, he drove back around to the bus stop and found a spot where he could watch the bus stop and the house at the same time. He waited. At 3:30 pm, the bus arrived at the stop on schedule.

Elizabeth hooped off the 3:30 pm bus. She walked with a couple of friends for a short distance before they peeled off to their respective destinations. She continued alone past the small, wooded area near the corner and onward to her house. Liz unlocked the front door and went inside as she did every weekday afternoon. Jasper wondered where the boy was. Maybe he was playing sports or something. He looked down the street towards her path and then back at the house. Tomorrow, he would stalk her again to ensure that this was her normal routine.

Chapter 24

The hunter is exposed

The banter between Susan and Jamie was good-humored as they guided her to the kitchen and helped her make a cup of Chai Tea. With her tea in hand, she went back to her office and started to assemble her proposal. Her first deadline was creeping up on her, and the pressure was on.

Sam worked the rest of the day and only stopped long enough to have a bite of a sandwich for lunch. By the end of the day, the proposal was complete. It just needed some final changes that she could easily finish the next morning. Sam placed her paperwork into her brief case so she could study it later. As she was leaving, Trevor stopped her at the door of her office and asked. "Can I come in?"

Sam stopped dead in her tracks and smiled at the sight of Trevor. She put on her corporate facial mask and took a step back. "Of course, it is your house. I'm temporary." Trevor understood, and softly closed the door behind him. He leaned casually against a small table next to the door and gazed at Sam. She felt slightly self-conscious and moved her briefcase in front of her, hiding behind it.

Trevor noticed the multi-colored notes on Sam's whiteboard. He cradled his chin in his palm as he analyzed it. Sam darted in front of him. "It is not ready yet. Come here tomorrow at 1 pm, and I will lay it all out for you."

Trevor looked down at her with a wicked smile. "You will lay it all out tomorrow?"

Sam immediately caught on to his clever semantics. "The proposal---I will explain the proposal tomorrow."

She tried to speak with conviction and portray it in her expression. Trevor's eyes lingered on her. "You left your hair down."

Sam nodded yes. "I don't understand what the fascination is with my hair."

"It's more than just your hair." With that, he turned and started to the door and stopped and turned to say, "One o'clock, I will be here." He exited.

Sam lingered for a moment and left. She dialed her home phone from the car through the Bose radio Bluetooth. Liz answered on the second ring, and Sam told her to start dinner as she made her way home.

Earlier, Liz had realized that the DVD drive was empty. She looked around and didn't notice anything else out of place. She headed to the bookcase, but something told her to stop and look around first. She saw nothing new and no hiding place for a camera. *Am I being paranoid? Why would anybody hide a camera in my house?*

The computer sat on a living room table in front of the window that displayed a beautiful view of the front yard. As she peered out the window, she noticed a large, black car sitting just a little way down the street. Liz grabbed her camera and chose a side window that gave her a clearer view of the front of the car. She zoomed in as much as she could and took a picture of the front license plate.

Liz slid out the back door and peeked around the corner, but she soon realized that she was within the driver's line of vision. She decided to go back inside and call Mathew. "Mathew, can you come over for a second?" When she saw him come up the steps, she opened the door and stepped out.

They calmly sat down on the bench with their backs towards the black car. Liz whispered, "Look, I might just be paranoid, but I need for you to take this camera, walk down the street past that black car, and take pictures of it. Don't turn around, but I need pictures of the license plate and the man inside. Don't let him know you are taking pictures."

Mathew complied. "Okay, but can we just sit here a little longer, so he doesn't get suspicious?"

Liz understood, so they sat back and talked about nothing for a bit. Mathew was ready. "I have to walk down the street." He got up, palmed the camera, and started down the street. The car was parked on the far side of the road, so Mathew crossed the street from the corner behind the car.

A sizeable hedge lined the sidewalk in front of the houses on that particular street. As soon as Mathew disappeared around the edge, he broke out running. When he reached the break in the hedge and he stepped through, an elderly female resident noticed him from the back yard. Mathew tried to hide his suspicious activities. "Hi, Mrs. Eckerd! No need to get up. I'm just passing through."

Mrs. Eckerd was a widow who liked Mathew and had known him since he was born. She looked up from her lemonade. "Okay, Mathew. Nice to see you."

Mathew ambled along the hedge so he could see where the car was. As the car became increasingly visible, he snuck the camera through the hedge and snapped a picture of the rear license plate---he even adjusted the camera to capture a different angle of the car. All of a sudden, the man in the car spotted him. Seeing the camera, he started the car and sped away. He made a sharp turn and was gone.

When Mathew returned to the house, Liz was examining the pictures on the camera. He gave her a rundown of the shoddy espionage. "Okay, I got him, but I think he realized what I was doing and got spooked. Liz smiled. "Take the camera home, copy the pictures, and safeguard them. Mathew confirmed the instructions and left. Liz heard the phone ring. She knew it was her mother and raced inside to grab it.

Jasper called Jimmy and told him that the boy had taken a picture of him. Jimmy was incensed. "You idiot! I told you to watch them. Why didn't you use a different car? Why didn't you park someplace else? Why did you make every stake in the handbook of an amateur sleuth? God damn it! I can't depend on you to do anything right."

Jasper hung his bulbous head in shame. "It's okay, boss. But I think we need to make moves sooner rather than later. I found something you might want to look at."

"Okay, but it better be good."

It wasn't long before Jasper reached Jimmy's office. He collapsed into the chair and wiped the drops of sweat from his forehead. Jimmy looked at him with his usual contempt. "Okay, what you got? It had better be worth it." Jasper pulled the DVD out of his coat pocket and tossed it over to Jimmy. Jimmy spun around and slid it into his computer DVD drive.

Jimmy exploded when he saw the incriminating contents. "That bitch got everything! She not only copied all my files, but she decrypted them. How did she do that? Arrrgh… wait until I get that bitch! I'm going to fuck her until she bleeds. That bitch!"

Jasper nodded, "Yea, I stuck it into my laptop in the car and saw what it was; I figured you might be interested." Jimmy gave him an angry look and turned to his computer.

Jimmy pulled Samantha's address into Google Maps. The entire neighborhood was suddenly at his sausage fingers. Jimmy was growing impatient and zeroed in on the tough questions. "The house is here, and from what you said, the bus stop is over here, so, she walks past this area twice a day?"

Jasper approved. "That's it. You got it." He was not known for his eloquence.

Jimmy scanned at the map. "Okay, it looks like we have some houses across the road, so parking a van there is out of the question. What we need to do is have one man here in the woods waiting, and when she is separated from the rest of the kids in this section, we get the van to pull up from behind. He grabs her, throws her into the van, and they drive off. We're talking 5 seconds tops."

Jimmy dialed a number. "I need for you to get the van ready; we will be making a pickup in a few days … Yea" He hung up the phone and looked at Jasper. "You let him get your picture, you idiot."

On Friday morning, Sam arrived at the "little house," and this time, she walked right in and down the hall to her office. After depositing her lunch and briefcase, she made tea in the kitchen and walked back to her office where she started to make the final adjustments to the designs on the white board.

Sam was wearing her navy pencil skirt with the slit halfway up the side. Since she would be walking back and forth in front of the whiteboard, it would make moving easier. This time, her blouse didn't button up to the neck, but she wore a scarf to feign prudence. With her 4-inch heels, she felt comfortable and in command. She was ready for him this time---he wasn't going to turn her insides to jelly again.

She finished the whiteboard, and at one o'clock sharp, Trevor knocked on the door and she allowed him to enter. He wore jeans this time a pale blue Guayabera shirt. *He must like those shirts. He looks good. Damn, he looks good!* Trevor walked in and closed the door. He looked at Sam as she stood before the whiteboard and couldn't help but smile at her. *That smile!* She was melting inside again.

Sam motioned for him to sit in the chair in the middle of the room facing the whiteboard, and he followed her instructions. She never turned her back to him---something Jennifer once mentioned as a "no-no". She gestured to one company, turning sideways with the slit towards him.

Trevor was mesmerized by her, but suddenly, he stood up.

Chapter 25

The Kiss

Trevor stopped her. "Can I ask one thing?"

Sam dropped her arms to her sides. "Are you comfortable? You look uncomfortable." He stepped forward, unbuttoned two buttons on her jacket, and pushed it off her shoulder. Sam looked down to see him unbutton her jacket, but made no attempt, to stop him. She watched his eyes as he removed her jacket and placed it on the table. Trevor was satisfied. "Okay, that's better."

An utterly confused Sam had taken a deep breath as he came closer. She again focused on her analysis of the whiteboard to get her bearings. As she explained the connection between the first and second companies, she paced nervously back and forth in front of him.

Trevor interrupted her again. "I'm sorry, but may I make a suggestion?" Sam froze this time and faced him. His velvety voice stopped her heart as she nodded yes again, seemingly in slow motion. Trevor approached her.

It was impossible to control her urge to gaze upon him like a blind woman seeing the sun for the first time. Trevor continued, "With the jacket gone, this scarf doesn't look right--- here." Trevor gently undid the scarf woven into her blouse and around her neck and tossed it onto the table along with the jacket before taking his seat again.

Sam felt exposed. Her jacket and scarf were gone, and her blouse felt like it was open halfway to her navel. She was still facing Trevor but nervously looked back at the whiteboard to pull herself together. She continued in her mannerisms to demonstrate the connection; between the third and first company, and how their effect on the second company would tie in together. In the middle of her presentation, Trevor stood and advanced towards her just as he had done before.

Sam clumsily retreated back against the whiteboard. *What is he going to take off now?* Her heart leapt into her throat when he extracted the pin from her bun again. He removed her glasses and tossed them. Trevor stared down at her and pushed her hair back behind her ears. Shivers radiated up and down her spine like an electric current.

He held her face in his hands as he leaned closer. "Please forgive me. I can't take this anymore." He gently pressed his lips against hers. She didn't realize what she was doing as her hands rose between them and gripped his shirt to pull him to her.

She could hear her inner voice screaming. *Stop, stop this right now! No good can come from this. He is your boss, or client---it doesn't matter. He is a man, and he won't stop. Get your arms from around his neck. Don't do this!*

Trevor wrapped his sinewy arms around her waist, picked her up, and pushed her into the whiteboard as his lips devoured hers. She involuntarily enveloped his waist with her legs. She was screaming inside to stop but making no serious effort. She threw caution to the wind and wrapped her arms around his neck.

She relished the fact for the first time in 15 years, she was kissing a man---and she was enjoying it. They kissed and held each other for a full minute before he gingerly lowered her to her feet again. She craved his support and could barely stand.

Trevor balanced her and admired the whiteboard. "It's perfect---the best I have ever seen. I have to leave on business for the next two weeks, but I would like to consult with you again…if you let me…when I return, if that is okay?" Sam struggled to catch her breath, but she managed to nod yes.

As Trevor backed out of the room, he looked at Sam once more. "Leave the contract on your desk, and I will read over it again this weekend before I leave." With that, he left her dumfounded and ecstatic. Sam was standing, barely, leaning against the whiteboard, pressing one hand against it to support herself, and the other against her chest to prevent her heart from leaping out, when Jamie and Susan walked in.

They were dressed in their workout clothes, which appeared to be their normal attire. After shutting the door, they looked at each other and laughed. Sam attempted to straighten herself before demanding, "What is so funny?" With that, both women burst out laughing again.

Jamie perched on the table while Susan leaned against the desk. Sam remained leaning the whiteboard. Jamie shot a mischievous look at Susan. "I think he finally did it. It only took three days, but he finally got the nerve to do it."

Sam was slightly irritated. "Did what? Three days to do what?" Sam walked behind her desk and gathered her paperwork as Jamie and Susan laughed in the background, seemingly at her expense.

Jamie slid off the table. "He kissed you, didn't he. He put a suck face, a lip smacker, tongue lock if you will, and if you weren't wearing those shoes, we would see your toes curling up. Admit it. Fess up, sis."

As Sam shook her head in denial, Susan noticed the smudged-up graphs and notes on the whiteboard. She pointed to it. "Before you start making a liar out of yourself, can I present circumstantial evidence number one?"

Jamie grinned knowingly and turned to Sam. "Well?" Sam dropped her head, sat down, and admitted defeat.

Susan clapped her hands together in victorious delight and turned to Jamie. "I won. Pay up."

Sam took slight offense to this. "Wait you two bet on when he was going to kiss me? How dare you!"

Jamie fished a dollar out of her bra and handed it to Susan. "No, not just us. Half the house was making bets. I figured two days, and Susan bet three. Everyone else said that you would be in his bed screaming by now."

Sam scrunched her face. "So what made you think he wanted to kiss me?"

Jamie took the lead on this question. "Ever since the first wave of presentations, were you able to finish this one? Think about it. From the look of the board, I would say no." Sam crossed her arms in defiance, but she knew Jamie was right.

Meanwhile, Susan eyed Sam's jacket and scarf. "Okay, I just have to know---how much clothing did he get_off you?"

Sam rolled her eyes. "You two are incorrigible; remind me not to bring my daughter anywhere near you."

Susan held her head back and laughed heartily. "Oh, why not? We could school her."_

Sam looked cross. "That is what I'm afraid of."

Jamie intercepted the impending tension. "Okay, so now that you got the kiss, what's next---Disney Land?"

Sam sprang from her seat abruptly. "No! He asked for another consultation, but I'm going back to Hutchinson on Monday. They probably have another account of me."

Susan and Jamie circled the desk from both sides, catching Sam in the middle. They embraced her and eased up on the teasing. "Really, you're not coming back here? Shucks, we are going to miss you!"

Sam realized that despite the harassment they doled out, she had a fondness for them. "Well, if Mr. Paterson needs more advice, I will be more than happy to assist in any way that I can."

All three ladies laughed in unison, and Jamie revealed, "I understand that he might be interested in some deposits."

At that, Sam pushed her back. "Now, wait! There will be none of that!" Susan and Jamie started to laugh again and walked toward the door.

Sam was embarrassed by their suggestion, but even though she knew it would never happen, it was intriguing. She suddenly remembered who she was. *I can't do that to Liz.* She gathered her things and left the contracts on the desk along with the GPS. They were useless now, and besides, she knew how to find her way back.

Meanwhile, dark clouds of evil were gathering in the east as in Jimmy's office, plans were in the making.

Chapter 26

The first move, a confession, a favor

Jimmy was briefing the two men on the plan. They flanked him on each side as he used Google maps to show them the plan. Jimmy instructed, "Okay, the bus should arrive at around 3pm. She will get off here, walk this way, and turn right to her house---here. Now park here. No one should see you, so you get out."

Jimmy pointed to one man. "And walk to here. Are you following? Hide in the trees out of sight. Jasper will park here and call the signals. After the bus leaves, he will signal for the van to come out. You will drive slowly, and when she gets to here, speed up. Make sure the side door is open so he can pop out of the woods and grab her. The van will be right there so you can step in and take off. The whole thing shouldn't take more than 5 seconds. By the time anybody realizes what is happening, you will be gone. Make sure you have the ether to shut her up. We can't have the little bitch screaming."

The two men nodded and walked out. Jasper was waiting downstairs, having already been briefed on the plan. As they walked over to the white Lincoln, the window slid down. One of the men asked, "What happened to the Caddy?"

Jasper answered, "Caddy's out. Made a change---now wait here for 10 minutes, and follow me. I don't want us both arriving at the same time. See you there." Jasper started the car and pulled out, and the two men followed suit in the dark brown van. They decided to grab a bite to create a delay.

Jasper arrived first and parked in a spot just down street where he had a clear view of Sam's driveway as well as the bus stop. The porker couldn't take the heat, so he kept the engine running for the AC. Also, he wanted his conversations with the other two men to be somewhat muffled. A few minutes later, the two men pulled past him and parked around the corner. One of the men walked back down the street and cloaked himself behind the clump of trees. Jasper picked up his cell and initiated the talk feature. "Check in." He quickly heard, "Check one." A second later---"Check two." They waited for their mark.

Just after 3pm, Jasper saw the bus round the corner and pull to a stop. Jasper picked up the cell. "Get ready. " He heard two blurbs and two more blurbs---it was go time. Jasper watched as the kids exited the bus and got eyes on Liz. Out of nowhere, he saw the white Volkswagen come down the street and turn into the driveway.

He began to panic. *Damn, damn, her mother's home*! He fumbled for his cell. "Abort! Abort!" The bus pulled away, and Jasper watched Liz walk alone past the point of attack and turn the corner. The brown van pulled out and picked up the second man then left. Jasper pulled out soon afterwards.

Jimmy he was livid! Once Jasper made it to his office, he really let him have it. "Why in hell did you abort, you fat fuck?! He could have grabbed the girl. What were you thinking?"

Jasper plopped down into the overstuffed chair. "Yes, we could have, but I felt we should play it safe. Her mother knows when she arrives home, and would be looking for her. Look, Monday she'll be alone, and no one will see us take her. It will be that much harder for them to figure it out.

Jimmy looked at him with distrust. "Okay, we go again Monday."

Liz saw Sam's car and ran to the house. She started her daily ritual of homework and helping her mother start dinner. Afterwards, they retired to the living room. Sam read her papers, and Liz buried her nose in a book.

As they indulged in the most recent addition to their ritual and sipped their wines, Liz looked at Sam inquisitively. "So…you going back to work on Monday, or are you going to see Mr. Paterson?"

Sam replied without looking up. "He is out of town for the next few days. I finished what I was doing, so yes, I will be reporting to work."

Liz grinned. "What did Mr. Paterson say when you said goodbye?"

"I am just an employee. There is no reason for him to come and say goodbye."

Liz closed her book, walked into her mother's bedroom, and returned with her blouse. She sat back and looked at her mother. "He didn't say anything?"

Sam's eyes remained glued to her paperwork. "No, he said nothing."

Liz tossed the blouse over to her mother. "Hmmmm…then why is there dry marker all over the back of your blouse. You know you ruined it, right?"

Sam half-glanced at her blouse. "I just happened to lean against the whiteboard---that is all."

Liz saw right through her and pressed on. "With that much marker on your blouse, you had to practically clean the whiteboard, wouldn't you say? Also, didn't you wear your dark blue outfit today---the one that has a jacket? There was no marker on that; apparently, you weren't wearing it."

Sam tossed the papers onto the coffee table and gave her daughter the response she was fishing for. "Okay! I took my jacket off! So what? Are you the wardrobe police?"

Liz smirked in satisfaction. "If I was the wardrobe police, you would be in a lot of trouble. When I came home, your hair was down. You weren't wearing your scarf, and your blouse looked like a dry eraser. What did he do, take your clothes off first?"

Sam retorted in indignant frustration. "So what if he did?"

Liz squealed with triumphant delight. "Okay, finally! Tell me what happened."

Sam's head was swimming with the influx of invasion on her carefully crafted bubble---first that pair at his house and now her daughter. Sam took generous swig of the wine and became somewhat emboldened. "All he did was kiss me. I was giving the presentation and trying to connect all the dots, and before I knew it, we were kissing. He left, and that's it. Nothing else happened."

Liz was not convinced. "He didn't say anything?"

The wine was lowering Sam's guard that she normally used to shield her daughter from the world's ills. "Alright…he said, 'Please forgive me.' Then he kissed me and left. It was as simple as that. Stop reading into it."

"Now it all makes sense! That's why you're out of sorts today! You wanted him to do more, and he didn't."

Sam scowled and stammered out her next words. "Of course not . . . don't be silly . . . I didn't even want him . . . to do that."

"Liar, liar, pants on fire. I saw the way you looked at him the day he came over. No other man would have been allowed to even stay on the property, but you let him stay. You even let him buy us lunch, which is so unlike you. And today, your last day there, you come home half-undressed and mopey. Mom, I may only be 15, but I'm not stupid.

He is a great looking man, and from what you have told me, a nice guy. You like him a lot, but you're afraid to admit it. Stop holding back."

Sam crossed her arms across her chest and stared daggers at her daughter because she knew Liz was right. Sam was self-programmed to forgo everything else in life for the sake of her daughter. No affairs, no men, and she dressed like a spinster.

She cut corners everywhere she could and sacrificed everything for her daughter. In spite of taking all of these extreme precautions, she was now struggling with a tricky decision of turning away a man that might be everything that she or any woman could ever want… but she wasn't willing to risk her daughter. She couldn't do it. Liz, however, knew her better than anybody and could see through the façade straight to the war raging within her.

Sam finally confessed. "Liz…yes, I like him … and today when he kissed me, I … I couldn't stop him, I didn't want to stop him. But Liz, I can't take the risk, of hurting you; I won't take the risk. If he really is the man of my dreams, he has….he has to prove it to me…I won't risk you."

Liz smiled and took her mother into her arms. Tears were pouring down both of their faces. "I love you, mommy." Liz went to bed. Sam sat there for a few minutes and went to bed as well. It had been a trying week.

Across town, Trevor sat at his desk reading over Sam's contract and proposal. He signed the contracts and put them into the out basket. He sighed and took a sip of his bourbon. Jamie and Susan walked in and sat in the two chairs in front of him.

Jamie knew he had been drinking. "No amount of whisky is going to ease that pain."

Trevor chuckled. "And what pain are you referring to?"

Susan and Jamie looked at each other and chuckled. Susan replied, "God, you must think we are stupid. You spent all that money to hire her to come here to do what you have already done, and now you're going to just let her slip away?"

Trevor waved his glass in the air. "No, I am not, but I need a favor from the two of you, since you are so worried about my well-being and hers. Keep an eye on her, and let me know what happens. Can you do that?"

Jamie nodded. "What do you want us to tell her?"

Trevor smiled. "I'm on my third bourbon, and you want me to come up with a convincing lie? Come on girls, I can't lie when I'm sober, which I currently am not, if you haven't noticed."

Jamie knew him like the back of her hand. "Boy, do you have it bad! Why not just tell her and be done with it?"

Trevor shook his head. "No, it has to be done right. You don't know her like I do. If I spring this on her like that, she will leave, and I will never find her again. I'm not taking any chances. It's like convincing a little squirrel to come over to you. If you make any sudden or grandiose gestures, you could scare it away." Trevor leaned forward in his chair so he could focus on both women. "And Sam is a complicated and cautious breed. You can't catch a raven until that raven wants you to. We have to do it right, okay? Understood?"

Jamie gave him her classic look of disgust. "Okay, we will do it your way. You're sure you won't need us on this trip?"

"No, no public appearances---just some quick in and outs. I hope to be back in one week, but it might take me two."

Jamie nodded. "Okay, we will keep an eye on them…and don't drink so much. You do stupid things when you get drunk, like taking on a bar full of bikers in the defense of a dyke."

Trevor grinned. "Yea! But that is one incredible dyke." The two ladies laughed, got up, and departed. Trevor killed the glass and retired for the evening.

Chapter 27

A departure, a surprise visit

Trevor owned a fleet of private jets that he leased out to other corporations in the Atlanta area. Sharing the operating costs reduced the cost of owning a private jet but also gave him the convenience of financial versatility. Keeping them at the DeKalb Airport meant that they could be serviced and ready whenever a member of the club needed one. All he needed was to make a call, and a private jet or helicopter would pick him up. The planes were owned by his company, Private Jet. Members paid a fee and could call for a plane to take them anywhere for the mere cost of the travel.

It was early Saturday morning and Jamie was driving with Susan in the passenger seat and Trevor in the back seat. They waited at the landing strip for the aircraft to arrive. Without turning around, Jamie asked, "You feel better?"

Trevor was clearly in dismay. "A little. God, why did you let me drink that much last night?"

Jamie chuckled over her shoulder. "Let you? Christ, you were gone by the time we got there. I didn't let you do a damn thing. That was purely a product of your self-loathing."

"Yea, you're right. I'm doing it to myself, but I still remember our conversation from last night. Can you do it for me?"

Jamie and Susan nodded in unison. "We will do what we can, but we can't do much with her living there and us here. So…unless we camp out on her front porch, our jurisdiction is limited."

"I know, but do what you can." They spotted the aircraft coming in for a landing and watched it touchdown before taxiing over to the SUV. The trio exited the vehicle, and as Trevor started to pull his large bag out of the back of the SUV, one of the pilots hurried over to retrieve it.

Trevor wrapped his arms around both girls at the same time. "You two are my best friends. We are a tripod, and a tripod requires all three legs to stand on its own. I know you will do your best." He turned and walked to the aircraft. The girls watched as the aircraft departed.

Susan asked Jamie, "Tell me, what excuse are we going to use when we show up at Sam's house?"

Jamie shrugged. "Corrupting her daughter?"

Susan laughed. "I don't think that will work, but it is worth a college try. How about we just tell her that we missed her in Trevor's absence, and we don't have anybody to pick on?"

Jamie watched the plane disappear into the morning sky. "That is a thought, and we can take them out to lunch. That way, we can plant some cameras and case the place." Jamie started the car and headed back to the house.

The girls returned to the Paterson house and assembled several cameras. Six actually transmitted via an encrypted Wi-Fi signal and the other six only recorded. They didn't know what they would need, but all had built in power supplies that would last 24 hrs. They stashed them in their purses, put on jeans and loose-fitting lace tops, and headed out. It was almost 9am, by the time they arrived at Sam's house in Winder.

They pulled in front and parked at the curb. Liz was sitting on the front-porch bench with Mathew. She noticed the two women exit the vehicle and start up the driveway. Liz called to Sam through the open window. "Do you know these women?" Sam was inside dusting the furniture and walked to window to see who was there. She was wearing jeans with her t-shirt tied in a knot in front and her hair in a ponytail. She noticed Jamie and Susan walking up the driveway and smiled.

As they reached the front steps, Sam stepped out to greet them. "So, you got bored and decided to come here to harass me some more?"

Jamie pulled a bottle of sweet wine from her large purse. "Yes, we did, and we brought some really good sweet wine to help." As they came up the steps, Mathew was sitting with Liz. He lowered his head and shook it no.

Liz looked at Mathew. "What's wrong?"

"I'm not sure if I can hang around you anymore."

"They're just mom's friends."

"Yea I know." He stood up, gave Liz a hug, and started to leave when Susan saw him.

Susan stepped over in front of him. "Now who is this?"

Jamie looked at Susan before eyeing Liz. "I know who mini-me belongs to, but who is this fine strapping fellow?"

Mathew's face turned red. "I'm Mathew. I live next door."

Susan toyed with him. "Next door, huh? Should we be concerned with you?"

Sam spoke up. "Mathew is good friend of Liz's."

Susan wrapped an arm around Mathew and put on her seductive voice. "So, Mathew, how good are you?"

Mathew's face reddened. He was at a loss for words and glanced at Liz, who rescued him from his discomfort. "He is plenty good. Now kindly unhand my friend."

Susan smiled. "Impressive. That's what I thought."

Mathew backed away, stepped around Susan, and quickly marched home. Sam scowled at Susan. "He is very shy, so you need to be gentle with him."

"Oh, gentle is my middle name."

Liz stood beside her mother. Jamie sized them up. "He was right---spitting images of each other! With this package, you get two for the price of one."

Sam chuckled. "This package is not for sale. Come on in, but you must behave."

As they proceeded back to the kitchen, Sam draped her arm around Liz. Liz whispered, "Who are these women?"

Sam stopped and realized that her worlds were intermingling. "Oh! Please, forgive me, Liz. This is Jamie Mathers, and this is Susan Walker. They work for Mr. Paterson." Sam left Liz to get acquainted with them as she busied herself in the kitchen.

Jamie smiled warmly. "It wasn't hard to figure out that you must be Elizabeth, Samantha's daughter."

Liz smiled. "Correct."

Sam placed a cold pitcher of lemonade on the table and turned to her two new friends. "Until I can determine what dubious scheme the two of you are working on, would you like some lemonade?"

Jamie understood Sam's hesitance to indulge in pleasantries. "Liz, I don't think your mother trusts us."

Liz confirmed that she was the type of girl who verified before trusting. "Well, have you given her reasons not to trust you?"

Susan started to laugh. "Yep, mini-me all right---is you sure she isn't a clone?"

Sam placed four glasses on the table and looked at her daughter. "Trust me, I gave birth to her."

Liz's curiosity piqued. "I assume that you two work for Mr. Paterson?"

Jamie looked at Sam for verification. "Really? You haven't told her about us? We are offended."

"I wanted to shield her from you as long as possible."

Susan looked at Jamie. "I told you she was smart."

The four women were now sitting around the table as Sam poured lemonade into each of the four glasses. She addressed her daughter. "Do you remember when I told you about the sparring match in the gym?"

Liz smiled. "The one where Mr. Paterson got his butt kicked?"

Susan piped up. "I wouldn't say he got his butt kicked; he put up a good fight."

Jamie nodded yes. "I would have said ass, but butt is good, and yes, you did kick it."

Liz's face lit up as she looked at Susan. "That was you?"

"Yea! I didn't want to do it, but someone had to."

Liz was highly amused with this banter. "Mom said you used to do cage fighting?"

Susan enjoyed Liz's flattery. "MMA---mixed martial arts is what it's called."

Jamie interjected, "She was ranked number 3 in the world at one time."

Susan added, "I would have been number two if it wasn't for that Rhonda Rousey bitch."

Sam decided to quell the upsurge of estrogen. "Language ladies! We have a young girl present."

Jamie nodded yes at Susan. "I guess PG is the rule here."

Sam had the situation under control. "Okay, it is time to fess up. Why are you here? I know this isn't just a random, friendly visit."

Jamie turned on her charm. "To see you, of course. We missed you."

Sam was unconvinced. "I saw you yesterday. It has been only one day."

Jamie looked at Susan and said, "Well that's at least 24 hours. That's a long time, isn't it?"

Susan spilled the beans. "Okay, Trevor asked us to check up on you."

Sam was not that shocked at this revelation. "I have been taking care of myself for some time now, and I don't need him looking after me."

Sam turned to Liz. "What are you grinning about?"

"I told you he liked you."

Jamie chuckled. "Did she tell you he kissed her?"

Sam was un-amused. "Jamie!"

Liz smiled in satisfaction. "Yes, she said it was just a peck on the cheek."

Jamie almost spit up her lemonade. "I don't think so!"

Susan chimed in on the banter with her prized line. "Yea, it was a suck face, lip smacker, tongue lock kiss that curled her toes."

Liz squealed, put her hands over her face, and looked at her mother, who was now shaking her head no. Sam was mortified. "I knew I shouldn't have allowed you two women in here."

Jamie smiled. "Too late."

"He knows you don't need him," Susan explained, "but he worries about the people he cares about. He just asked us to swing by, so with him gone, we're using it as an excuse to come over and harass you."

Sam's expression softened at the kind gesture. "Thank you."

Liz had additional questions. "So what do you do for Mr. Paterson?"

Jamie took the lead on this subject. "We are his bodyguards."

Liz's face lit up. "Really?!"

Susan found Liz's reaction adorable. "What, you don't think we can guard his body?"

Liz looked at her mother. "That must be fun, Mom. Wouldn't you like to guard his body?"

Sam gave her daughter a stern look and started to say something when Jamie interjected. "Now there's a smart girl."

Jamie and Susan started to laugh. Sam went into mama bear mode. "This is not proper conversation for a young lady."

Jamie replied, "Well, she is the only young lady here. I like to refer to myself as a seasoned woman, if you don't mind."

Susan hailed from the peanut gallery, "Here, here!"

Sam shook her head. "She is too young for this kind of conversation."

Jamie tried to change the subject. "Ah shucks, you're right. Okay, let's go shopping."

Sam refused the offer. "That's okay. I don't need anything."

Jamie would not take no for an answer, and she had promised Trevor to keep eyes on Sam. "Neither do we, but shopping doesn't necessarily mean spending money. We just look at the clothes, try on a few items, and have lunch---a girls' day. Besides, how often do you get to go shopping with a couple of catty women like us? Now both of you go put on some dresses, and off we go!"

Sam started to protest, but Jamie stopped her. "If you don't come peacefully, I will have Susan throw you over her shoulder, dressed as you are, and take you anyway."

Liz piped up. "Come on, mom. It could be fun."

Sam looked at the two women and then at her daughter. "Okay, give me a minute. I need to clean up a little."

Jamie replied, "Take your time, we aren't leaving without you." Sam and Liz went into their bedrooms to clean up and change. Jamie and Susan looked at each other and moved quickly.

Susan noticed that the white refrigerator was directly across from the back door, and she pulled a small, white box from her purse with a long power cord. She placed the magnetic box beside some other items on top of the refrigerator and ran the power cord down behind the refrigerator to a wall socket. Jamie pulled a small viewer from her purse opened it and turned it on; she hit a couple of buttons and gave a thumbs up.

They walked into the living room and spied a dark, wooden bookcase against the far wall. It faced toward the hallway that an intruder would walk down after entering the front door. They placed a book with a small camera in the binder among the books. It contained a built-in battery that would last a month.

They found the DSL modem and installed a small Wi-Fi receiver into one of the Ethernet jacks. The receiver would automatically connect to the two cameras and transmit the video through the DSL modem to their server.

They could use the connection to view both cameras. Just as they were finishing up with the small receiver, they heard Liz exit from her room. Susan sent a text saying the cameras were in place. Meanwhile, someone at the Paterson house keyed in some numbers, and two pictures appeared. They could see anyone who entered through the rear or front doors. It was all tied to a DVR for recording.

Sam came out wearing a light, one-piece, lace dress with thin straps over the shoulder, a small V-cut at her neckline, was hemmed just above her knees. Liz was wearing a tulip-cut skit that came midway between her hips and knees and a tank top that showed a little cleavage. They both had their hair down held the back with ribbons.

Jamie looked at Susan, and had one of their brief, nonverbal conversations. "Wait! Is this the same woman that dresses like a school marm, all week long? Hold it right there. I must capture this moment in time! She pulled her phone out and took a picture."

Sam put her arm around her daughter. "That was business, and this is pleasure."

Susan and Jamie shared a sly smile before they drove off in the SUV. They spent the rest of the afternoon checking out the shops in downtown Winder and also hit up the mall on 316. As Jamie promised, they didn't buy anything, but they tried on several dresses and picked on each other.

Trevor was almost to the west coast when he received a phone call. "Hello, how many cameras were …only two . . . that is better than none, okay good. Keep an eye on it … and … thank you." He hung up the phone.

Sam arrived at work on Monday morning and parked in her spot. She was wearing her black pencil skirt and button-up blouse with a jacket. As she made her way to the elevators, she noticed the parking garage guard watching her again, but that was normal. She proceeded to her cubicle on the 15th floor.

Her goal today was to send files to storage. The copy boy had delivered two boxes for her, and one was to go to The Country Town Bank. In the second box, she put the bulk of the information for

Fletcher industries, but she always kept a few files out for reference purposes. Once the files where in the boxes, she labeled each box according to content and stacked them on the chair inside her cubicle. She continued about her daily duties, and soon, the copy boy arrived with a cart and headed off to storage with the boxes. Sam noticed the email from the Chief of Security about taking files off premises, but she paid little attention to it. She never did that sort of thing anyway.

Sam updated the files on Paterson with her proposal and contracts and entered her notes from the last three days. Jennifer arrived, placed a file on her desk, and sat down in the chair in her cubicle. Sam picked up the file and saw the name: Bormann Industries. She looked at Jennifer and asked, "So, we have a new client all ready?"

Chapter 28

Sam is trapped

On Monday morning, Jennifer stopped by Sam's cubicle. "One of the other teams has this Steve Bormann account and wants to do a hostile takeover on Paterson Corporation. Since you just spent three days going through his books with a fine-toothed comb, they wanted to know if you would help."

Sam stared at the file and back at Jennifer. "I didn't go through all of his books; there is more to him than Paterson Corporation alone. Besides, he only allowed me access to assist the connection between his company and two others. I spent my time working on that, not Paterson."

"So…your answer is no."

"Of course, it is no. If it every got out that I shared the private information of one company with another, we would never be trusted again."

"I agree, but I was told to ask and to press. I agree with you; we can't assist them." Jennifer left.

Sam stared at her monitor and thought about that encounter with Jennifer---it wasn't like her. But she said she was told to ask and press.

She would meet in Jennifer's office away from thirsty ears so they could talk again.

Sam had some other technicalities to deal with. For example, there were some forms that required Larry Fletcher's signature, but first, she had to put them together. It was 12 by the time she assembled everything, and she took them to Jennifer for approval. They were standard forms that all clients would sign at the end of the marriage between Hutchinson Merger and Acquisitions and the company in question. It insulated the accounting firm against any lawsuits that might arise after everything was completed. What a company did after Hutchinson parted ways was not Hutchinson's problem.

Once she completed the forms, she rushed them over to Jennifer's office for the final approval. Jennifer signed the bottom and handed them back. Sam placed the documents into a folder and looked at Jennifer. "Okay, so what was that earlier?"

Jennifer looked up from her computer. "What was what?"

Sam looked confused. "Earlier…when you came and asked me to violate a client's confidence to assist another company who wants to engage in a hostile takeover."

Jennifer's expression didn't change. "I did what I was told to do---that was all."

"I need to run these over to Fletcher's and get Larry to sign them. I will be back tomorrow if that is okay?"

Jennifer remained stoned faced. "That is fine. See you tomorrow."

Sam left well enough alone. She gathered her things, placed the documents that needed to be signed into her briefcase, and peeked into Jennifer's office on her way out. Jennifer would normally look at her---this time, she didn't. Sam didn't understand but continued.

It was a sunny day with a clear blue sky, so Sam let the top down on her convertible as she wrapped a scarf around her head and started towards the exit. As she approached the exit ramp, the gate was down, and the young guard blocked the lane.

She pulled up, and he walked around to her side. "Sorry ma'am, but we have been ordered to inspect all vehicles leaving the garage."

Sam nodded. "Okay, as you can see, other than my briefcase, I have nothing in here."

The guard inspected the front and rear seats. "Could you open the trunk, please?"

Sam hit the button, and the trunk lid popped up. She saw him raise the lid and talk to someone on his radio. As if on cue, several people appeared on both sides of the car. Sam was confused as to what was happening.

One of the guards opened her door. "Can you exit the car, ma'am?"

Sam unlocked her seat belt and turned off the car. "What is the problem?" The man guided her to the rear of the car, and there in her trunk were the two boxes she had sent to storage.

Sam was in shock. "What are they doing in there? I just sent them to storage."

One of the guards asked, "That is what we want to know. Can you come with us?" Sam was baffled but complied and followed the man to a room on the 14th floor. The room was bare with light grey walls and a white ceiling---it was clearly staged for interrogation. There were two cameras in opposing corners near the ceiling and a table in the center. The guard motioned for her to sit in one of the chairs facing the large, one-way glass and left her in the room by herself. *How on earth did the boxes get into her trunk, and why were they there? The car was locked.*

She waited for about an hour before a man walked in with a briefcase and some files. He was accompanied by another guard who carried the boxes on a hand truck. He parked the hand truck with the boxes at the end of the table and departed. The other man sat down and laid the files out before him. He glared at Sam. "How much were you expecting to get for these files that you were stealing?"

Sam's jaw dropped. "Sell?! I sent those boxes to storage this morning. They are supposed to be in secure storage, not in my car. I don't know how they got there."

The man nodded and turned a page. "Do you have a receipt?"

Sam shook her head no. "I have never needed a receipt before. I just give them to him, and he takes care of it."

The man lowered his head and wrote something on a pad. "No receipt."

Sam was getting nervous. "Look, if I wanted that information, I could have made copies and taken them home. There is no reason for me to steal them. Let's be logical here."

The man's stoic expression was unwavering. "Do you have backups at home?"

"No! No! I don't! I just meant, why would I want to steal them? For what reason?"

"But you just said you had copies at home."

Sam was now beyond frustrated. "No, you misunderstood me. I just said that hypothetically, why would I steal them now when I had plenty of time to copy them? It doesn't make any sense."

The man seemed to completely dismiss her explanation. "Okay, we will have some people go to your house and find those documents---unless you are willing to tell us where they are."

Sam was now upset. Regardless of what she said, he was twisting it into some sort of incriminating confession. "No! No! I don't have a copy, that is what I'm saying! Are you even listening to me? I don't need to steal them or anything else."

The man nodded and turned the page. It was at this time that another man walked into the room, but instead of sitting at the table, he sat in a chair by the wall and listened. The first man started again. "So... you don't have any reason to steal and sell classified documents. Is that what you are saying?"

Sam nodded frantically. "Yes! Yes!"

"What did you pay for that car you're driving?"

"It was a deal I worked out with Mr. Bushier of The Country Bank."

"So, the car was payment for what--- information or sexual favors to Mr. Bushier?"

Sam shouted, "No! No! He wanted to meet me, and the deal was that we would trade cars."

"Interesting...he traded a 2005 Volkswagen for a 1986 Prism?"

Sam explained, "It was for his father. He wanted that car for his father."

The man's nodding was now bordering on misogynistic condescension. He clearly didn't believe a word she said. "His father died while he was in college."

Sam shook her head back and forth. "Wait, I don't understand, everything I have done has been above board. I have never cheated or lied to anyone. I don't know how those files got into my car. Understand? I didn't cheat anybody, so why are you doing this to me?"

"The reason is simple---files have been disappearing and comprising the security of our company and clients. Ms. Raven, you have been caught red-handed with the files; you're driving a car you can't afford; you're living in a house that is completely paid for; and on your salary, there is no way you could maintain this lifestyle. From a practical and logical standpoint, we have enough evidence to charge and convict you with corporate espionage and prostitution; you are looking at 10 years."

Samantha Raven almost went into shock. She was innocent, and now she was going to jail---she didn't understand. Sam looked at the man sitting across from her and kept saying, "No! No! I didn't do that---it is NOT me. I can't go to prison. I have a daughter. No!" She was in tears and rapidly unraveling.

The man that was sitting to one side suddenly moved his chair next to her and put his arm around her. "Ms. Raven, my name is Roger Dawson, and I'm the Chief of Security here. Maybe I can help." He turned to the suspicious interrogator. "Look she is one of the best people on our team. If she agrees to counseling with me, and I monitor her, can we delay these legal proceedings? She is far more valuable to this company working than sitting in prison."

The man protested. "Mr. Dawson, I have an airtight case here. If we get a search warrant for her house, I'm sure we will find more documents to prove her guilt."

Roger removed his arm from Sam and leaned towards the man. "As I said, she is still worth more to us working than in prison. If you send her to prison, she is worthless to us. Now if you want to proceed fine, I can't stop you. But if she agrees to counseling sessions with me, she will be more of an asset to the company than she would be in prison. I have no problem explaining this to your superiors, and we can see were the axe falls."

The man gave Mr. Dawson a long, hard look and nodded reluctantly. "I haven't heard her agree yet."

Roger turned to Sam and put his arm back around her. "Sam, agree to counseling sessions with me, and you won't go to jail. Your house and car won't be seized, and your daughter won't go into foster care---please agree. "

Sam was stuck between a rock and a hard place, and her world was crumbling all around her. "I would go to jail…my daughter would go to foster care? No, that can't happen! I didn't do anything!"

Roger repeated himself. "Agree that he is the witness and will testify that you agreed. Just say yes." Sam's mind was muddled, but she couldn't go to jail---she knew that. She took the only course of action open to her and silently nodded yes. Roger was unsatisfied. "No, we need to hear you say it."

Sam wiped her tears. "Yes, I will go to counseling sessions with you---just please don't take my daughter."

Roger nodded and turned to the man. The man looked furious, tossed the files into his briefcase, and slammed it closed. "This is ludicrous. She should go to jail." He pointed a finger at Sam. "You miss one meeting or I get one report from Mr. Dawson that he is not satisfied with you, trust me, you will be in jail. Do you understand?" Sam nodded yes, and the man left.

Sam looked at the Mr. Dawson. "Why did you do that? I don't know you."

"But I know everyone here, and I know who is worth it and who isn't. I meant what I said before: you are worth saving."

Sam was still wiping her tears. "Thank you, but what do I have to do now?"

"You will meet with me twice a week, let's say Tuesday and Thursday. Here is the address." He handed her a card. "Be there at 3pm tomorrow. The room number is on the back, and I will be waiting." Roger checked his watch. "Go home and count your lucky stars that I was here. I will see you there tomorrow." He left Sam to her own devices.

Sam was now crying alone in the interrogation room. She slowly rose onto her shaky legs and tried the door---it opened. She exited and headed home.

Jasper arrived at the meeting point and parked. He waited for the brown van to appear and watched it pull down the street and around the corner. He watched as one of the men walked up the street and crept into the woods. Jasper picked up his cell." Contact." Soon he received two contacts in return. They waited for 45 minutes before the bus rolled around the corner. They watched as it pulled to the stop and let the kids off. Finally, he spotted Liz.

But along with Liz was Mathew. Jasper slammed his fist against the steering wheel and picked up his cell. "Abort, Abort!" He watched as Liz and Mathew walked past. He noticed as Mathew took a long, hard look at the white Lincoln. Jasper put the car into gear and sped back to Jimmy Dittle's office.

Jimmy was once again infuriated. "What was the damn problem this time?! That is twice you went to get her and twice that you brought me nothing back. He could have killed that kid, and we would have been out of there. My patience is wearing thin."

Jasper plopped down into the chair. "Look Jimmy, if we grabbed her and the kid escaped, he would be able to pick me out of a lineup. He definitely spotted the car. You're letting your hard on for that bitch cloud your common sense. If we grabbed her today, the police would know it was a kidnapping. They would immediately start an Amber Alert search. Now if we wait, the police won't know it's a kidnapping, and they will have to wait 3 days before they do anything. By that time, you will be able to have your fun and sell her ass for everything it's worth. "

Jimmy knew that Jasper had a point. "So, when you going back?"

Jasper was quiet for a minute. "We need to wait until Friday. That way, they won't see us, and hopefully that kid won't be with her this time. Okay?"

Jimmy agreed. "I expect that little bitch in my office Friday afternoon. Do you understand?"

Jasper understood. Jimmy turned back to admire the wall of monitors.

Chapter 29

Roger Dawson

Sam didn't eat much that night. The entire event had her all out of sorts. She was trying to put it all together: the boxes in her trunk; the lawyer threatening her with jail; the loss of her home. The worst aspect would have been the loss of her daughter. She spent 15 years doing everything right, not breaking any rules or laws and having everything under control. Now she was looking at jail time---this was not right! She was at the mercy of someone else who was in complete control. Sam didn't like it. After dinner, she went to bed, but she didn't sleep much.

Liz watched her closely and knew there was something wrong, but Samantha wouldn't tell her what the problem was. Sam just went to bed, and Liz stayed up for a while reading.

The next day, Sam isolated herself in her work cubicle. She didn't want to talk to anybody about anything. Jennifer stopped by and delivered some folders---the Bormann files. Sam looked at the file." What's this?"

Jennifer's reply was somewhat robotic. "I have been asked to have you look at this."

"You want to go to your office, or do we talk here?"

Jennifer looked at Sam, looked up and scanned the top of the cubicle walls and back to Sam. She took a deep breath. "This is bigger than the two of us. I was asked to ask you to look at it." She bowed her head and peered up at Sam. "Please, for me."

Sam knew there was something else going on here. Jennifer had been a good friend for several years, so until she could figure it out, she would play along. Sam picked up the file. "I will look at it, but I'm not making any promises. I'm just saying I will look at it." Jennifer mouthed a silent "thank you" and left. Sam opened the file and started reading.

Sam couldn't even choke down her lunch, which was only a small sandwich. At half past two, Sam gathered her things and stepped out. She looked into Jennifer's office and they shared a quick nod of understanding and solidarity. She turned and walked out.

As Sam looked at Roger Dawson's card, she realized that she was familiar with the address. It was only 3 blocks away. When she arrived, her fears were confirmed---it was a hotel. That made her nervous. *Why would a counseling session be held in a hotel?* She breezed through the lobby to the elevator and pressed the 11th floor button.

As she exited the elevator and proceeded to room 1101, the last door on the right. She stood in front of the door for a second and knocked. *No answer.* She knocked again, and the door opened---there stood Roger Dawson.

Roger Dawson stepped back to allow Sam entrance. The room was actually an efficiency. Immediately to her left was a bar separating the living area from the small kitchenette. A large couch sat in front of a TV, and in the corner, a table with four chairs was surrounded by glass windows. Behind the couch was a door that obviously led to a bedroom.

Roger pointed to the couch. "Why don't you put your briefcase and jacket on the couch?"

Sam laid down her briefcase. "I'd like to keep my jacket on."

Roger nodded. "This way." He motioned towards the table in the far corner. Sam followed him to the table and sat opposite of him.

Roger grabbed two wine glasses from the credenza and place one in front of each of them. He picked a bottle and poured some wine into each glass.

Sam refused. "No thank you. I don't want any."

Roger placed the bottle back onto the credenza. "On the contrary, I didn't ask if you wanted any. I want you to drink because it will help you relax. Besides, you're tighter than a snare drum."

Sam looked at him and slowly picked up the glass before taking a small sip and setting it back down. *What kind of counseling is this? Is there something in this wine?* Roger smiled. "The purpose of this is for us to get to know and understand each other. I need to know what you like and/or dislike, and you need to understand what I expect. Understood?" Sam nodded.

Roger picked up a notepad. "We will start off by you answering some questions. Is that okay with you?" It was not okay, but Sam felt that she had no choice but to agree.

Roger looked at his notepad. "You live in Winder Georgia?" Sam nodded yes.

"You live there alone with your daughter?" Sam nodded yes again.

"How did Mr. Paterson finance his latest acquisitions?"

Sam jerked her head up. "Since I didn't get into that part of his books, I don't know."

Roger nodded and wrote something on his notepad. "Your daughter is 15?"

Sam replied reluctantly. "Yes."

"She was a product of a college fling?" Sam looked away and nodded yes.

"How long did you date her father?"

Sam sighed. "We dated almost nine months."

Roger scribbled something else on his notepad. "How long had you been dating before you became intimate?"

Sam looked at Roger for a second before answering. "Three months."

Roger had a sinister grin on his face. "So, you held off for three months before giving it up?"

Sam sensed a creepy vibe from him. "If that is how you want to portray it, then I guess that's right."

Roger marked the ledger again. "When did you realize you were pregnant?"

Sam revealed no emotion in her facial expression. "Early June, after I came home from school."

"So, you were fucking him for almost six months before he got you pregnant?"

Sam found this line of questioning invasive and vulgar. "Are these questions necessary?"

Roger smiled again like the Joker from the Batman movies. "Whatever I want is necessary, now answer."

Sam didn't like this skewed portrayal of herself. "We were intimate for six months before I got pregnant, yes."

"You don't like the word Fuck?"

Sam was irritated. "When characterizing what we---yes!"

"So how did you keep from getting pregnant--- birth control, condoms, timing, oral, or anal?"

Sam was disgusted but continued, "Condoms and timing."

Roger nodded. "What about oral sex?"

Sam didn't want to answer. "What about it?"

Roger's creepy smile sent shivers up Sam's spine. "Do you like giving it or receiving it?"

"I guess both."

Roger continued to take notes. "When was the last time you where intimate with a man?"

"What do you mean by 'intimate'?"

Roger clarified his inquiry. "When was the last time you fucked a man?"

Sam turned red. "I haven't been with anybody since Tip in college."

"Was he your first?"

Sam was silent for a second. These were inappropriately personal questions. "No." She looked away.

Roger smiled again. "Take your jacket off."

"I'm fine."

Roger leaned in closer. "That wasn't a request."

This made Sam nervous, but she knew she had to comply---it was only a jacket. She removed the jacket and tossed it over to the couch.

Roger sat back and looked her up and down. "So, which do you prefer---having your pussy licked or sucking dick?"

Sam had reached her limit of being objectified. "Excuse me. but is there a point to these vulgar questions?"

"There is, now which one?"

Sam didn't know how to answer. With Tip, she enjoyed pleasing him as much as she enjoyed him trying to please her, and it wasn't a question of which one was better. Both were great. Sam took a gulp of wine. "I can't answer that."

"Okay. Pick up your wine and follow me." He got up from the table, grabbed the bottle of wine, and headed for the bedroom. Sam didn't know what to do. She didn't want to go into the bedroom; the questions were bad enough.

Roger stopped at the bedroom door and repeated himself. "Excuse me, but that wasn't a request." Sam got up slowly, picked up her wine glass, and walked towards the bedroom. When she arrived at the door, she looked up at Roger, and he gestures for her to go in. Sam entered the bedroom. Just inside the door to the right was a dresser with a large mirror over it. About three feet away was the king size bed, and to the left was the entrance into the bathroom. She took a couple of steps in and heard the door shut behind her. It sounded loud and heavy like a jailhouse door.

Roger circled her and set the bottle on the dresser. He motioned for her to come to him. Sam's heart was in her throat. *Please not sex, please!* She stopped in front of him still holding the glass of wine with both hands in front of her. Roger took the glass of wine and placed it on the dresser.

He started to unbutton her blouse, and Sam put up her hands to block him. "What are doing?"

Roger had ensnared his prey. "What do you think I'm going to do to you?"

"I thought this was a counseling session?"

"It is whatever I say it is."

"I didn't agree to have sex with you."

Roger stopped closer. "You can walk out whenever you want to, but remember if you do, hire a lawyer. You will need one, and trust me, you will end up in jail. As for your daughter, well, you know what happens in foster homes."

Sam wasn't confident that she could beat him in court, and she didn't have enough money to hire a lawyer sufficient to beat anybody the firm could hire. If she gambled with the feigned integrity of the justice system, she could lose everything---or she could wait, and hopefully she could talk her way out of it. She allowed him to unbutton her blouse.

He turned her to face the mirror and stood behind her. She felt him undo the clasp on her skirt and pull the zipper down slowly as she begged, "Please don't." Her skirt drifted to the floor.

Sam shuddered. *I don't want this, but how can I stop it?* Roger reached around finished unbuttoning her blouse. He pulled it slowly off her shoulder as he savored the expression on her face. She didn't want to watch him undress her, so she turned and looked away from the mirror. The blouse was gone. She felt him touch the clasp to her bra, and she again begged, "Please don't do this." She was on the verge of tears.

Roger whispered into her ear, "I'm with one of the most beautiful women in the office, and you expect me to not have sex with you?"

Sam gave in because she had no choice. With a flick of Rogers's fingers, the shoulder straps on her bra disappeared as it dropped to the dresser. She was now naked except for her panties. *This can't be happening! Am I trapped in a nightmare? Someone wake me up!*

Roger picked up a pillow and stood beside her. "So, you don't know which you prefer--- giving oral sex, or receiving it?" Sam shook her head in utter dismay. Roger dropped the pillow between them, grabbed her face, and turned it to him. She didn't want to look at him. *I don't want to see his face.*

He placed both hands on her shoulders and forced her to her knees. "You know what to do---now do it!"

Chapter 30

Things get ugly

Thus, began her introduction to Rogers's world of sexual coercion. Sam was now on her knees before him with tears running down her face. She watched in horror as Roger unzipped his pants and presented his penis. Placing his hand on her head, he forced her to perform fellatio. She was appalled at what he was making her do. *He is forcing me to let him rape me.* The worst part of this real-life horror show was that Samantha Raven was no longer in control. She was helpless had no say in this matter.

Roger didn't stop with the fellatio---he continued to other positions. Once she completed the first task, Roger stepped to the bed and yanked the duvet from the bed. He forced Sam onto the bed where he proceeded to have sex with her. After more fellatio and cunnilingus, he rolled her onto her stomach and took her from behind. He wasn't finished with her just yet. He rolled her onto her back started to mount her in the missionary position.

Sam cried out in agony, "Please don't! I don't want to get pregnant." It was the first time she had been penetrated in 15 years, and this was not how she envisioned her next sexual encounter.

Roger continued on with his forced submission as if he got some sort of sick pleasure from Sam's desperate protests. "Please don't get me pregnant…please!" As he reached a crescendo Sam went numb mentally and physically. She became lost in the inferno of his rapture. *If he gets me pregnant, how will I explain it? How can I justify what just happened? This type of thing doesn't happen to women like me. I planned my life so carefully.*

Roger invaded her thoughts with sick justifications for his vile behavior. "Don't worry, I shoot blanks."

Sam did not trust him, so she had to ask, "What do you mean?"

"I had a vasectomy several years ago. I don't want kids either, so I won't get you pregnant." A wave of strange relief came over her. Roger suddenly got up and walked to the bathroom. Sam laid there for several minutes. She felt tainted and dirty submitting to this pig that she barely even knew. Yesterday, she had been in the driver's seat of her life. Now, she was merely a passenger.

For a woman, it is not what the man does but who is doing it that matters. When a woman willingly gives herself to him, she is not only giving him access to her body. She is giving up the key that unlocks her heart and her soul.

A woman gives everything, and a man grants her access to his resources. She is the prize that men vie for. Men learn how to act, to dress, and eat with utensils just to earn the privilege of being with a woman.

In the complex mind of a woman, sex is more of an investment into a relationship rather than an attempt to quench the thirst of carnal desire. Most women derive more pleasure from satisfying their man's needs than from the sexual act itself. When their men are happy with all of their basic needs met, women derive a sense of purpose. Women don't think about sex as often but thrive on its implications.

Because of the mechanics of heterosexual genitalia, men tend to think of themselves as the givers and the women as receivers. On the contrary, a woman gives up a precious gift during intimate relations. And when she is robbed of this ability through force, it creates a ripple effect of crippling loss of control that permeates all other aspects of her existence. Seeking help from others is not always an option because the fear of being judged and blamed is simply too much to bear.

Roger exited the bathroom and started to get dressed. He pulled an envelope from the inside pocket of his suit coat and laid it on the dresser before placing Sam's panties in his pants pocket. He motioned for Sam to approach him. She was sore, so she moved slowly towards him. He touched the envelope and said, "In here is 6 hundred dollars and 2 business cards."

Sam insisted, "I'm not a whore."

Roger grabbed her by her hair and pulled her close enough to feel his hot, putrid breath on the nape of her neck. "You are what I say you are---understand? And if you don't like it, there is the door. Now the money is to pay for certain expenses you will incur. There is a card to an OBGYN in our building, and I scheduled an appointment for tomorrow. She will prescribe birth control, so take it. There is also a fashion store on the first floor you will need to secure outfits of my choosing. And when we meet here again on Thursday, this had better be clean shaven." Sam winced as he grabbed her pubic hair and yanked it.

Roger released her and stepped back. "You've done well today---don't blow it. I'm satisfied with our first consultation." He started to leave but stopped at the door and looked at his watch. "It's 4 o'clock. Take the rest of the day off." He stormed out, letting the door close softly behind him.

Sam felt like a used dishrag. She felt that everyone who looked at her knew what she just done, but she didn't want to remain in the hotel any longer. As she hurriedly dressed quickly, she cursed the fact that he had stolen her panties. With her hair restored to its bun, she gathered her remaining belongings and headed for the door, but she looked through the peephole to make sure that the hallway was clear before leaving.

She breezed through the lobby and exited without saying a word. As she walked back to past the guard in the parking garage, she became paranoid. *Can the guard tell that I just had sex? God, I hope not!* Once she reached her car, she left the top up and proceeded home.

When Sam was 30 minutes out, she called home, as was customary, and talked to her daughter. She informed Liz of her impending arrival, but this time, there was no talking of getting the boys out. Just that she would be home.

The missing banter did not go unnoticed by Liz, but Liz didn't know what to make of it. When Liz walked home in the afternoon from the bus stop, she noticed the white Lincoln Mathew spotted before wasn't there. She entered her house and proceeded to finish her homework. She secretly wanted to return to this Jimmy Dittle project, but first, work!

She checked her E-bay account, and several of her items had sold. She entered the address into the Click-n-Ship program and packaged up the items for shipment. She calculated her profit margin and realized she made roughly $10 that day.

Next, she signed in as Tweenie on Facebook and noticed that Jimmy Dittle was online. Almost immediately, a window popped up with a message from him. "Well, you are very nice looking. What is it you like to do?"

Liz smiled. "I like to watch TV, mostly love stories, and hang with my friends. As Jimmy asked more questions, Liz continued to give vague answers. Suddenly the phone rang, and it was her mother. Liz decided to end the conversation.

Sam arrived home and showered immediately. She had to get the filth off of her. She joined Liz in the kitchen for dinner and began cleaning up. Sam tried to read the Bormann file but found it difficult. Finally, Sam rose from the couch and went to bed. She tried to sleep but kept visualizing Roger's menacing grin above her. It was a rough night.

On Wednesday, she was still trying to concentrate on the Bormann file. She was able to get some work done, but it wasn't easy. The file seemed to be full of fluff and misinformation, so she Googled the company to find more. She found their website, but unlike other sites, it didn't go into any of its history. She had to dig deeper.

Sam perused the web page but didn't see a thing. Her mind was elsewhere, and she was having a hard time concentrating. Suddenly Mary, the receptionist, appeared in the opening of her cubicle. She smiled and asked, "Are you okay?" Sam instinctively nodded yes, but she was lying, and Mary knew it.

Mary took a step into the cubicle and perched on the edge of the chair. "You know, what you did in that presentation was phenomenal. No one expected you to do that. You finally stepped out of your comfort zone and tackled an impossible situation." Sam liked hearing the words of praise, especially right now when she felt like trash after allowing Roger Dawson to rape her. But silence was her only option.

Sam thanked Mary for her words. She was doing her best to prevent the tears from coming. Mary stood up and patted her on the back. "Just keep doing what you do best, you hear me? You have friends, friends you don't even know about, so just keep doing what you do best. That is what will get you through this."

Sam was dumbfounded. *Did Mary know what was going on?* Before she could ask anything, Mary walked out. Sam looked back at her computer screen. Mary was right---her strength came from knowing what was going on, and right now, all she knew was that she was being forced to submit to rape. And yes, this technically was rape. She wasn't resisting, but it was not what she wanted. If given the choice, she would say no, but she couldn't. Saying no would be the proverbial nail in her coffin, and she would lose everything. She wouldn't dare take that chance.

She had to make her appointment with the OBGYN on the 10th floor, but first she had to stop by the drug store---all things she was being forced to do. Sam concentrated and decided that at this time, she had no power over what was happening to her, but she kept her wits about her. Her intelligence would get her out of this---it had to. She just had to bite her lip and save face for now. She logged off her computer and exited for her doctor's appointment.

The plane had just leveled off at 30,000 ft, and Trevor picked up the phone. It wasn't long before he reached the person he wanted. When they picked up, Trevor asked, "Okay, what's happening?' He listened to the other person for a minute and asked, "When was this . . . as she was leaving?" Trevor listened to the response on the other end before inquiring, "Where did they take her … what do you mean you don't know … 14th floor? Whose offices are there . . . who is Roger Dawson? . . . Okay, I'm listening."

Trevor went silent; he was visibly upset. The in-flight stewardess walked over and placed a small glass of Maker's Mark on the table beside him. Trevor nodded thank you and resumed his phone conversation. "Okay, what happened … what do you mean you lost her … when did she reappear?" He nodded. "What do you mean she looked … Okay? So how does she look today?" He took a swig of his bourbon and continued to listen.

Suddenly, Trevor spoke in an authoritative tone. "Listen to me--- we can't let this happen again, understand? There is some real shit getting ready to come down. I have to know where she is and what is happening. I need her protected. Okay … in her briefcase … good idea. Can we get a tap on her phone?" Trevor's seemed irritated this time. "I don't give a damn if it's illegal! I want to know she is safe. I'm depending on you, so please don't let me down. Okay, thank you. I will call the day after tomorrow. Goodbye." He hung up the phone, picked up the shot glass, and killed it.

The stewardess approached him. "Would you like another, sir?"

Trevor mulled over whether he should have another and decided that he needed one. "Make it a double."

Chapter 31

Sam is rapped again

On Wednesday evening when Sam arrived home, she spotted Jamie and Susan's car at the curb. She enjoyed seeing them, but today had been a dumpster fire. She didn't really feel like she could handle their deprecating banter right now, but they were here, so what could she do?

She entered the house to find Liz and the two ladies sitting in the living room talking and put on a fake smile. What surprised her was that the banter was refreshingly positive. Sam laid her briefcase onto the dining room table and excused herself to go change into sweats and a t-shirt. She came out and found Jamie sitting by the computer with Liz, and Susan was coming out of the kitchen with a glass of water.

Susan looked at Sam, and in a depressed tone said, "Now how can we take the two of you out to dinner with you dressed like a homeless person?"

Sam shrugged. "I'm not in the mood---it has been a long day."

Jamie nodded. "Okay, so you're in the mood to make dinner, and since you forgot to call that means you get to make it…or we can go out, your choice."

Sam was in no mood to cook and she was famished from skipping lunch. "How fancy?"

Jamie and Susan looked at each other. "Jeans and a nice shirt, that's all."

Sam nodded and went back into her bedroom. Jamie looked to Liz, "Go change." Liz nodded and pranced out of the room.

The girls quickly went to work. Susan pulled a small black box from her purse that looked like a DSL filter and switched it out with the one in the wall jack before reconnecting the phone. The DSL filter had two jacks---one for the phone and one for the DSL modem. This adapter transmitted a WIFI signal into the WIFI receiver already plugged into the modem then relayed to a server at the plantation. That way, any phone call, incoming or outgoing, would be transmitted to the server.

Jamie picked up her cell and made a call. Susan picked up one of the cordless phones and dialed another number. Jamie asked, "You got the connection?" She nodded and hung up. Susan then hung up and returned the phone to the cradle. Jamie spun the briefcase around and opened it. Susan brought over her case, which was identical, and they quickly swapped the contents of Sam's case into Susan's. Susan then swapped the stickers between cases that made them look different so Sam wouldn't notice. They shut the case and walked back into the living room.

On Thursday, Sam had no desire to go to work. She wished she could have called in sick, but she didn't think that would be a wise idea. She knew what was going to happen at 3pm and dreaded it with a passion. She tried desperately not to think about it.

Suddenly, Jennifer appeared at the door of her cubicle and presented her with a FedEx folder. "This just arrived via courier for you." Sam nodded. She didn't know how to deal with Jennifer these days. They had been friends for several years, and suddenly Jennifer being secretive and barely speaking to her.

Sam opened the folder and removed the papers. As she read them, she realized this was the information on how Mr. Paterson engineered the purchase of the furniture and moving companies---information that has been asked of her, but she didn't have. *Why did these appear out of nowhere all of a sudden? Who sent them?* She looked around suspiciously. *Trevor was out of town, so he wouldn't have sent it.* She read the documents and found the contents interesting, but at this time, it wasn't relevant.

She couldn't eat lunch, so at 2:30 pm, she picked up her things and started towards the door. Jennifer was in her office, just sitting there staring blankly at the wall. She appeared lost, but Sam didn't know why. Sam turned and headed for the door. As she passed reception, she waved to Mary and left.

When Sam arrived on the first floor, she turned to head for the parking garage. She had considered what she was going to have to do and didn't want to return to the garage. She would want to get into her car and leave---the fewer people she would have to meet the better. She drove the few blocks to the Marriott hotel, parked in the parking lot and headed through the lobby to the elevators. Once she arrived at room #1101, she stopped outside the door, took a deep breath, and slowly knocked. The door opened.

Roger stepped aside to allow her to enter. She was wondering. *Are we going right into having sex, or do I have to succumb to another litany of asinine questions?*

Roger brought her a glass of red wine. "Right on time. Are you looking forward to our little consultations?" Sam toke a sip and didn't say anything. She dropped her briefcase onto the couch and walked to the table in the far corner. She gazed out on to the Atlanta skyline. Roger stepped up behind her and refilled her glass. "How was your day?"

Sam kept her stone face. "How long will I have to do this?" *Is he serious? Why is he trying to exchange pleasantries?*

Roger smiled. "Until I get tired of you, now come."

He took her by her free hand and pulled her into the bedroom. Her mind was racing. *I guess it will be like last time. I will give him a blowjob, and then we will have sex. Then he will leave---okay, I can handle this.* As they entered the bedroom, Roger grabbed the duvet and pulled it off the bed onto the floor. He then took Sam's wine glass placed it onto the dresser. "Now strip."

The words landed like a slap to her face. Sam moved slowly, unbuttoned her jacket, and removed it. She then unzipped her skirt and allowed it to drop to the floor. Next, she unbuttoned her blouse and pulled it off her shoulder. Reaching behind her back, she undid the clasp to her bra and allowed it fall off. As she bent down, she picked up her skirt and laid it with the rest of her clothing on the dresser. She was now naked except for her panties. Roger stood and smiled. He pulled her hairpin out and gathered her hair into a ponytail using rubber bands to hold it.

Roger stepped over to the bed, picked up a pillow, and dropped it between them. He then took off his shirt and laid it onto the dresser. Sam slowly knelt before him, unzipped his pants, and started to perform fellatio. She tried to take her mind elsewhere. *Go to my happy place. Go to my happy place. Mind over matter or member in this case.* Sam wanted to vomit.

Roger started to moan, and she felt him getting larger when suddenly, she heard a door slam and a man yelling, "We don't allow prostitutes in this hotel!" Sam rotated and ended up sitting on her butt looking up at a stranger standing inside the door to the bedroom. He was looking at the envelope containing $600 and pointing at Roger, "How dare you bring this whore into our hotel! We don't tolerate prostitution, and I'm arresting her right now."

The stranger reached down, grabbed Sam by the wrist, and pulled her up. In that same motion, he pressed handcuffs onto her wrist, turned her around and started to place them onto her other wrist. Sam looked at Roger, "Roger!"

Roger stepped forward. "Wait, you can't do this."

The man pulled some credentials from his pocket. "I'm house security, and yes I can arrest her for prostitution."

Sam looked at Roger and shook her head. She felt her mind going into a tailspin. *Oh God, can this get any worse?* Sam pleaded through her tears, "Can I at least get dressed?"

The stranger laughed. "You make your living taking your clothes off---might as well let everyone see you without them."

The stranger started to pull her from the bedroom and through the living room towards the door. Sam looked at Roger and yelled, "Roger! Do something!"

Roger then stepped between the stranger and the door. "Listen here, if you walk out that door with her, you will be fired."

The man scowled at Roger. "Excuse me?"

"My company keeps several rooms here on retainer. If you leave with her, we will pull those retainers, and that will be a major loss of revenue for this hotel."

The man stopped what he was doing. "You don't have that power."

Roger didn't back down. "I'm the Director of Security, and if I say it is not safe here, we will remove our retainers."

"I just can't ignore this. It's illegal. I wish I could arrest you, but it is not illegal to be a John---just a whore."

Roger nodded. "Let's make a deal. What if she gives you a blowjob? Trust me, she can pull a vacuum on a tanker---you won't regret it." The man looked back at Sam, whose expression was now shock. She had gone from being arrested to giving this stranger a blowjob. *I guess it can get worse.*

Sam looked at Roger, who was now dragging her back into the bedroom. "What are you doing?"

"You have a choice, give him a blow job or he can parade you through the lobby naked and have you arrested for prostitution. That means jail, the loss of your job, and everything else. So…what do you want?" Sam couldn't believe her ears. She had never imagined that she could hate another human being this much.

Chapter 32

The uninvited guest

Roger turned to the man. "Get these handcuffs off." The man searched his pocket and produced the key to remove her handcuffs. Sam was looking at Roger with pure contempt. He disgusted her, and she whispered, "I hate you."

Roger smiled and silently mouthed, "I know." Sam was trapped, and he knew it. She was now being forced to service another man, a man she has never even met before.

While she was servicing this man, she felt Roger taking advantage of the situation, and soon she had both men on her. She tried to push him off, but it was pointless. There was nothing she could do. She was being taken by two men at once, and she was revolted and ashamed at what she was being forced to do. They forced her onto the bed where they continued to rape her. She continued to exist in her mind. *I have never felt so helpless.*

After a while, Roger went into the bathroom, and the security guard forced her onto her stomach so he could sodomize her. She was trying to fight him off, but she wasn't strong enough. He was taking her anyway. As she was being forced, face down on the bed, crying with one man on top of her, she saw Roger.

Roger lingered by the door of the bathroom as he watched the stranger violate her. When the stranger finished, he pulled out and got dressed. He departed without a word. Roger rolled her onto her back and finished her off.

She of course allowed it; did she have a choice? She lay like a limp fish as he rutted on top of her when she asked, "He wasn't really Hotel Security, was he?" Roger stopped and looked down into her face. Her expression was devoid of emotion.

He started to deny it but realized that she had figured it out. "No, he wasn't."

Sam was irate. "I have to fuck you, but don't ever do that again. I'm not a whore, and I will not be treated like a piece of meat!"

Roger rested himself on his elbows. "You will be what I want you to be. Understood?"

Sam didn't say a word---she just turned her head away. She couldn't handle looking at him---it was revolting. Once he finished, he rose and walked into the bathroom. Sam felt dirty, used, and cheap. She thought about what they did to her today, and it horrified her. She thought about a line from college that she remembered in Edgar Allan Poe's, *The Cask of Amontillado,* "Revenge is a dish best served cold." Sam vowed that when the time came, it would be cold, ice cold. Most importantly, he wouldn't even see it coming.

After Roger left, Sam dressed. She made sure the hair was back into its customary bun, grabbed her briefcase, and exited the room. She proceeded to walk with as much dignity as she could muster when she crossed the lobby out to the parking lot where her car was parked. She started it, sat for a second, and then turned it off.

She had to cry first and let the emotion out after what she had just done. There was no way she could go back to the office, much less drive a car. She had been meticulously careful for so long to ensure the protection of herself and more importantly, the protection of her daughter. Without Samantha, Elizabeth would become a ward of the state, and be cast into the foster care system. She couldn't fathom what would happen to Liz there.

This--- Samantha was not going to allow. She would do anything to protect Elizabeth, even having sex with the pig, Roger Dawson. If this is what she had to do, then so be it. But right now, she had to get control of her emotions, and that required a cathartic cry.

Liz had arrived home, and after finishing her homework and E-bay sales, she focused her energy on researching Jimmy Dittle. She fired up the computer and logged into Facebook. As she expected, there was a message from Jimmy. "When do you plan on leaving home?

Liz contemplated her answer for a moment. "I don't have anywhere else to go." She knew Jimmy would make her an offer, and she would have to continue to tease him. She was interrupted by a call from her mother.

Liz answered the phone. "Hi mom! When are you going to be home?"

Sam was still trying to compose herself, so she steadied her wavering voice. "Hi honey! I will be there in about 50 minutes. Can you have dinner ready? I am going to be exhausted tonight."

"Of course. You okay mom. You sound a bit off."

Sam caught her breath. "I'm fine honey---I'm just tired. See you soon." She disconnected and then pulled off the road. She had to stop and cry again. This was too much, and it was never what she wanted to be or become. She was being used like a whore for some psychopath's perverse amusement. She had no control over anything anymore, and this realization was eating her up from the inside out.

Once the private jet reached 30,000 ft, Trevor picked up the phone again. It had been a harrowing two days. He had accomplished a lot, but he now needed a thorough briefing on events back home. Soon the party he wanted came on the line, and he was eager to speak,

"It's me…Okay that was good." Suddenly he sat up and asked, "She went where? You have to be kidding me! I don't believe it. Who did she meet?"

Trevor shook his head and continued. "Did we … good, how did she sound? … Like that huh? … Maybe it is not what we think. Look, I want to know what happened Monday. Find out … that is when everything went to hell. Okay, do what you can. I have one more stop I have to make … no, I don't have a choice. I will be there on Sunday. Can you help her keep it together? Okay." Trevor hung the phone up and tossed it across the cabin in frustration. He normally didn't lose his cool in this manner.

The stewardess stepped out of the small kitchen, picked up the phone, and handed a shot glass of Woodford Bourbon whiskey to Trevor. He looked up at her. "Thank you."

She remained professional. "Dinner will be ready in a few minutes. Would you like some wine with your meal?" Trevor nodded yes and said nothing else.

Jamie and Susan were sitting in the control room as they listened to the phone. Jamie looked at Susan. "Did you hear that in her voice?"

Susan nodded. "She is under stress---even her daughters heard it and look at the screen. She pulled off the road, and now she is sitting on the side of I-85--- just sitting there. That's not a safe or normal place to park a car."

Jamie studied the screen. "Let's think about this. She left work and went to the Marriot. What room did she go to?"

Gary then hit some keys, and her path emerged. "She went to the 11th floor and walked to this room---1101."

Susan thought for a minute. "Trevor is right. We are approaching this all wrong. Who was in that room with her?"

Jamie and Gary looked at each other before Gary said, "We don't know."

Susan turned to Gary and demanded, "I want to know who rented that room and who was in there with her upsetting to Sam so much. We need to find out who is doing this and what they are doing." Gary nodded and turned to his computer.

Jamie walked over to Susan and asked. "You want to go see her?"

Susan nodded, "I would love to go, but I don't think we would be welcome at this time. We need to figure out what is going on so we can get ahead of it. Right now, we are playing catch up."

Susan looked at Jamie. "The most exasperating thing about Trevor is that he senses that shit is going to happen. How does he know these things?"

Jamie nodded in agreement. "I have known him too long to ignore his feelings. I don't know how he does it, but he has been right too many times to ignore it."

Jimmy was sitting at his computer reading the last message from Tweenie. In his office sat Jasper and the two muscle men to drive the van. Jimmy announced, "Tomorrow is a go. She thinks she is stringing me along and that I don't know anything. We have been stopped the last two times---I want her this time. You know the plan. Once the school bus leaves and she is passing the wooded area---grab her! You will be pulling up in the van to pick them up. Do you get it?! I don't want any fuck ups this time. Let's do it right."

Jimmy paused. "Oh! Jasper, one more thing. I want you to get there earlier and go back into that house. See if you can find any more DVD's, okay! Now get the hell out of here, you imbeciles."

The three men left. Jimmy turned to looked up at his screens and then leaned back and smiled. He brought up the GIF of Tweenie and played it repeatedly. He thought to himself, "By this time tomorrow, I will be fucking the shit out you, little Tweenie---and I'm going to enjoy every second of it."

Chapter 33

Liz is kidnapped

Friday morning Liz went to school and Sam drove to work. Sam's routine was the same: park the car, put her hair up, and then walk to the office. She was working hard to keep her shit together. She wasn't going to fall apart in public.

Sam arrived at her cubicle and sat down. She pulled the folder out that had arrived yesterday from Paterson and studied it. Why would someone send me this? It doesn't make any sense. She didn't want this incriminating information. It could only mean danger for her and her daughter.

She picked up the Bormann file, and started her research again. She had to figure out who this Bormann was and why the company wanted to perform a hostile takeover. She checked to see if the SCC and IRS had authorized access to those files---and they had. At least she was getting somewhere. Over the next few hours, she managed to paint a picture of who and what Bormann was.

Bormann was actually Bormann Ltd., and they were listed as an investment group. However, they were actually Corporate Raiders. Corporate Raiders is a group that tries to take over companies, whether the group is viable or not was never important. Their goal was to seize the company, gut it, and sell off the parts for a quick profit. Sam thought about this. *Apparently, what Bormann sees here is a company whose parts are worth more than the whole. But what makes them think they can overtake Paterson and then butcher it for its parts?*

Sam pored over the influx of information for a while longer, and then it occurred to her to inspect the Paterson file she had just received. Even though the company was making good profits, it didn't have the cash to swing the purchase of the two companies. They must have used their war chest as collateral for a large loan to make their recent purchase. Even though they have plenty of money in savings, they can't use it to fend off a hostile takeover. In a relative sense, they were broke---at least for now until the new investment started paying off.

But how did Bormann know, and if they already knew, why were they asking her questions about Paterson? They were asking because they suspected but also wanted confirmation. Sam came to a logical conclusion. *If you attempt a hostile takeover and fail, then the company goes bankrupt.*

The stock market has many benefits and just as many pitfalls. To begin with, if you are able to sell stock in your company that means every stockowner owns that much of the company. The Securities and Exchange Commission (SEC) works with the company to determine the value of the company. The company then decides the number of shares they want to sell, and the SEC determines the price of each share. The advantage here is that for every stock sold, that is investment money available to the company for expansion. That is good, but each share also constitutes a vote. Whoever owns the majority of the shares also possess the majority of the votes. To take over a company, all they need is to control the majority of the shares.

In a hostile takeover, the hostile party attempts to purchase enough stock to become the majority shareholder. When they start purchasing the stock, the value of the stock will go up. This is basic Econ 101---when the demand of an item goes up and there's a limited number of items, so does the value. And as purchasing of the stock continues, the value inflates in direct correlation with the cost. Situations like this cause an abnormal jump in stock price, to the great joy of their owners. Therefore, many will sell. The Hostile then purchases them at the inflated rate until they emerge as the majority owner.

Contrary to popular belief, it is not always necessary to own 51%. If the largest stockowner possesses only 25% of the shares, then all the Hostile needs is 26% to seize the company. Most of the stockowners never vote, so the vote typically comes down to those that do vote on a regular basis. As a line of defense, the target company can fend off a hostile takeover by purchasing their own stock to maintain their superior numbers, but that requires money. If they don't have it, then they sustain a crippling loss. Essentially, it all comes down to a purely democratic vote---he who has the most votes wins.

So...if Paterson can't purchase more stock than Bormann can buy, then Bormann takes the company. That is why they wanted to know how Paterson was able to swing the purchase of the furniture and moving companies. They had been tipped off that he had used his War Chest as collateral for the loan, which means Paterson can't use any of that money to purchase stock; thus, making them sitting ducks.

Sam sat back in her chair with the sudden realization of what she had just learned. *But why give me this information?* She was bound by client privilege to not disclose anything to about a client's financial standing. First off, this information was not necessary for the proposal she put together. Secondly, now that she had it, she still couldn't reveal it to anyone---and why would she want to? She liked Trevor Paterson and wouldn't do anything to hurt him---at least not by choice. Sam stuffed the papers into her briefcase for safekeeping. She wanted to keep them close to her and protected.

Jennifer stopped by to pry, as she usually did these days. "Did you find out anything about Bormann?"

"Yea! They are corporate raiders, and I think they are intent on taking over Paterson. First, I don't want to help them, and second, I can't."

Jennifer nodded. "Okay, I just had to ask."

"Look, I worked through lunch on this. Do you mind if I go home early?"

Jennifer was silent. "That's fine, and you've done a great job. See you on Monday." Sam gathered her things and started to leave. It was three o'clock; by leaving this early, Sam would be home in 45 minutes.

Jasper arrived in Winder at 2 pm. He went for a walk and entered the house through the rear door. As he walked around, he first checked the cabinets in the kitchen and found some cookies. He removed the box and started eating them. He then checked the DVD drive, and it was empty.

Jasper channeled his inner policeman and thought, "If I was a DVD, where would I hide?" He walked into the living room and spotted two bookcases. One was opposite of the front door, and another was close to the desk just inside of the front door.

Jasper turned to the bookcase and scanned the titles. He was not a savvy_man, but he did have experience with human behavior. He spotted "Pride and Prejudice" and thought, "That's something a teenage girl would like," and pulled it from the shelf. When he turned up it upside down, the DVD fell out. Jasper smiled and silently congratulated himself. "I am just too good."

He had to kneel to pick it up before he stood and headed for the back door. He fired up the engine to his white Lincoln and checked the time. It was almost 3pm, and the bus would be arriving soon. He pickup his cell and made a broadcast, "Get ready." On cue, one of the men bent the corner, walked down the street, and stepped into the woods.

At 3:05 pm, Jasper saw the bus turn the corner and pull to a stop. He watched Liz exited the bus and began her daily path towards home. She stopped for a second to talk to friends before they parted ways and continued. The bus pulled away and disappeared around the corner.

Jasper picked up the cell," Step 1, now." He saw the brown van pull around the corner and creep towards Liz with the side door open. He waited---just as Liz reached the target zone, he gave the second command, "Step 2, now." The man sprang out of the woods just ahead of Liz. Liz stopped and looked at him---she started to back up when the man jumped and grabbed her.

The van pulled up with the door open, and there was not much of a struggle for a 200 lb. man abducting a 15-year-old girl weighing less than 100 lbs. He deftly yanked her into the van, tossed her book bag onto the sidewalk, and slammed the door shut. The van sped off. Jasper looked at the clock on the dash---3:08pm. The mission had only taken three minutes from the time the bus arrived, and no one saw a thing. Jasper put his car into gear and drove away slowly.

Jamie and Susan walked quickly into the control room. "What's going on? Why'd you call us?"

Gary pointed to the monitor. "Here, watch this." He started the play back, and they noticed a portly man enter the rear door.

He searched the cabinets and disappeared from their view. He then reappeared with a box and started to eat the contents before leaving the kitchen. Suddenly, he appeared in the living room, and they watched as he rummaged around and pulled a book off the shelf. Something fell out of the book, and he had to struggle to pick it up using the corner of the desk to help him. He left.

Susan turned to Gary. "Please tell me you're running him through face recognition?" Gary pointed to another computer to his right with faces flashing on the screen.

Gary turned to Jamie. "I restricted the search to the local area. It will take a while, but we should find him." Jamie looked at Susan, and no words were said---this wasn't good.

They stood watching the video, and Jamie asked, "Go to real time." Gary hit some keys and it jumped to real time.

Jamie looked at her watch. It was 3:10 pm. She turned to Susan. "Where is Liz? Shouldn't she be home?"

Susan asked Gary, "Go back to 3 and come forward." Gary did, but there was no sign of Liz.

As Sam headed home, she picked up the phone and dialed the number. She heard it ring---no answer. *This is odd. She normally picks up by the second ring. Maybe she's in the bathroom or something; I will wait a few minutes and call again.* Sam tried again and again, but there was no answer. Sam put the pedal to the metal and raced home.

Sam arrived at her house at almost 4pm and noticed the door was closed. Normally Liz would be sitting on the front porch with Mathew. Sam grabbed her briefcase and walked up to the house; the door was locked. As she stepped in, she looked around and didn't see Liz anywhere. She called her name---no answer. She stepped into the living room and spotted a box of cookies on the desk in the living room. This was not right; Liz wouldn't leave a box of cookies on the front desk. A debilitating wave of panic rushed over her, but she had to focus.

Sam grabbed the phone and called Mathew's mother next door. "Hi, this is Samantha. Is Elizabeth there?" The woman said no and asked if there was anything wrong? Sam replied, "I'm not sure yet, but thank you."

Sam disconnected the phone call and proceeded to scan her living room, the front yard, and anywhere that Liz may have possibly gone. A feeling shot down her spine like someone was dragging the sharp edge of a knife down her back. She had to think. *What if I'm wrong? What if she just went to a friend's house? She always tells me where she's going, but what if she forgot this one time. Teenagers sometimes do that.* Sam looked back at her phone and experienced a shudder that shocked her to her core. She pulled herself together and began thinking of phone numbers to call.

Chapter 34

Coming to terms with reality

Jamie looked at Susan. "I think we better get over there now. Sam will be arriving home soon, and Liz isn't there."

Susan turned to Gary. "If Liz appears, call us."

They started out. Susan was about 15 minutes into the 40-minute drive when Gary called Jamie. "Sam just got home, and she is looking for Liz." Jamie informed Susan and accelerated.

Jamie called Sam, but the phone was busy---she waited. Jamie called again, and Sam came on the line. She was frantic. "Liz?"

Jamie replied, "Sam, this is Jamie. Are you okay?"

Sam was shocked that Jamie had called, she nodded without thinking. "Yes, but Liz isn't here. I don't know where . . ."

Jamie spoke quietly. "Sam, I need for you do something for me--- this is very important. I need for you to do exactly what I say. Go out and sit on the porch. We will be there in 20 minutes."

Sam was confused. "Okay. Wait, why do you want me outside?"

"Sam, I can't explain right now but please, go outside and call the police about your daughter. We will be right there."

Sam stepped outside onto porch with the phone as Jamie disconnected, but she didn't want to call the police. *Is Liz with a friend? Oh my God; what if she was kidnapped?* Sam decided to call the police.

Jamie and Susan pulled up first, and then a police cruiser pulled up. Jamie and Susan walked up and hugged Sam. Jamie spoke first. "Go tell the policeman that she isn't home. We will be inside."

Sam became even more frantic. "No! Please stay with me…I don't know." Jamie and Susan looked at each other and nodded in unison.

The policeman walked up and started asking questions. "Can you tell me what she looks like?"

Jamie took this one. "Take this and subtract 15 years. "

The policeman smiled and asked, "How about a picture?"

Sam shook her head, and Jamie helped her out. "You got a phone number, big boy?"

The policeman smiled, but he looked confused." Excuse me?"

Jamie had her phone out and showed him the photo she had taken of Sam and Liz. "I can send it to you, if you like?"

The policeman slowly responded, "Okay, but remember I'm married … happily married." Jamie nodded and started to send the photo with a fiendish smile. Susan shook her finger at Jamie.

The policeman continued, "Okay ma'am, here is how this works. Because you can't report that she was kidnapped, we have to assume your daughter just forgot to come home. After three days, we can pronounce her missing and start looking for her. Sorry ma'am, its policy."

Susan turned to Sam. "Where does Liz get off the bus?"

"Well, the bus lets them off around the corner--- it's a one-minute walk."

Susan looked at Jamie and then said, "Show me." Sam and Susan headed for the bus stop closely followed by the officer and Jamie. As they rounded the corner Sam spotted Liz's backpack lying beside the sidewalk. She ran to it, and Susan had to stop her from touching it. Susan put on rubber gloves and slowly turned it over. She then peeked inside, reached in, and removed Liz's cell phone. Jamie looked at the officer.

The officer looked at the three women. "Look, this is not proof, but we will come by tomorrow morning to check, okay?" Jamie nodded as he turned and left.

The women walked back to the house. Susan picked up a kit from the rear of the SUV. As they entered, Jamie turned to Sam. "I need for you to do something for me. Just sit on the couch with your phone in case she calls … okay? Sam didn't like the feeling she was having, and she didn't like not knowing where Liz was. However, she trusted Jamie and Susan and did as she was asked.

Sam was still in a fog and sat down. Susan grabbed a kit and headed back to the kitchen. Jamie put on rubber gloves then picked up the cookie box with her fingertips and dropped it into the large bag. Susan returned with some powder and dusted the edge of the desk where they had seen the large man place his hand. She used wide, clear packing tape to capture the figure print. Susan came back from the kitchen with the kit. Sam started to come out of her shock and realize what the girls were doing. "What are you doing?"

Jamie looked at Sam. "We saw a man enter here at about 2:40 pm. He entered through the rear door and took that box of cookies from your cabinet. Then he found something in a book over here. We are taking fingerprints so we can identify him.

Sam nodded and allowed the information to sink in. "What do you mean you saw him enter through the rear door?"

Susan stepped forward. "We planted cameras and we have been monitoring your house for the last week."

Sam was still processing the chaos. "You have been watching us for a week!"

Jamie tried to calm her down. "Sam, before you get angry let's see what we find out from the face recognition we're currently running and from these fingerprints. Then you can chew us out. Deal?"

Sam nodded slowly, not really comprehending or understanding why or what to say. Then it dawned on her that if there had been a man in the house, the likelihood of Liz being kidnapped was very real. Her heart almost stopped.

Jamie looked at Susan. "You got the kitchen."

Susan nodded and faced Sam. "Sam, if you want, you can come back to the house with us." Sam shook her head. "What if she went off with a friend, and she returns and I'm not here? I have to wait for her to return." Susan and Jamie nodded, packed up their gear, and headed to the SUV.

All Liz could remember was seeing a strange man stepping out of the woods. She tried to run, but before she could, he wrapped his powerful arms around her with one hand over her mouth pressed her head into his chest so she couldn't scream. He ripped her book bag from her grip, tossed it toward the woods, and forced her into the van. Suddenly, a soft cloth came over her face, and everything faded to black.

As she slowly regained consciousness, she found herself in a strange room. Her head hurt when she tried to sit up. She pushed herself up despite the pain and realized where she was---she was in Jimmy's office. She was on the couch she had seen through his camera. As she sat up, she heard someone say, "She's up boss."

She looked to her right, and there was the man who grabbed her along with another man. On her left was an enormous man sitting in a chair. Jimmy sat across from her at his desk, and behind him she saw 16 monitors of 16 rooms, many of them occupied with people having sex. She was shocked and appalled. How gross!

Jimmy turned and faced her. A sinister smile came over his face. "Good, she is awake. How do you feel, sweetheart? I have been looking forward to meeting you."

Liz gave a weak nod. "I need some aspirin." Jimmy snapped his fingers, and one of the men on her right approached her with two pills and a glass of water.

Jimmy stared at her. "Yea, I know that stuff can leave you with a massive headache, but these will help." Liz thanked the man who then backed away as she took the pills and drank the water. Jimmy stood up and walked from behind his desk. "I have a question. We found your DVD with all my personal data. How did you get it?"

Liz wasn't going to reveal her tactics. "I just hacked in and took it. Your security is almost nonexistent."

Jimmy chuckled, "Well maybe I will get you to design me a new one in your spare time."

Liz smiled nervously. "Spare time, I don't understand."

"It's simple---you now work for me."

"What would I be doing?"

Jimmy pointed at her and looked at the men on both sides, "See, she is quick." He took a step forward. "You see the girls in those rooms? By the time we are finished with you, you will be one of them."

Liz almost lost it. She stood up slowly, looked at the monitors and then at the men in the room. "I can't do that; I have never done ..."

Jimmy guffawed. "Don't worry honey. Some of them never did that before either but look at them now. They're pros!"

Liz was sizing up the room. She figured there was no way she could get past the two guys on the right, but the big fat man in the chair wasn't ready, and she just might get past him. She took a quick step forward, leaped over the big man, and headed for the door. But before she reached it, Jimmy was right there chuckling and blocking her. She felt the heavy hands of the two muscle men on her as they dragged her back into the room and tossed her on the rug in the center.

She tried to fight them off, but it was two large 200 lb. men against one little girl. This struggle was futile. It wasn't long before her clothes were gone, and she was naked. First fellatio, then fellatio as someone took her from behind.

She then heard Jimmy yell out, "Don' fuck her in the ass until she can handle a 2.5 butt plug! I don't need you assholes ripping her new one. "One of the men replied, "Aw come on boss, she has such a nice ass." Jimmy replied, "I don't care."

By the time the third man was on top of her, she had given up. It was pointless. She couldn't stop them, and they didn't care about her at all. She was a piece of meat placed here for their personal enjoyment. All of her tears and pleading had little to no effect on them. Liz was in hell, and her senses were flooded with the foul smells of the men rapping her: their breath, their body order, the smell of the room. There was nothing, she could do about it.

Liz realized she couldn't stop them from doing what they wanted. In a sense, she had surrendered, but she quietly availed herself of the one thing they couldn't own---her mind. Just because Jimmy Dittle took her virginity and forced to satisfy every carnal whim of these pigs, that didn't mean that they were going to own her. Her survival was entirely dependent upon her intelligence, and she had to wait until the right moment.

They forced Liz to perform fellatio on everyone at least twice. They now had her face down on the table. One muscle man was holding her hands while Jimmy prepared to sodomize her. Once he was finished, the other three men took their turns. Liz was bruised, sore, and tired. It was well after midnight when Jimmy finally ordered the men to take her and lock her up in room 10. As they were taking her out, he said, "We will put her into rotation tomorrow. Let her sleep tonight--- she will need the rest."

The jet was still in the air when the phone rang, and Trevor answered it. He listened to the call for several minutes and didn't say a thing. Finally, he replied, "I saw this coming. I didn't think it would be this, but I knew something was going to happen---I just knew it. Who do you think is behind it?" He listened some more and then asked, "Jasper Grebes! Who the hell is that? Okay, I'm cancelling the rest of this trip. I will be there tomorrow, and I would like some good news if you can deliver it."

Chapter 35

The rules to abide by

Jamie looked at Susan. "I think we better get over there now. Sam will be arriving home soon, and Liz isn't there."

Susan turned to Gary. "If Liz appears, call us."

They started out. Susan was about 15 minutes into the 40-minute drive when Gary called Jamie. "Sam just got home, and she is looking for Liz." Jamie informed Susan and accelerated.

Jamie called Sam, but the phone was busy---she waited. Jamie called again, and Sam came on the line. She was frantic. "Liz?"

Jamie replied, "Sam, this is Jamie. Are you okay?"

Sam was shocked that Jamie had called; she nodded without thinking. "Yes, but Liz isn't here. I don't know where . . ."

Jamie spoke quietly. "Sam, I need for you do something for me---this is very important. I need for you to do exactly what I say. Go out and sit on the porch. We will be there in 20 minutes."

Sam was confused. "Okay. Wait, why do you want me outside?"

"Sam, I can't explain right now but please, go outside and call the police about your daughter. We will be right there."

Sam stepped outside onto porch with the phone as Jamie disconnected, but she didn't want to call the police. *Is Liz with a friend? Oh my God; what if she was kidnapped?* Sam decided to call the police.

Jamie and Susan pulled up first, and then a police cruiser pulled up. Jamie and Susan walked up and hugged Sam. Jamie spoke first. "Go tell the policeman that she isn't home. We will be inside."

Sam became even more frantic. "No! Please stay with me…I don't know." Jamie and Susan looked at each other and nodded in unison.

The policeman walked up and started asking questions. "Can you tell me what she looks like?"

Jamie took this one. "Take this and subtract 15 years. "

The policeman smiled and asked, "How about a picture?"

Sam shook her head, and Jamie helped her out. "You got a phone number, big boy?"

The policeman smiled, but he looked confused." Excuse me?"

Jamie had her phone out and showed him the photo she had taken of Sam and Liz. "I can send it to you, if you like?"

The policeman slowly responded, "Okay, but remember I'm married … happily married." Jamie nodded and started to send the photo with a fiendish smile. Susan shook her finger at Jamie.

The policeman continued, "Okay ma'am, here is how this works. Because you can't report that she was kidnapped, we have to assume your daughter just forgot to come home. After three days, we can pronounce her missing and start looking for her. Sorry ma'am, its policy."

Susan turned to Sam. "Where does Liz get off the bus?"

"Well, the bus lets them off around the corner--- it's a one-minute walk."

Susan looked at Jamie and then said, "Show me." Sam and Susan headed for the bus stop closely followed by the officer and Jamie. As they rounded the corner Sam spotted Liz's backpack lying beside the sidewalk. She ran to it, and Susan had to stop her from touching it. Susan put on rubber gloves and slowly turned it over. She then peeked inside, reached in, and removed Liz's cell phone. Jamie looked at the officer.

The officer looked at the three women. "Look, this is not proof, but we will come by tomorrow morning to check, okay?" Jamie nodded as he turned and left.

The women walked back to the house. Susan picked up a kit from the rear of the SUV. As they entered, Jamie turned to Sam. "I need for you to do something for me. Just sit on the couch with your phone in case she calls … okay? Sam didn't like the feeling she was having, and she didn't like not knowing where Liz was. However, she trusted Jamie and Susan and did as she was asked.

Sam was still in a fog and sat down. Susan grabbed a kit and headed back to the kitchen. Jamie put on rubber gloves then picked up the cookie box with her fingertips and dropped it into the large bag. Susan returned with some powder and dusted the edge of the desk where they had seen the large man place his hand. She used wide, clear packing tape to capture the figure print. Susan came back from the kitchen with the kit. Sam started to come out of her shock and realize what the girls were doing. "What are you doing?"

Jamie looked at Sam. "We saw a man enter here at about 2:40 pm. He entered through the rear door and took that box of cookies from your cabinet. Then he found something in a book over here. We are taking fingerprints so we can identify him.

Sam nodded and allowed the information to sink in. "What do you mean you saw him enter through the rear door?"

Susan stepped forward. "We planted cameras and we have been monitoring your house for the last week."

Sam was still processing the chaos. "You have been watching us for a week!"

Jamie tried to calm her down. "Sam, before you get angry let's see what we find out from the face recognition we're currently running and from these fingerprints. Then you can chew us out. Deal?"

Sam nodded slowly, not really comprehending or understanding why or what to say. Then it dawned on her that if there had been a man in the house, the likelihood of Liz being kidnapped was very real. Her heart almost stopped.

Jamie looked at Susan. "You got the kitchen."

Susan nodded and faced Sam. "Sam, if you want, you can come back to the house with us." Sam shook her head. "What if she went off with a friend, and she returns and I'm not here? I have to wait for her to return." Susan and Jamie nodded, packed up their gear, and headed to the SUV.

All Liz could remember was seeing a strange man stepping out of the woods. She tried to run, but before she could, he wrapped his powerful arms around her with one hand over her mouth pressed her head into his chest so she couldn't scream. He ripped her book bag from her grip, tossed it toward the woods, and forced her into the van. Suddenly, a soft cloth came over her face, and everything faded to black.

As she slowly regained consciousness, she found herself in a strange room. Her head hurt when she tried to sit up. She pushed herself up despite the pain and realized where she was---she was in Jimmy's office. She was on the couch she had seen through his camera. As she sat up, she heard someone say, "She's up boss."

She looked to her right, and there was the man who grabbed her along with another man. On her left was an enormous man sitting in a chair. Jimmy sat across from her at his desk, and behind him she saw 16 monitors of 16 rooms, many of them occupied with people having sex. She was shocked and appalled. How gross!

Jimmy turned and faced her. A sinister smile came over his face. "Good, she is awake. How do you feel, sweetheart? I have been looking forward to meeting you."

Liz gave a weak nod. "I need some aspirin." Jimmy snapped his fingers, and one of the men on her right approached her with two pills and a glass of water.

Jimmy stared at her. "Yea, I know that stuff can leave you with a massive headache, but these will help." Liz thanked the man who then backed away as she took the pills and drank the water. Jimmy stood up and walked from behind his desk. "I have a question. We found your DVD with all my personal data. How did you get it?"

Liz wasn't going to reveal her tactics. "I just hacked in and took it. Your security is almost nonexistent."

Jimmy chuckled, "Well maybe I will get you to design me a new one in your spare time."

Liz smiled nervously. "Spare time, I don't understand."

"It's simple---you now work for me."

"What would I be doing?"

Jimmy pointed at her and looked at the men on both sides, "See, she is quick." He took a step forward. "You see the girls in those rooms? By the time we are finished with you, you will be one of them."

Liz almost lost it. She stood up slowly, looked at the monitors and then at the men in the room. "I can't do that; I have never done ..."

Jimmy guffawed. "Don't worry honey. Some of them never did that before either but look at them now. They're pros!"

Liz was sizing up the room. She figured there was no way she could get past the two guys on the right, but the big fat man in the chair wasn't ready, and she just might get past him. She took a quick step forward, leaped over the big man, and headed for the door. But before she reached it, Jimmy was right there chuckling and blocking her. She felt the heavy hands of the two muscle men on her as they dragged her back into the room and tossed her on the rug in the center.

She tried to fight them off, but it was two large 200 lb. men against one little girl. This struggle was futile. It wasn't long before her clothes were gone, and she was naked. First fellatio, then fellatio as someone took her from behind.

She then heard Jimmy yell out, "Don' fuck her in the ass until she can handle a 2.5 butt plug! I don't need you assholes ripping her new one. "One of the men replied, "Aw come on boss, she has such a nice ass." Jimmy replied, "I don't care."

By the time the third man was on top of her, she had given up. It was pointless. She couldn't stop them, and they didn't care about her at all. She was a piece of meat placed here for their personal enjoyment. All of her tears and pleading had little to no effect on them. Liz was in hell, and her senses were flooded with the foul smells of the men rapping her: their breath, their body order, the smell of the room. There was nothing, she could do about it.

Liz realized she couldn't stop them from doing what they wanted. In a sense, she had surrendered, but she quietly availed herself of the one thing they couldn't own---her mind. Just because Jimmy Dittle took her virginity and forced to satisfy every carnal whim of these pigs, that didn't mean that they were going to own her. Her survival was entirely dependent upon her intelligence, and she had to wait until the right moment.

They forced Liz to perform fellatio on everyone at least twice. They now had her face down on the table. One muscle man was holding her hands while Jimmy prepared to sodomize her. Once he was finished, the other three men took their turns. Liz was bruised, sore, and tired. It was well after midnight when Jimmy finally ordered the men to take her and lock her up in room 10. As they were taking her out, he said, "We will put her into rotation tomorrow. Let her sleep tonight--- she will need the rest."

The jet was still in the air when the phone rang, and Trevor answered it. He listened to the call for several minutes and didn't say a thing. Finally, he replied, "I saw this coming. I didn't think it would be this, but I knew something was going to happen---I just knew it. Who do you think is behind it?" He listened some more and then asked, "Jasper Grebes! Who the hell is that? Okay, I'm cancelling the rest of this trip. I will be there tomorrow, and I would like some good news if you can deliver it."

Chapter 36

Violation of Rule # 1

It was just before noon on Saturday when the aircraft came in for a landing and then taxied over to the SUV parked on the side. Jamie and Susan exited the vehicle and walked around to open the back. Trevor and the pilot carried the bags to the car and tossed them into the trunk. Trevor thanked the pilot and shook his hand. They then parted---the pilot to the aircraft and Trevor to the vehicle.

As Trevor settled into the back seat, he was quiet for a moment. "Okay give it to me."

Susan was sitting in the passenger seat; and handed two pieces of paper over her shoulder to Trevor before speaking. "We believe these two men are involved. We spotted Jasper Grebes on the camera inside Sam's house the day Liz disappeared. We talked to the neighbor boy, and he confirmed that Jasper has been watching the house. The boy was able to get me pictures of his first car, a black Cadillac, but he was last seen in a white Lincoln. We are currently verifying that he owns or rents either car."

Trevor nodded and then asked, "You don't have an address on him yet?"

Jamie spoke up, "We didn't before we came out to get you. I wouldn't be surprised if Gary has an address on him by the time we get back."

Trevor nodded. "What about this Jimmy Dittle guy?"

Susan smiled, "He's a piece of work. He has a long history of rape, assault, and prostitution. He was the Union Boss at Fletcher Industries."

After Jasper left the police force, he teamed up with Jimmy Dittle, and they are known associates. Other than the fact that they have been seen together a number of times, we don't have anything on them. But honestly, if you're not into that lifestyle, why would you even want to associate with these two?"

The SUV turned in front of the house, and two men scurried out to grab the bags from the back. Trevor and the ladies walked in and down to Trevor's office. Trevor sat down behind the desk and laid the papers onto the desk. He looked at the two women before him and asked, "How is Samantha doing?"

Jamie spoke up, "She's a basket case, but she is holding up."

Trevor nodded and then asked, "What happened to her this last week? According to your reports, she's been under stress. Why?"

Susan and Jamie looked at each other before Susan took a deep breath and started, "Last Monday, she was exiting the building before she was stopped and taken to the 14th floor by Hutchinson Security. She was kept there most of the afternoon. We're still trying to find out why."

Susan continued, "On Tuesday, she walked to the Marriott Hotel. We weren't prepared for this, so we couldn't track her. After this, we installed the cameras and phone tap into her house. We also swapped her briefcase out with one that is equipped with a tracker. On Thursday, she drove to the hotel, and we tracked her to the 11th floor---room 1101. We checked, and this is one of several rooms, that Hutchinson retains for company use. It appears that their Director of Security, a Roger Dawson, has been using this one."

Trevor was twirling a pencil in his hand. "Do we know why he is using them?"

Jamie gave Susan a glance then replied, "It appears that he is meeting women in them. He has a Jennifer Wills in there on Mondays and Wednesdays, but last week, he had Samantha in there on Tuesday and Thursday. It was reported that they are having consultations."

Susan and Jamie looked at each other. Susan cleared her throat. "We don't think what is happening in there is platonic. We suspect that he is forcing them to have sex." The pencil in Trevor's hand suddenly snapped, and the two girls noticed the look of anger on Trevor's face. Susan piped up, "May we make a suggestion?"

Trevor continued to stare at the pictures on his desk then nodded slowly. Susan took the floor. "I know that look---you want to set fire to his face and put it out with a hatchet, but let's leave this Roger Dawn thing alone for now until we can get confirmation. We need to concentrate on Elizabeth first. Once we have her, then Jamie and I would like to deal with Roger."

Trevor leaned back in his chair and looked up at her for a moment. "If he is doing what I think he is doing, you're correct. But you are also correct about Liz---she is priority right now. Do whatever you have to do to find him. I will decide later if I need my hatchet."

Jamie stood up beside Susan, "I say we go see Gary and see what he has for us." All three headed to the control room.

As they entered, they spied Gary at the computer console, and he was typing. He smiled, "Hi Trevor. I hope the trip went well?"

Trevor wasn't smiling. He was in a bad mood because of what had happened, so he simply nodded and replied, "It was productive. What can you tell me about our current predicament?" Trevor walked between the console and 60" LCD screen while the girls flanked Gary.

Gary nodded towards the large screen on the wall, and the three watched as Gary moved a page of Jasper Grebes to the screen. He then started to explain, "Okay, I'm sure the ladies have already introduced him to you. As it turns out, he owns a company called JG Investigations---not very imaginative but his company, nonetheless. Until recently, was leasing a black Cadillac."

Gary displayed a picture of the car and a copy of the lease on the big screen. "Now one of the pictures that the neighbor boy took was of the license plate, and that plate matches the plate on the lease. Yes, I think it is a safe bet that he was the one who not only broke into Ms. Raven's house but was also spotted parked on the street that day. On Thursday, he turned that car in for a white Lincoln. Please take notice of the license plate."

Trevor looked at Gary, and Gary nodded, "Yes, I know what the next question is. Do we have an address? Well, yes, we do in parts. All paperwork for his company is sent to a post office box owned by one of those private companies, and it is located in Lawrenceville. I have attempted to find a subsequent address, but everything that he has is in his company's name, and this is the address. As you can see, even though it is listed as a suite, it is nothing more than P.O. Box."

Trevor stewed over this. "What about this Jimmy Dittle guy? What do you have on him?"

Gary moved the picture of Jimmy to the large screen. "Jimmy is a squirrely little fellow, and he has nothing in his name. However, he is listed as an officer of several different companies. I'm currently running a search on those companies, but they are all incorporated out of Delaware---this process is slow. But I will find him. I just can't say when, sorry."

Trevor nodded, "You did good, keep at it."

He turned and faced the ladies and Gary then started to speak again, "I think we can safely identify what has happened here. Apparently,

Jimmy Dittle found Elizabeth---how or why we don't know. But I bet he has her holed up in a house somewhere and is forcing her into prostitution. I can't imagine the hell she is going through right now, but these people have no morals and no conscience. If they think she will become a liability, they will kill her and bury her body in the woods. They don't care."

Trevor looked at Gary. "Gary, stay on those addresses. We need to know where they are." He then looked at the ladies, "You ladies go and stake out that post office box. With any luck, Jasper will come or send someone to collect his mail. I'm heading to Winder. I think Sam could use me support." They all nodded and continued on to their respective missions.

It was nearing 2 in the afternoon on Saturday when a green pickup truck pulled up in front of the Sam's house. Trevor exited and walked up the driveway to the house. He reached the porch then pressed the doorbell and waited. After a few seconds, the door opened slowly, and there stood Sam.

Her hair was a rat's nest in a half-up/half-down style that in no way resembled her bun. She was still wearing the clothes from work on Friday, and her eyes were red and swollen with leftover mascara splayed over her cheeks like a preschooler's painting project. Sam was trying her best to look composed. "Mr. Paterson, what can I do for you?"

Trevor smiled, opened the screen door, and stepped into foyer. Sam stood her ground and looked up into those beautiful brown eyes when Trevor instinctually wrapped his arm around her waist. He picked her up and pulled her close. Without realizing what she was doing, Sam circled her arms around his neck and buried her face into it. She started to cry again, but she desperately needed this release.

Trevor stepped forward and kicked the door closed behind him. He scooped her legs up into his arms and carried her like a baby back to the bedrooms. After peeking into the first one, he continued into the second, surmising that it looked like the bedroom of a grown woman.

Trevor sat down on the corner of her bed, rested Sam in his lap, and held her for several minutes. Sam relished in having someone to hold, but when she finally opened her eyes, she noticed that they were in her bedroom, her safe space. She pushed away and stood up quickly before teetering a little. Then looked at him and drew back in a defensive reflex of shock and fear.

Trevor walked into her bathroom and started the shower. "You take a shower while I start breakfast." As he exited the bathroom, he spotted the bathrobe hanging on the door. He then turned and closed the door.

Sam stood there for a minute and looked around. She loved seeing him, holding him, and having him hold her. But when she realized where he brought her, she was frightened. She already had one man taking advantage of her, and she didn't need another.

Sam started to disrobe. She looked back at the door to her room and thought, *should I lock the door?* She decided to leave it. After all, if he wanted in, he could just kick the door down. Then she realized that the lock probably didn't work anyway.

Sam entered the shower and felt the warm water cascade down her body. She quickly washed her hair, bathed, and then exited. In fresh underclothes and her terrycloth robe, slipped into her slippers and peeked out of the door.

She could hear Trevor in the kitchen bustling about and peered around the corner into the kitchen. Trevor had removed his jacket, laid it over the back of a chair, and put on one her frilly aprons. He was now comically searching for something.

She watched Trevor and giggled quietly. He was trying to orient himself as to what was where. There were two frying pans on the stove while the coffee brewed. He suddenly pulled a spatula from a drawer with a big smile as if he had found a prize. Then he opened the refrigerator and scanned the items. She watched in amusement as he pulled the eggs, bacon, and butter out and set them on the counter.

He removed a breakfast towel from the cabinet and set it on the stove. Trevor clumsily turned the knobs until he got the gas stove working and placed a pan on each burner before starting the bacon. When he broke the eggs and dropped them into the bowl, one of the shells fell in. He struggled to get it out but somehow ended up pouring it into the pan and had to pick out the shells anyway.

The bacon pan was getting too hot, Trevor burned his fingers when he tried to move it. Sam smiled warmly for the first time in days as she watched him fumbling around in the kitchen. He wasn't familiar with it or cooking for that matter, but he was doing the best he could.

The flame was too high, and the bacon started to burn. The eggs were also cooking too fast. Trevor did the only thing he could think of---he picked up both pans off the burners and held them up. He was looking around when he suddenly noticed Sam standing in the doorway.

Trevor smiled, "I guess my culinary skills aren't that good."

Sam walked around the table and turned off the burners. "You have the burners too high." He had made a mess of her kitchen, but she was eternally grateful for his genuine efforts. He could have easily hired someone to do this, but he didn't.

Trevor nodded. "What else do I need to do?"

Sam glanced up at Trevor. "Put the pans back. Without the flame, there is no heat. You know---science."

Trevor nodded, lowered the pans onto the burners again, and pitifully said, "I... I made coffee."

Sam glanced at the coffee pot, and then leaned against the counter. "I noticed." Trevor stepped over to Sam, put his arms around her shoulders, and pulled her into his chest. This was exactly what she needed. She didn't care about the breakfast catastrophe, because the thought that he put into it meant everything.

Sam had her arms up between them then she slowly started to extend them until they eventually encircled his waist.

Trevor felt relieved that she wasn't irritated by the circus he had created in the kitchen. "I started breakfast kind of."

Sam nodded against his chest. "I noticed."

"I think I made a mess."

Sam smiled. "I noticed that too."

"What can I do to make it up to you?"

Sam squeezed him tighter and sighed. "You're already doing it."

Ah, the enigma of women. Men try hard to be logical, balanced, and able to do what is necessary regardless of the cost. They toil in the fields and tolerate jobs they hate for years to supply their women and families with what they think they want or need. Men build large skyscrapers and dams. They invent machines that perform numerous, miraculous feats. They purchase jewelry and adorn them with all kind of beautiful trinkets to win their hearts. Ironically, sometimes all women really need is to know is that the man they choose will be honest, faithful, and most importantly, be there to hold their hand and weather all of the storms of life.

They can be so hard to understand!

Chapter 37

Taking the bait

Late Saturday afternoon, Jimmy was leaning back in his chair watching the monitors. He already had a few customers, but Saturday night was the busy shift. He had already thrown a couple of clients into room 10. She was clumsy, but she was doing the job, and as long as she did, he was happy. In fact, he was thinking of paying her a special visit later. He saw a couple of steady customers coming in, so he decided to just watch the show. This would be an interesting afternoon.

Liz was lying on the bed when she heard the door unlock and open. An older man walked in and said, "Well well, what do we have here? They said I would like you, and they were right. He started to take off his clothes and then removed two chips from his pocket--- one blue and one red. Liz shuddered but knew what she had to do. This was not her first customer---she was getting into the stream of things. She hated what she had to do, but she knew that if she didn't do them, the consequences would be dire.

Trevor stayed with Sam the rest of afternoon. Sam knew she was violating rule number one: no men in the house. But she didn't invite him in---he just walked in and thank God for that. He delivered her from the brink of insanity. She had lost control; and was in danger of slipping into a mental abyss. She felt like a complete failure, but Trevor made her feel better about herself. She didn't know why or how he did it but having him there made her feel that things would get better.

Trevor didn't touch her other than carrying her to her bedroom. They just sat in the living room and talked or slept on the couch while he held her. She felt safe and warm in his arms---she couldn't explain it, but she kept telling herself that it wouldn't last. Regardless, she needed him right now, and she was enjoying his presence.

Jamie and Susan found the store where the P.O. Box was and went in to talk to the clerk. They found him behind the counter doing paperwork. Jamie flashed her badge. "Can we ask you a few questions?" The clerk looked up at the two women, slowly nodded, and then continued what he was doing.

Susan produced a picture of Jasper. "You recognize this man?"

The clerk glanced at the picture and chuckled. "JG, yea I know him. What has he done now?"

The ladies gave each other a quick glance before Jamie asked, "Does he have a box here?"

"Yea, he comes in a couple of times a week to get his mail, and no unless you have a warrant to go with those badges, I won't show it to you."

Susan took over. "When was the last time he came in?"

The clerk shook his head and replied, "He hasn't been in here in a couple of days, so I won't be surprised if he comes in soon."

Jamie grilled him. "Do you have a billing address you can show us?"

The clerk smirked. "You got that warrant? Look ladies, I wouldn't be surprised if he comes in soon. You can ask him then, but without a warrant, the only thing I will admit to is that he does have a box here. Now unless you two beautiful women want to take me out later and torture me like in the movie "Bandidas" with Selma Hayek and Penelope Cruz, I have work to do."

Jamie and Susan glanced at each other and Susan replied, "You sure you could handle us?"

The young clerk gave a large smile. "I have no idea, but I'm willing to die trying." Jamie and Susan chuckled at the irony and started to leave. Jamie glanced at her watch. It was late in the afternoon. They proceeded to the parking lot and watched the store.

At 6 pm, they watched as a white Lincoln pulled into the store parking lot across the street. A humongous man struggled to exit and lumbered over to the shop. He had to turn sideways to get through the door, but he made it and retrieved his mail. Jamie and Susan followed him as he walked to a bar close by.

They took a seat in a booth and watched as Jasper actually sat on two stools at the bar. Jamie and Susan ordered iced tea and watched. The news came on and it reported an Amber alert for a young girl abducted the previous Friday. The ladies watched as Jasper drank, and Jamie turned to Susan. "You know, I have an idea. This is risky, but I'm going over there to plant a seed.

Susan eyed Jamie but trusted her. "Am I going to regret this?" Jamie smiled and slid out of the stall, motioning for Susan to follow.

Normally, the news repeats itself, so Jamie had to time this move right. She pulled herself onto a stool within earshot of Jasper and waited for the news to repeat. After the national news, the local news came on. It featured an extended piece on the disappearance of the young lady from Winder and showed the picture of Elizabeth and her mother. Jamie motioned for the bartender to come over. "Jimmy, a shot of Tequila, please? And turn that up. Wow, they look like twins! When did she get snatched?"

Susan replied, "Friday."

Jamie continued," Boy, that is one cute little girl. If that were my daughter, I would walk through hell and high water to get to her." Jasper didn't move and just sat there.

Susan looked at Jamie and realized what she was doing. "Boy, they really are spitting images of each other."

They left the bar and stood outside for a second before Susan spoke. "This is something really stupid or really smart, but if it works, he will lead us right to Liz."

Jamie winked at her. "I agree. All we have to do now is hope he takes the bait." As they headed toward the parking lot, they spotted Jasper's Lincoln. Jamie pulled a small black box from her purse and searched under the rear bumper until she found some solid metal. She attached the box, which had a strong magnet to grip the metal, and they left.

On Tuesday, Jasper went over to the see Jimmy. After stumbling up the stairs to his office, he slumped into the chair and looked up at the monitors. Jasper asked, "So how is our newest acquisition doing?"

Jimmy turned to look at Jasper. "She is doing fine. She was clumsy at first, but she is performing well."

"Boy, it would be nice to have her mother too."

Jimmy smiled and said, "That would be nice, but there is no way we grab her."

"Actually, you don't need to grab her."

Jimmy turned and looked hard at Jasper. "What the hell are you talking about?"

"We have her number. I bet she is going to call in sick on Wednesday, and when she does, we'll call her, have her meet me, and I'll bring her here. Her car will be left somewhere else. No one will know where she is, and we'll have both mother and daughter."

Jimmy listened and then asked, "So what do we say to get her come?"

Jasper proudly replied, "What is the one thing Samantha Raven would walk through hell or high water for?"

Jimmy winked at Jasper. "Her daughter." Jasper smiled. The seed had been planted successfully.

Jimmy turned and looked up at the monitors. "Let's do it. We call tomorrow morning and arrange for her to meet you. Then we put her in the back seat of your car with one of my guys. We blindfold her so she won't know where this place is and bring her here---then we have a party."

"You're a genius, boss!"

On Wednesday morning, Sam called in sick again. Despite having Trevor over each day, she needed her daughter and couldn't go to work knowing that Liz wasn't at home. Trevor was gone--- she wouldn't allow him to spend the night---she almost had to push him out of the front door.

It was good that he resisted. She was taking control again; or what little control she could claim. But she had control of her house at least, despite Trevor's insistence of her coming to the plantation. She refused to leave her house just in case Liz was able to get to a phone and call home.

And when or if she did, Sam would be there to take that call. She put on a pot of coffee and dressed in her jeans and t-shirt. She was doing the only thing she could do, which was clean the house.

At 9 am, the phone suddenly rang. She picked it up and answered. Jimmy was on the line. "Well well Ms. Raven, how are you doing today?"

Sam was shocked and slowly answered, "I could be better. Why are you calling me, Jimmy?"

Chapter 38

Making a deal with the devil

Jimmy chuckled. "Because it appears that we both have a similar love, Ms. Raven."

Sam huffed, "Oh, really---and what is that?"

"Why, your daughter of course. I must say she is a sweet little thing. I have really enjoyed her." Sam's blood pressure erupted. She knew her daughter had been kidnapped, but now she knew who took her---he had her. She wanted to maim him.

Gary heard the call come in from Jimmy Dittle. He first started a trace, and then he hit the emergency button. Gary then pushed his chair over to a bank of computers, pressed some keys, and suddenly a map appeared on the 60" display monitor. The program immediately determined that Jimmy was calling from a cell and started to triangulate his position from the cell towers.

Sam was incensed! How could this animal take her daughter?! She calmed herself and collected her thoughts. As she listened to his voice, she steeled herself and calmly asked, "You have my Elizabeth?"

Jimmy had no regrets. "Of course I do, bitch---a sweet little thing like that, how could I resist?"

Gary talked her through it. "That's right, keep him on the line---just a little longer and we will find him."

He heard Trevor speak from behind him, "Who you talking to?"

Gary didn't turn around because he was busy manipulating the search pattern to narrow down the location. Gary replied, "To her damn it. Just keep him on the line." Trevor nodded and stayed quiet.

Sam replied, "If you touch one hair on her head, I will ..."

Jimmy interjected, "Oh please lady. I not only touched her hair, I fucked her until she screamed. She was fine stuff, and I enjoyed every minute of the time I had with her. I went back for thirds yesterday."

Sam wanted to reach through the phone and strangle him, but she needed to remain calm and asked, "So why are you calling me?"

Jamie and Susan arrived from the gym. Susan looked at Jamie and smiled. Jamie said, "It worked." Trevor looked at them intently and started to say something but stopped. He wanted to listen.

Jimmy chuckled. "Well the problem with a sweet little thing like your daughter is that I get bored, and after a time, I don't want her anymore. "

Sam continued to steady herself and asked, "So what do you want with me?"

Jimmy responded, "Well apparently with the news media coverage of your daughter, I can't dispose of her in the normal manner. So, in an effort to show my compassion, I would like to know if you would like her back?"

Sam's heart leaped with the hope of getting her back. "Of course, but what do I have to do?"

"Come get her of course---what else?"

"How do I know she is still alive?"

Jimmy chuckled. "Excellent question, would you like to talk to her?"

Sam's heart leapt. "Of course."

Jimmy turned to Liz, who was sitting between him and one of the thugs and put the phone on speaker. Holding the phone in front of Liz, he then said, "Go ahead and speak to her." The thug removed his hand from her mouth to allow Liz to speak.

Sam asked, "Honey, are you there?"

"Hi mom. I'm okay." Sam's heart soared.

"Have they hurt you, honey?"

Jimmy came online. "Okay, you have talked to her. Here is the deal: if you say she just ran away for the weekend and take the heat off, we will give her back. Do we have a deal?"

Sam nodded. "Okay, I can live with that, but how can I trust you?"

Jimmy laughed. "To be honest, you can't, but I need the heat off. If you take her back, then that will do it."

Sam sighed. "Okay, what do I have to do? "

"Today at noon, drive to the mall near you on 316. There is a Staples store. Park as far out as possible and wait---a white car will pick you up." Sam agreed to the terms, and then the line went dead.

Jamie and Susan checked their watches simultaneously. It was 9:30 in the morning; they had to get ready and get there before anyone, and it was an hour's drive. They started to leave the control room when Trevor yelled, "Halt!"

Both girls turned and looked at him with straight faces as Trevor approached. "Are the two of you executing some kind of plan that I'm not aware of?"

Jamie put her innocent puppy look on. "Now boss, he called her. We didn't even know where he was."

They all looked at Gary and he confirmed the information. "He's in a car cruising down I-85."

They both looked back at Trevor. "Look, we don't have much time. Can we go?"

Trevor slowly nodded yes, and they ran out. He knew they had done something, but at this time, it wasn't important. He trusted them completely.

They dressed and headed for the SUV. Trevor stopped them at the vehicle and said, "I'm going with you."

Jamie shook her head. "This is girls' night out honey. No man will be safe on this one, but you can be our Calvary."

"I'm your Calvary?" Trevor smiled. He knew there was a GPS in the SUV, so he would know their location. He also knew what "girls' night out" meant.

They arrived at the mall parking lot at 10:40 am driving a black Toyota Land Cruiser with blacked out windows and parked amidst a group of cars. They waited, and soon they saw the white Lincoln pull in at 11:30 am and park two rows over. A man got out, walked over, and sat in the grass at the far end of the parking lot.

At 11:55 am, they saw the white Volkswagen pull in and park at the far end about ten places down from where the man was sitting. The white Lincoln slowly circled the block, pulled in front of the white Volkswagen, and stopped. Sam exited her vehicle and approached the white Lincoln. Sam didn't' see then man come up behind her and force her into the rear seat. He climbed in after her, and white Lincoln sped away.

As Jamie pulled out to follow, Susan hit the button on the dash, and a GPS display appeared. She then hit a couple of other buttons, and soon the tracking device that Jamie had planted appeared. They relaxed---with the tracking device; they didn't have to get too close.

It took another hour as Jasper displayed his paranoia to ensure he was not followed before they reached Jimmy Dittle. They ventured to the outskirts of Alpharetta before Jasper finally turned off and veered down a dead-end alley.

Jamie pulled the SUV to the opening of the alley and watched as the thug pulled Sam from the white Lincoln and then approached a metal door. Sam's hands were tied behind her back, and she was blindfolded.

They watched as Jasper knocked on the door, which opened after a minute. They went in. Jamie parked the SUV at the curb, and they exited the vehicle.

The thug held Sam's arm tight as he dragged her up the stairs to the office before opening the door and shoving her in. Sam wore jeans and a loose-fitting t-shirt. The thug pushed her into the room, and she fell to the floor. Jimmy and another thug laughed maniacally as they watched her fall to the floor. Jasper struggled to the top of the stairs, out of breath and sweating. He made it to his chair and fell into it.

Jimmy laughed again. "Untie her." The thug who brought her pushed her onto her stomach and held her down with his knee as he cut the ties to her hands before moving away.

Sam jumped up and looked around. She was in the middle of the room in front of Jimmy's desk. To her right was a large, muscular man standing by a door. To her left was Jasper recovering in a chair along with the thug that tied her up by that door. *No way out.* Sam glared at Jimmy with utter disdain. "Okay, the deal was if I come and get her, I can have her." Jimmy nodded and laughed as the other three men joined him.

Sam repeated herself. "I thought we had a deal?"

Jimmy had both feet on his desk and said, "We did, we did, but the optimal word there is 'did.' I have changed my mind."

Sam's heart sank. *Why did I trust him? What choice did I have?* "I want to see my daughter?"

Jimmy smiled and looked over his shoulder at the monitors behind him. "Sure, no problem. She's right there in number 10, and as soon as she is finished with this customer, we will go get her. I have no reason why we should keep her from the party. You know I believe that a family that fucks together stays together."

Someone really needed to eradicate this demonic menace to society.

Chapter 39

Liz is found and it's Girls night out

Sam took a gulp after suddenly seeing Liz on the screen. She was in room 10, and some old man had her on a bed humping her. Sam gasped at the sight. She looked back at Jimmy Dittle, and God, she wanted to kill him! She stood before him. "So… you lied. What a shock. What do you intend to do with me now?"

"Remember when I told you I was going to fuck you? Well guess what baby; today is my lucky day. In fact, after I finish fucking you, my friends are going to fuck you. You see, I like to share in my good fortune." Jimmy looked at the man standing by the inside door to his left. "As soon as the little bitch is finished, bring her in here."

Jasper spoke up. "Hey boss, since you got to pop the cherry on that little bitch, can I have first on her mother?"

Jimmy looked at Sam and said, "Sure, I don't mind sloppy seconds."

Jamie and Susan exited the vehicle and started down the alley. Susan was dressed all in black with steel-toed boots; loose, black, 511 tactical pants; and a black, Under Armor, skintight shirt. On her forearms, she had black, leather, steel-reinforced protectors. Her hair was in a tight braid down to her shoulders, and she was wearing tactical gloves. The fingers were cut off after the first digit. The area over the knuckles had a hard fiberglass covering them. She looked imposing, as if she were going to war.

Jamie, on the other hand, was very different. She had a short, plaid, pleated schoolgirl skirt with a white tank top open around the waist. On the tank top, it said, "Yes! I'm Trouble!" Her hair was in two ponytails with pink ribbons. She wore white bobby socks that hid two throwing knives and black and white shoes. She had a bra holster attached under her bra with a Ruger LC9 pistol in it. She had the same leather forearm bands, only white and the same gloves that Susan had in pink. Jamie looked like she was going to a party.

They walked up to the metal door, and Susan stepped to one side out of site. Jamie knocked on the door and stepped back. The window slid open, and Jamie went into her dumb valley girl act. "Hi, sir! Mr. Dittle told me if I ever wanted to party, I just needed to come here and ask. So, can I come in?" She gave her best 'young girl' impression.

The old man inside was pleasantly flabbergasted. "Holy googly moogley! I hate this job." They heard the heavy bolt slide back, and the door started too opened. With that, Susan slammed into the door, forcing it back against the old man inside. He slammed against the wall and bounced back. Susan made quick work of him. They closed the door and started quietly up the stairs.

They could hear Sam screaming from the room upstairs. Liz had finished with her customer, and the smaller of the two thugs had retrieved her. Liz was naked, and the thug held her from behind by her arms, just inside the far door.

The larger of the two thugs was holding Sam by her wrists. She was face down on the table while Jasper pulled her pants down. She was trying to kick and scream, but to no avail. Jasper had just dropped his pants when the door suddenly opened up. Jamie and Susan casually stepped into the room.

Susan looked at Jasper. "Oh! My! God! As I live and breathe, it's Juba the Hut and Princess Lea." Jamie and Susan spotted Liz on the other side of the room and Jimmy Dittle behind his desk. Jasper yelled, "Who the hell are you?" Jamie moved towards Jimmy as Susan drew the attention to herself by stepping forward. "With that belly, when was the last time you saw that thing?" Liz started to scream, but the man holding her gave her a jerk. "I told you to keep quiet."

Susan bent down to look under his belly and mocked his manhood. "Don't worry lady. I've seen bigger dicks on a Chihuahua. You probably won't even know he is in you." Jasper was enraged. He was holding Sam down with this left hand as he attempted to backhand Susan with his right. Susan easily dodged the swing. "You got to weigh more than 350 lbs. ---now how can a fat tub of lard like you stand on one leg?"

Jasper looked at the other thug then back at Susan and said, "Why? I got two legs." With that, Susan leaped up and came down hard with her boot on the outside front quarter of his leg just above the knee. Immediately, a loud crack could be heard as he came down and he landed on the stump. Susan spun and landed a back kicked into his face as he was going down.

Jimmy Dittle sprang to the top drawer of his desk, but he failed to notice Jamie, who had quietly moved to cut him off. It only took 1 second for her to pull her pistol and hold it to his head while she slammed the drawer hard against his hand with her knee. Jimmy was grimacing from the pain and knew she had just broken a bone.

Jamie gave him a big smile and asked, "You must be Jimmy?" Using her best teenage cheerleader voice, she then pointed to his weapon. "Now, is that your gun? Jimmy nodded yes, as he gawked at the barrel of her gun. Jamie then asked, "Can I see it?"

Jamie put one hand on his wrist and pulled it out of the drawer while holding her gun to his head. Jimmy allowed her to withdraw his hand, and Jamie then retrieved the pistol from the drawer and took a step back. She was the holding the pistol by the barrel.

Jamie laughed at the gun. "Oh! Jimmy, it is so big!" With that, she started to beat him with it, and when he fell out of his chair, she started kicking him until he was on the floor unconscious.

Jamie focused on the man holding Liz and leaped over the desk as she locked eyes with him. With a wicked smile, she cooed, "What's a big man like you playing with a little thing like her? You don't think you can handle a real woman. Why don't you let her go so you and I can dance?"

He looked at Jamie, who still had Jimmy's pistol. Jamie flashed her most comely smile as she slowly stepped away from the desk. "Oh this? You let her go, and I promise I'll give her the guns, okay?'

The thug pinning Sam on the table let her go as he saw Jasper hit the floor and started to move to his right around table towards Susan. Susan squished Jasper's bulbous gut as she stepped over him and patted Sam on her butt as she proceeded to the same end of the table.

Susan was smiling at the thug. "Oh, now you're more like it. I like a man who takes care of himself." The thug smiled. "Good, because I'm going to enjoy fucking you." Susan smiled even bigger. "Oh, really?" With that, she leaped forward and slammed her forehead into his nose.

The man holding Liz asked, "What about the other one?" Jamie pulled the Ruger LC out and shrugged her shoulders. "Oh, this? Sure! Come here, Liz." Liz glanced up at the thug, moved cautiously forward, and ran to Jamie. Jamie leaned over and gave her both guns. "Get in the corner with your mother and wait there." Liz nodded and ran to her mother, who had slid from the table and was now sitting on the floor in shock watching what was going on. Liz helped her get up and pull her jeans back up so she could move. They retreated into the corner away from what was happening.

The big man took a step back from the head butt and recovered. Susan grinned. "I'm going to enjoy fucking you up." The man shot a quick left jab to her chest, which knocked her back. He then stepped forward and punched again with his right, but this time, Susan ducked under his jab and delivered an upper cut with her left palm into his nose. She followed up with an overhand strike to his right eye, which drew a slow, rich stream of warm blood.

He attempted a roundhouse punch with his left, but Susan again wasn't there until…bam! Two more hard punches to his left eye and a knuckle strike to his throat. The man stumbled back and tried to grab her, but Susan had already stepped back. This time she served him with a powerful roundhouse kick to his solar plexus. He stumbled back again holding his chest. With the speed and agility of a lemur, she gave two quick kicks to his right-side rib cage, and when he tried to cover it with is arm, she drove a strong kick into his left rib cage.

Jamie continued toward the thug after he released Liz. Jamie had a big smile on her face. She wiggled a little. "Oh! I'm so excited!" With that, he stepped forward to deliver a right-hand punch, but Jamie caught his punch. Their 4-inch height difference allowed her to easily pull him up onto her hip and over---she guided him to land directly on his head. While he was lying on his back with his head against the floor, she followed with several hard punches to his eyes.

He rolled over to protect himself and tried to jump up, but Jamie jumped to one side and delivered a hard kick to the side of his head. She backed off and remained a safe distance as she chided him by saying, "Ahhh! What's wrong? Finding a real woman difficult to deal with?"

The thug rolled away from her and used the wall to struggle to his feet. He wiped the blood from his face and reached into his back pocket to retrieve a switchblade holding it up and said, "Okay, bitch let's see you dance with this?"

Jamie jumped up, patted her hands together, and replied, "Oh! We are going to play with toys?" There were pink bows at the top of each knee-high stocking. Jamie knelt down, and when she rose, she was holding two double-edged throwing knives, with the blades back against her white, leather wristbands.

The thug lost his smile but remained determined. He was holding his knife in his right hand by the handle with the blade pointing towards Jamie. He lunged forward with slight swing and tried to cut Jamie's midsection, but Jamie instantly drove her left hand down. Using the blade to block the swing, she struck his cheek with the pointed butt of the knife in her right hand and then swept the blade in across his cheek causing a gash. Jamie wasn't finished with him---she stabbed his chest, and dragged the razor-sharp edge back across his chest from his right to his left and then stepped back. The entire move took only a second.

In an instant, the thug had blood pouring from his forearm, chest, and cheek. He lunged, driving the knife blade straight forward to puncture Jamie's abdomen, but this time, Jamie brought her right arm down in a circular motion. She pushed his thrust past her and spinning to her left and to his right side, brought her left hand around. She deftly sliced the blade across his other cheek then stabbed at his throat where his cardiac artery was. Jamie pushed him forward like the trash that he was, where he dropped to one knee at her feet.

Sam and Liz were holding each other in the corner, watching as these two women dismantled the huge, sinewy men. Sam noticed Jasper starting to move, so she picked up the small gun and handed it to Liz. She grabbed Jimmy's gun and stepped over to Jasper, who simply groaned. Sam then noticed Jimmy's feet move. She looked at Liz and said, "Cover him," and walked over behind the desk where Jimmy was starting to regain consciousness. When Jimmy looked up and saw Sam standing with his gun, he muttered, "Ah shit!"

Instead of kicking him a second time in the left side, Susan chose to bring the kick up and deliver it to the side of his head. He was betting on the second kick going low and was looking to grab her foot. He stumbled back and fell onto the couch. He felt his jaw and knew it was broken. Moreover, he was bleeding from the other side of his head, and his right side felt like a rib had cracked.

Susan extended her left hand. "Here, let me help you up." He figured, if he could pull her down and overpower her, so he reached up with his right hand to take hers. As he started to pull her, she put a foot onto the couch and pulled him up, using his body weight against him. She then took his hand high then spun under his arm, forcing him to turn with his arm behind him---but she didn't stop there. She threw all of her weight to pull his arm away from his body and dislocated his elbow. She could hear the bone break, and he let out a piercing shriek.

After she pushed him down onto the couch and pinned him with his only good arm under him, she started to pound on him with vicious lefts and rights. As she rained punches, he shrank to the floor. He suddenly yelled, "I give, I give damn it!" Susan stood up and backed away.

He looked up and Susan. "No more, no more, please." Susan looked disappointed and said, "But I was just getting warmed up. I haven't even broken a sweat yet." He looked up at her and said, "Lady I don't know who you are, but I'm not paid enough to take this kind of punishment." Susan's face suddenly got very serious. "If you get off that couch, I will beat you so bad your grandchildren will feel it." The man nodded. He remained there holding his side and trying to breathe.

Jamie took a couple of steps to her left so the thug wouldn't know where she was. She saw him toss the knife away, and when he rolled onto his back, she realized her thrust to his jugular was more accurate than she had realized because blood was gushing out into his hand. She stepped forward so he could see her and asked, "Problem?" He nodded. "I need a doctor."

Jamie shook her head and shrugged. "Sorry, don't see one." He was now pleading. "You can't leave me like this?" Jamie took another step forward. "I can't? As the last drops of blood slowly drain from your body, I want you to think about all the girls, you helped drag in here and how you treated them. The only thing you deserve is to be castrated." Jamie glanced up to see Susan backing away from the man on the couch. Liz was standing near Jasper pointing a gun at him, and Sam was pointing a gun at Jimmy. She looked around, spied Jimmy's jacket, and picked it up. Jamie reached over to the door near her and engaged the dead bolt.

Sam was holding the gun on Jimmy and asked, "So Jimmy, what about that deal? You still in the mood for a good fuck? I think I am." Jimmy was bleeding from his head, and he started to push toward the wall trying to gain distance---as if two feet would make a difference. Jimmy looked up again. "Go ahead and take her. I don't want her anymore." Sam's expression went cold, as she looked him dead in the eyes. "You think that is it? What is there to prevent you from trying to kidnap her again, huh?"

Jamie tossed the suit coat over to Susan, who wrapped it around Liz. Susan eased the pistol out of Liz's hands. Jasper was lying in the floor whimpering, and Liz asked him, "Does it hurt?" Jasper looked at her. "What the hell do you think, you little bitch?!" With that, Liz stomped on his already broken leg, and he wailed in agony.

Jamie stepped up in front of the desk and said, "Sam we're finished here. They won't be bothering us anymore---come on, let's go." Sam hadn't taken her eyes off Jimmy and continued, "Living is too good. You raped all these girls; and worst of all, you touched my daughter. You raped her. What do you deserve Jimmy, what?" Jimmy looked up and Jamie and begged, "You gonna let her kill me? You can't do that!" Jamie looked down at Jimmy and said, "Sorry if you have a problem with that, but I don't."

Jimmy looked back at Sam and begged, "Please don't kill me." Sam said, "Roll onto your back." Jimmy asked, "Why?" Sam gave two reasons: "First, I want you to see it coming just like all those girls saw it coming, and second, because I said so." Jimmy slowly rolled to his back; his hands were up as if he could catch the bullet. Sam lined up the sights then suddenly lowered the gun and started firing at his crotch. Jimmy reached down with his hands to protect his groin, but

Sam didn't stop firing. She emptied the 15-round clip firing through his hands at his crotch.

Jamie grabbed the gun and looked around. She spied a bag, picked it up, and shoved the gun and her knives into it. Susan tossed the Ruger to Jamie, who returned it to her holster. They wrapped Liz in Jimmy's jacket, and Susan picked Liz up as the four women headed down the stairs. They could hear banging on the other door.

As they walked out to the SUV, it beeped twice as Jamie pulled the dongle from a small pocket and hit the button. Jamie jumped behind the wheel, and Susan rode shotgun. Sam and Liz jumped into the rear seat.

Sam immediately pulled Liz into her arms and held her. They looked at each other and began to cry. The SUV pulled away slowly, and Jamie drove calmly as they watched as a couple of police cars speed past and turn down the alley.

They drove in silence until they reached Winder. Instead of parking at the curb, Jamie pulled all the way down the drive so they could enter the house by the rear door. Sam took Liz back to her room and put her into the shower.

Susan and Jamie remained long enough to make sure Sam was okay, when Sam suddenly asked, "My car, what about my car?" Susan said, "Give me the keys." Sam reached into her pocket and handed them to Susan. Susan reassured her. "We will go get your car and park it in the driveway. We'll push the keys through the mail slot. Sam nodded.

Susan and Jamie went back to the mall where the Staples was and retrieved the car. She pulled it into the driveway and then walked up to the house, when the door suddenly opened, and Sam appeared.

She looked at Susan and asked, "Can the two of you come in, please?" Susan looked at her for a second then turned and waved for Jamie to come in as well. Jamie exited the SUV and trotted to the house.

As they entered, Liz was standing in the living room wearing her robe. She had taken a shower and washed her hair. As the two women entered the house, she ran to them, threw her arms around both of them, and held them. Among all the tears and blurbs, all that could be understood was the thank you.

Sam stood back with her hands over her mouth and tears running down her face as she watched, not wanting to interfere. It was Susan and Jamie who rode to their rescue---and what a rescue it was! Finally, Jamie reached over and pulled Sam into the melee of arms and tears.

Finally, Susan pushed back. "Alright, you people are going to make me cry and I don't like to cry. So, stop it." Liz looked up at her. "Sorry, too late?" Susan smiled. "No, I just got something in my eye."

They started to laugh, then Jamie said, "We've got to get back to the house. Trevor will be pissed at us for not reporting in yet." Sam looked at Jamie and asked, "He cares about you?" Jamie chuckled. "Yea! He can be like an old woman sometimes." They laughed, and Susan and Jamie left. Sam and Liz made dinner, sat on the couch, and talked. They ignored the elephant in the room and concentrated on being together again. There would be plenty of time to discuss what happened, but right now, they needed to just be together.

Chapter 40

Athens police gets involved

On Thursday, Sam decided she had to go to work. She told Liz to sleep in and not go to school. She would deal with the school later. Sam felt that Liz needed a day at home to re-acclimate herself to normal life before braving the circus that would inevitably be there upon her return to school.

She left for work in Atlanta at 7am and the day as usual. She remembered that today she had a consultation with Roger Dawson, and the fact that her daughter had been kidnapped wouldn't matter to him.

At 8 am on Thursday morning, a green tuck pulled up in front of the house and parked in the driveway. Trevor exited the truck and walked to the house. When he arrived at the porch, he looked at the front door, but instead of ringing the doorbell, he walked over, sat on the floating bench beside the front window, and started gently rocking in it.

It didn't take long, but soon the window beside the bench slowly rose. He heard Liz ask, "You going to ring the doorbell?" Trevor smiled and shook his head no. Liz then asked, "Why?"

Trevor answered, "Because you can't let me in."

Liz was quite for a moment. "Then why are you here?"

Trevor looked over at her through the window. "Whatever happens, don't open the door until I say so. Do you understand?"

Liz looked quizzically at him. "Not really ... but okay."

Trevor smiled. "But while we wait, we can talk. How you doing?"

"I'm fine ... I guess. Why are you interested?"

Trevor knew she was lying. There is no way any young woman who had just spent a week being raped would be fine, but the fact that she could carry on a conversation with him showed her strength. Trevor smiled at her through the window. "Because as your father I'm concerned. Is that okay?"

This hit Liz like a ton of bricks! She almost fell backwards but instead, she stood up in shock. She didn't know how to deal with this, so she knelt back down at the window. "O ... Kay!" She was shocked, excited, and confused all at the same time. The man that she had instinctively liked from day one just revealed that he was her father. Now what was she supposed to do---trust him, run to him, ask him questions? And if he really was her father, why did he wait so long to come forth?

Their moment was interrupted when an unmarked vehicle drove up and parked in the driveway. Two men exited and walked to the front door. They looked over at Trevor, who was sitting on the front porch bench smiling. They rang the doorbell as they opened the screen door. From inside the house, they heard Liz ask, "Who's there?"

The first man spoke. "I'm Police Detective Farmer, and I would like to ask you some questions."

Liz answered, "I'm sorry, but I can't let anyone inside the house---especially men."

The detective looked back at his friend and then at Trevor. "Look young lady, I'm the police. You can let me in."

"I'm sorry, but I can't."

With that, the man hit the door with his fist and yelled, "Young lady, open the damn door now!"

Trevor stood up. "May I see your credentials?"

The two policemen took a step back, allowing the screen door to close as they watched him. The lead detective asked, "Who the hell are you?"

Trevor walked towards them. "I'm her friend, and she is not allowed to open the door to strangers; besides, you can't interview her without a parent. So, you being here is a waste of time. I suggest you leave."

The two detectives glanced at each other and replied in unison. "Oh? Who is going to make us?"

Trevor smiled. "Well since you haven't produced any credentials to prove you're actual detectives, I am."

The detective was not convinced. "Can you prove you are a friend?"

Trevor chuckled. "I don't need to, but you do." One detective then showed his badge, and Trevor took it before replying, "Terrific, you are an actual detective, but can you tell me why two detectives from Athens, Georgia are investigating a case in Winder?"

The detective who had shown his credentials then snatched them back. "We don't have to."

"Well…what if I call the Winder Police Department and tell them there are two Athens detectives here attempting to usurp their authority? What do you think they will do?"

The lead detective looked nervous as he glanced at his partner. "By the time they get here, we will be long gone."

Trevor smiled again. "But without the girl."

The lead detective started to say something when the other broke in. "What if we just talked to her through the screen door with you supervising? Would that be okay? We only have a couple of questions."

Trevor leaned against the door and asked, "Liz, did you hear that?"

Liz was standing just inside the door. "Will you stay with me and not let them take me away?"

Trevor stared daggers at the two detectives as he answered Liz. "They will take you nowhere---you have my word on that. If I say 'now,' you are to slam the door, lock it, and call 911. Okay?"

"Oh-oh....kay."

The detectives smiled and looked at each other. Liz slowly unlocked and started to open the door. One of the detectives reached over to the screen door to open it, but Liz slammed the door shut. Trevor stepped in front of him. "Don't touch the door."

The detective did not like his authority being challenged. "Look pal, if we want to take her in for questioning, we can."

Trevor's smile disappeared. "Don' try it. She will open the door, and you can ask her only appropriate questions through the screen door---then you will leave."

The two detectives looked at each other and nodded. Liz slowly opened the door again and stood behind the screen partition. Trevor leaned against the outside of the screen door to prevent them from opening it.

One detective took out a notebook. The lead detective then addressed her, "So Liz." Trevor interjected by saying, "Her name is Elizabeth." The detective looked at Trevor then asked, "Okay, Elizabeth? Where did you run off to?"

"I didn't run off."

The detective shook his head and asked again, "No you ran off. Where did you go?"

"I didn't run off."

The detective glanced at this partner. "Look, we know you ran off ..."

Trevor spoke up. "She said she didn't run off. Go to the next question."

The detective looked at Trevor then asked, "So where did you run off to?" Trevor interjected again, "She already told you she didn't run off, so move along, or I'm ending this."

The detective's eyes rested on Trevor before he turned and asked, "Elizabeth, can you tell us who you were with these past few days?"

"I was kidnapped by Jimmy Dittle and forced to prostitute for him."

The detective looked at Trevor then back at Liz. "So, Jimmy Dittle is a friend?"

Trevor took over. This was getting out of hand. "She didn't know Jimmy Dittle until he kidnapped her, and I can't see how you would call anyone a friend who forced you to prostitute for them."

The detective was running out of patience with Trevor. "Look, I am done tolerating you. I think it is time we take her down to the station for interrogation."

Trevor suddenly stopped leaning against the door. "You will take her nowhere---Liz NOW!" Liz slammed the door and locked it.

The detective smirked. "Listen hot shot, there are two of us and one of you ..." Trevor cut him off mid-sentence. "Well that isn't fair---you need two more men." The detective looked back at his friend and took a swing at Trevor.

Trevor blocked the swing, hit the man in the nose with his palm, and grabbed him by his hair. He pulled the detective forward to a rising knee, and as he fell backwards to the floor, he stepped to the second detective, who was going for his gun. Trevor slapped both of his hands over his ears then pulled his head forward, delivering it directly to his rising knee. The detective pulled back so hard he fell hit his head on the porch. Trevor then turned to the first detective and delivered a brutal punch before grabbing him and tossing him into the second man. He then took both of their guns and backed off.

Both men found themselves lying on the front porch, bleeding and dazed. Trevor gave them a final warning. "Now get off this property before the Winder Police arrive."

The detectives asked, "What about our guns?"

"Tell your chief to come to Paterson Corporation, and I will give them to him. If I were you, I would be leaving since Liz has already called the Winder police. Now git!" The two detectives scurried like rats to their vehicle and peeled out of the driveway.

Liz watched them leave before slowly opening the door. She peered up at Trevor through the screen door. "Is…is it true?"

Trevor was standing on the sidewalk and turned to Liz. "Is what true?"

Liz pushed through the screen. "You said you were my father---is that true?"

Trevor nodded and looked down. "Yes, I'm your father, and I have been looking for you for 12 years." Liz hesitated for a moment then stepped to the edge of the porch as Trevor approached the steps.

Liz looked up at him wistfully and slapped his face with the rage of warrior avenging her pillaged homeland. The slap came out of nowhere and shocked Trevor as he stumbled back. Liz stepped to him and demanded, "How could you do that to her? Do you realize what my mom had to do to keep us together?" Trevor saw the tears come to Liz's face and dropped to his knees on the porch before her as if he were accepting defeat. Tears welled up in his sorrowful eyes.

Liz's rage had not yet run its course. "You don't know how many times I have heard her cry in her room because she didn't have the money to buy me a birthday card or the number of time Social Services came to our apartment and threatened to take me away if she didn't get me a bed! We had two Christmases when the only presents I received were from charity. Do you have any idea how much that destroyed her? She deserves better---much better!"

Trevor watched her as she poured out her woes. The sudden realization of their pain hit full throttle and shocked him to his core---he reached for her. She pushed his hand away and continued, "Do you know she has a picture of you hidden in her bedside table?"

Trevor nodded in defeat. "And the terry cloth robe hanging from her bathroom door is the one she stole from me. I'm sorry I wasn't there. I will never forgive myself for disappearing and I'm so sorry. I can't correct what happened in the past, but I can put all of my efforts into creating the future that you and your mother deserve. Can you give me chance, please?" Liz finally took a breath and wiped the tears from her cheeks. As she stepped closer to Trevor, he used the opportunity to pull her into his arms and wrap them around her. Liz let him hug her and slowly circled her arms around his neck.

Trevor held her and explained his absence. "What I did was wrong, and I have been looking for you for twelve years. I thought I found you twice before, but by the time I got there, you were gone. I'm so sorry." Suddenly, they heard someone clear his throat and they both looked up to find the same officer who had come out the day Liz disappeared looking at them.

The officer was standing with his arms crossed. "Sorry to break up this love fest, but we got a call that two men were trying to break into your house?"

Liz took a step back, wiped the tears from her cheek again, and replied, "I'm sorry officer, but he drove them off."

The officer looked at Liz for a second. "You're Elizabeth, aren't you?"

Liz took the handkerchief from Trevor and answered, "Yes."

The officer nodded and regarded Trevor as he stood up. "I take it you know Mr. Paterson here?"

Liz gave a weak smile as she glanced up at Trevor. "He just told me he is my father."

The officer looked at both of them and smirked. "Well, if there is nothing I can do, I will leave---unless you want me to arrest him for hugging you and crying all over your shirt?"

Liz looked up at Trevor and shook her head. "No . . . thank you officer. I'm better now." The officer nodded then turned and walked away.

Liz turned to Trevor still wiping her eyes with his handkerchief and asked, "So what do we do now?"

Trevor asked, "Well that depends on you. Do you want to sit here and hide or get even with Jimmy Dittle?"

Liz's face lit up. "Wait right here." She ran inside, came out, and locked the door. She had a DVD in her hand.

"What is that?"

Liz answered with a smile, "I'm hoping you have a computer at your house, and if you do, then you will see."

Chapter 41

Liz goes to the Plantation

They walked out and jumped into Trevor's truck. As Liz wiped her tears, she said, "This is a cool truck."

Trevor beamed at his resilient daughter. "It belonged to my grandfather. I had it restored, but I made a few modifications."

"Like what?"

Trevor's smile grew larger. "Well, I put in a bigger engine and a better transmission along with some other fancy stuff."

Liz looked around the cab. "Well I think it is cool."

Trevor looked over at Liz. "So, you still hate me?"

Liz sat back and studied Trevor. "I never hated you. I just felt bad for mom, she still loves you, you know?"

Trevor sighed. "Look, we don't know each other, so I'm not going to be upset if you don't want to confide in me--- but I do worry about you, and I don't want to see anything bad happen to you."

Liz was leaning against the door watching Trevor cycle through the four gears. "Did you love my mom?"

Trevor was lost in the throes of nostalgia. "I loved her so much and wanted to take her home myself, but she wouldn't let me. Then I had to leave. When I returned, I learned that she was pregnant. That's why I have spent the last 12 years looking for the two of you. I had to find you."

Liz looked pensively at Trevor. "Are we what you expected?"

Trevor grinned from ear to ear. "Your mother is so much more than what I expected. She was a remarkable woman before, but she is so much more now…and you, well you are just full of surprises. I'm looking forward to finding out who you are." Trevor was testing his jaw where Liz had slapped it when he spoke. Liz chuckled as she watched Trevor.

Liz's face was serious now. "Where did you go?" Trevor had stopped at the red light at the corner of W. Stephens and Broad St. Across the intersection to the left was the Hardies and across the road to the right was a US post office building.

As they waited for the light to change, Trevor sat back in his seat and looked over. "This isn't a fun story---you sure you want to hear it?"

Liz needed to know what took him away. She and her mother had struggled for so long. They persevered but they had experienced some hard times. "Yes, I think we deserve it."

The light turned green, so Trevor pushed it into first gear and turned left. "I remember the day like it was yesterday. I was upset with your mother because I wanted to take her home. She would never tell me where she lived, and I wanted to meet her parents. She demanded that I take her to the bus, so I dropped her off. As I was saying goodbye, I received a call telling me that my parents were murdered."

He glanced over at Liz, who was still trying to read him. He continued, "I had to leave and drive home to get the full story. I had spent the previous two years working in Pakistan for the Peace Corps, and I convinced my father to invest money into a glass factory in Rawalpindi."

"What were you doing in Pakistan?"

Trevor was quiet for a second. "I was working for the Peace Corps in Gujranwala with a furniture maker and learned to speak Urdu the language of Pakistan. I learned of an investment possibility and told my parents---they decided on my recommendation to invest. They decided to return to Pakistan and tour the plant. Afterwards, they received and invite to a restaurant in Rawalpindi. They were sitting with the plant manager, when three men showed up and shot both of them four times."

Liz put her hands up to her face. "Oh my God!"

Trevor nodded as he passed through another stop light and accelerated towards the Ingles and out of Winder. He glanced over at Liz. "The Pakistani government said they would investigate, but you have to understand something about Muslims---they don't consider killing an infidel a crime. So, their investigation would be cursory at best."

Liz gave Trevor an incredulous look. "You're kidding! They weren't going to do anything?"

Trevor bore left onto 53 and accelerated. "Different countries and different cultures have unfamiliar value systems. No, they had no intention of catching the men, so I knew it had to be me. I went back to Pakistan and met with the RSO at the U.S. Embassy, and he had not spoken with the police. Because the murder of the infidel occurred in Rawalpindi and not Islamabad, they didn't care. The only reason they were even pretending to look into it was because Americans were murdered. I teamed up with a friend of mine from the Embassy, and he helped me. I spent the next three years looking for the men…and I put four bullets into them like they did to my parents." Trevor continued his tale as they drove. They finally arrived at the Plantation.

Trevor emerged through the gates of Paterson. He headed up the drive when Liz asked, "So that's why you disappeared?"

Trevor nodded as he slowly navigated the path through the woods. He glanced at Liz. "What I should have done was place a bounty on the head of the men instead of going myself. I should have been with your mother and you."

It was at that time, that they broke out of the woods; and for the first time, Liz got an eyeful of the house. She looked up and squealed, "Jesus Louis, momma lied!"

Trevor slammed on brakes. "What?"

Liz was looking at the house with her mouth wide open. "That's not a house---that's a hotel. Is that where you live?"

Laughing, Trevor nodded and joked, "Yea it's a tiny dump, but I call it home."

Liz gave him a look of disbelief. "Tiny? You call that tiny?"

Trevor cranked up the truck and steered it into a garage on the other side of the mansion. As they walked around to the front door, Trevor explained, "I was so filled with hate and revenge that I didn't think clearly. What if they had killed me? Paterson Corp would have no leader, and thousands of people would have lost their jobs. I realize now that I was wrong." Liz looked up at him and nodded.

Trevor stopped in the foyer then turned to face Liz. "I have one more favor to ask."

Liz looked at him curiously. "What is it?"

"I would like for you to see a friend of mine."

"Oh?! Who's that?"

"Dr Cynthia Winston. She is an OB/GYN, and all of the women here at the Plantation see her."

"So why do you want me to see her?"

Trevor ran his hand through his hair. "Well, considering what you have been through this past week, I was thinking it would be wise if a professional checked you out to make sure that you are okay."

Liz studied Trevor and asked, "Does Mommy know about this?"

Trevor smiled and said, "Noo ... not yet----I haven't had the chance to ask her. If you say no, I will not force you. And if you would like Jamie or Susan with you, that will be fine. I know I've sprung this on you kind of quickly, but as I said, with your recent experience, it's better to be safe than sorry."

Liz looked down for a second. Trevor had a point. Her mother had told her she needed to contact her OB/GYN, but she hadn't had a chance to do it. Liz agreed and followed Trevor to the medical center in the basement of the Plantation. She stood beside her estranged father and sized up the female doctor. She felt comfortable with her. She looked back up at Trevor. "I guess it couldn't hurt." Trevor walked out of the room.

At 10am, Sam decided to call home to check on Liz. The phone rang several times with no answer, so Sam hung up. This bothered Sam, but she didn't know what to do. She sat back and thought about it. Sam wanted to go home, but she had already missed one session with Roger. If she missed another consultation session with Roger Dawson, she could lose Liz again plus everything else. She had to make the meeting at 3pm, and that was actually the only reason she came in.

As Sam was calling home, two women walked up to the security guard at the entrances of the parking garage. The taller one flashed a badge and asked, "Can we ask you some questions?"

The young man smiled and said, "No problem." It wasn't long before they determined that he was the guard on duty the day Sam was stopped. He was able to identify the two guards that took Sam upstairs. They were also the same two that put the boxes into the trunk of her car to begin with. For that matter, they found out that one of the company's lawyers, a Mr. James Sykes, and another security man by the name of Dave Worthington were part of the conspiracy. The lawyer attempted to play hardball, but the two detectives quickly located his Achilles heel.

He had always wanted to be a defense lawyer but was scared of the courtroom. He couldn't argue a case in court and because of this, he was resigned to doing research. The little act he played getting the women to fear for their lives was perfect. It gave him a sense of power and made him feel like real lawyer. Once the detectives were aware of this, they were able to break him down and make him realize that he was in real danger of going to prison, where he would end up as some guy's bitch.

The security man was easier---his problem was that he had no self-confidence, and to have a chance to have sex with a beautiful woman was simply a dream. The detectives were able to show him that even though the lady in question was able to say no, but didn't, it wasn't necessarily rape. That carried on for 10 years, and the security flunky was begging for forgiveness, willing to do anything.

Sam was getting upset and didn't know what to do. Liz wasn't answering at home, but Sam couldn't leave to find out what was happening. She knew her closest neighbors were the Chambers, and both parents were at work. She didn't have a neighbor she could call and was dreading the meeting with Roger Dawson. She now wished she had called in sick as well but didn't know what to do.

Suddenly, Jennifer walked into the cubicle and sat down. She was still looking depressed and asked Sam about her research on the Bormann account. Sam didn't really want to talk about it, but what else would they talk about? A tidal wave of stress washed over Sam again.

Finally, Jennifer asked Sam, "Do you know how Trevor Paterson was able to swing the purchase?" Sam was fraught with desperation and not in her right mind. She told Jennifer that he used the corporate savings as collateral for the loan. Jennifer didn't smile as Sam expected-

--she just nodded and left. Sam had missed lunch because she couldn't eat, and she had just unintentionally revealed sensitive information.

Sam rose from her desk and exited the office. She drove to the hotel and walked through the lobby to the elevators. She scanned the area to make sure that the security guard was nowhere in sight and continued. Sam exited on the 11th floor and proceeded to room 1101. She knocked on the door, and Roger opened the door.

Sam entered the room and noticed a man sitting at the table near the windows. She looked up at a smiling Roger and asked, "What's going on?" Roger just nodded for her to enter, and she complied. The man got up and walked towards Sam. He stuck out his hand, and Sam shook it with no hint of a smile.

Roger closed the door and joined them. "May I introduce Steve Bormann of Bormann LTD? He wants to sign on as our newest client." Sam looked up at Steve Bormann. At least 6' 3", he wasn't fat, but he definitely wasn't thin. Sam didn't like his cologne or his smile and was ready to leave. Roger continued, "I invited Mr. Bormann here today to show him some of our southern hospitality and the charm of our company in hopes that he avails himself to become one of our clients."

Sam nodded. "Mr. Bormann, would you mind having a seat here? Please enjoy some of Mr. Dawson's fine wine while we have a quick chat?"

Mr. Bormann smiled. "As long as it doesn't take too long---no, I don't mind at all."

After seating Mr. Bormann, Sam turned and gave Roger a look. "Come with me."

Chapter 42

Sam tries to regain control

They exited into the bedroom, and after Sam closed the door, Roger stepped up to her menacingly. "You better remember the legal problems you have; if you don't do this, I will make sure you rot in jail!"

Sam crossed her arms and looked up at him. Her face was filled with anger. "Fine, go ahead. I told you the last time that I'm not some whore that you can hand out to your friends in order to impress them. I am willing, as disgusting as it is, to have sex with a pig like you to save my daughter, but you are not to involve anyone else. Understood?"

Roger placed his hands on his hips. "You're getting to be a real pain in the ass."

Sam's expression was unwavering. "Pain in the ASS! You try being fucked in your butt once and then tell me about it! And if you push this, your little house of cards here will fall so quickly that your head will spin. I told you before---I'm not a whore, so don't treat me like one. Now explain to me why you want me to do this guy?"

Roger glared defiantly at Sam. "I don't like your attitude … but this is important. If I get his signature on the contract, I get a big bonus. I will share the bonus with you if you do this."

Sam was heated. He was now selling her like some piece of meat, but it was money, that was important to Roger not women. *Ha, I'm going to make him pay dearly for this.* Sam stepped forward aggressively and demanded, "So If I get him to sign, we get a bonus?"

Roger took a step back, shocked by Sam's newfound aggression. He slowly nodded yes and said, "50/50."

Sam shook her head no. "If I'm doing all the work, I get the majority share. How much is the bonus?"

Roger looked at her for a second. "$2500."

Sam stared at him for a moment. "Knowing you, the bonus is $5000, so I suggest 80/20, which means you will pay me $4000. Roger shook his head no and countered with a 60/40 split in his favor. Sam shook her head and said, "Fine, go fuck him yourself." Roger looked at her in shock but quickly complied. Sam then said, "So you owe me $3000. Do you have the contract?"

Roger growled but nodded and pulled the contract out of his coat pocket, and handed it to Sam. Sam opened it quickly and checked it. "If I ever get the chance to fuck you like you're fucking me, I will. This will be the last time I do this, understand?" Roger simply accepted defeat and thanked her. Sam only shook her head and leaned against the dresser. She perused the contract and instructed, "Send him in."

Samantha was taking a calculated risk. She knew of Mr. Bormann and his history. He was corporate raider, but from what she had learned, he was a moral family man. She was betting on the assumption that she could get his signature on the contract without having sex with him. She knew she was playing a high-risk game here.

Roger guided Mr. Bormann into the bedroom with Sam and closed the door. Roger smiled, sauntered over to the table, and poured another glass of wine. He looked out over the Atlanta skyline and smiled at his good luck. Suddenly, the door to the apartment opened, and Mr. Hutchinson walked in.

Mr. Bormann remained fully dressed in his 3-piece business suit and walked to the bed. He sat on the edge of the bed and looked over at Samantha Raven. "I hear that you are one of the best forensic accountants in Georgia and possibly the country. Is it true?"

Sam looked up from the contract at Mr. Bormann. "Is what true?"

Mr. Bormann studied her for a second. "Is this how you do business?" Sam let out a breath and shook her head no. Mr. Bormann then asked, "How many success stories do you have now?"

Sam looked up again. "Three."

Mr. Bormann nodded and walked over to the dresser. He leaned against the edge of it two feet away from Sam and asked, "Three success stories? How long have you been doing this?"

"Six years."

"You know, I have been doing this for over 20 years, and I have worked with numerous accountants. Many only count 3 success stories in their entire career, but you did it in 6. Impressive."

Sam nodded. "This contract---what was the deal with it?"

Mr. Bormann smiled. "Mr. Dawson told me if I signed the contract, he would get me you. I figured I would get you as a forensic accountant, not like this."

Sam smiled. Her hunch had been correct. "So, you weren't expecting all of this?" She waved her hand around the room.

"It is unexpected, and it is making me nervous."

"Why?"

Mr. Bormann looked Sam in the eyes. "You have had 3 wins in 6 years---why are you doing this?"

Sam looked away. "It's a little complicated, but no, this is not my choice."

Mr. Bormann nodded. "So, if I sign that contract, I get to have you?"

Sam looked down at the contract and then back at Mr. Bormann. "That depends…do you want my accounting abilities or my sexual favors?"

Mr. Bormann smiled. "Ms. Raven, as much as I would love to have sex with you, I think I would prefer your accounting talents to this."

Sam breathed a sigh of relief. "Mr. Bormann, this is not the way to do business. If you want me as your forensic accountant, all you need to do is ask. That way, you won't have to lie to your wife or daughter."

Mr. Bormann realized she had researched him. "Actually, I would prefer it that way. I would prefer to keep you as a friend than to lose my family with you as a lover."

Sam grinned and shook his hand. "So, tell me about the bonus Roger was supposed to get." Sam felt good. She was in control again and didn't need to have sex with Bormann. *I am regaining control of my life.*

Suddenly, the door opened, and Susan walked in. Sam jumped up in shock and horror as she uttered, "Oh God!"

Susan walked over and stood in front of Samantha. She flashed a badge to Mr. Bormann. "Can I ask what is going on here?" Sam was speechless, and as she looked up at Susan, she covered her mouth with her hand and started to cry.

Mr. Bormann stepped forward and explained, "We were talking about this contract." He picked up the paper and showed it to Susan. "We're discussing it."

Susan nodded as she continued to look at Sam. She turned to Mr. Bormann. "Can you leave us alone for a minute?" Mr. Bormann stood up and quickly walked out.

Sam's eyes brimmed with tears as clasped her face with both hands. She couldn't look at Susan---how could she? She started to shake her head no when Susan looked at Sam and said, "I already know what's going on." Sam jerked her head to look at Susan and sat back onto the dresser as if she were hit by a punch.

Susan moved closer. "Okay, here is what we are going to do. You are going to get your things and go to the mansion. Don't go home! Go to the mansion! Liz is there." Sam's jaw dropped. She opened her mouth to say something when Susan urged, "Go!"

Sam closed her mouth and exited the bedroom. When she stepped out, she found Mr. Hutchinson standing by the table with crossed arms and a scowl on his face. Roger, the lawyer, and the security boy were sitting on the couch. Jamie was standing in front of all three. Sam grabbed her things and left. As she exited the apartment, she noticed what looked like two large female bikers in the hallway.

She stopped to look at the two women, who were standing just outside the room looking ominous and deadly. She started slowly then continued past, only glancing back to see if anybody was following. She quickened her pace to the elevator.

Sam exited through the lobby and jumped into her VW. She stopped for a minute to process what just happened. How did Susan and Jamie know where she was, and whom she was with? How did they know what was going on? She thought back to their confession of a camera in the house with the picture of Jasper Grebes.

She then thought about how these women had suddenly appeared at Jimmy's place and rescued her and Liz. How where they able to accomplish all they had done? She needed answers to so many questions, and she needed them right now.

She started the car and proceeded north on I-85. As she drove, she contemplated everything that had happened: Roger Dawson, Jimmy Dittle, etc. Just as she was just getting control of her life, it imploded again. Damn it, she was fuming!

If Susan and Jamie knew, then so did Trevor, but how? She was lost in thought and before she knew it, she was approaching the Plantation. As she passed through the entrance and drove down the path to the house, she was still unable to make sense of everything.

Sam pulled into a parking spot and knew she had to get some things straight. Sam was going to take control of her life and keep it this time. Ever since that man came into her life, having control was a fleeting proposition. Sam sat in the car for several minutes mulling over these issues.

Sam finally exited the car, slammed the door, and didn't bother locking it. She stomped right up to the house and charged through the front door without knocking or ringing the bell. She turned left and started toward Trevor's office. As the front door slammed closed behind her, an SUV came out of the woods and accelerated to the front of the mansion. Susan and Jamie slammed on the brakes as soon as the SUV stopped. They jumped out of the vehicle and ran to the door.

Sam was now ready to get control and hold onto it by making it clear that she was the boss. No one was going to dictate to her anymore.

Chapter 43

The Show down

Trevor had just finished meeting with Gary and left Elizabeth with him. Susan and Jamie moved on Roger Dawson and dealt with that problem. Furthermore, Liz received a clean bill of health from the doctor after her ordeal. All in all, things were coming together. He had decided to finally tell Samantha who he was.

Trevor entered his office and removed a framed picture from the bottom drawer of his desk of him and a woman laughing from sixteen years ago. He hid the picture several weeks ago and smiled as he looked at it while he walked to the bookcase and placed it back onto the shelf. This was where it belonged.

Trevor returned to his desk and started working on some papers. He heard the door slam and looked up to see Sam walking towards him with an angry expression. He jumped up and came around his desk with a big smile on his face and arms outstretched saying, "Sam, how are …"

Sam stormed up to him and punched him in the stomach as hard as she could. He winced and cried, "Ouch!"

Sam was unsympathetic. *No mercy.* "How dare you… you bastard!" She waved her fists of fury in the air and barely missed his face.

Trevor cried out, "Ouch!" He stepped to one side. "Wha … What?'

Sam angrily demanded, "Susan showed me a picture of Jasper in my house---can you tell me how in the hell she got that picture?"

Trevor thought *Oh shit, she knows*!

Trevor struggled to find his words. "Ah, well I … I ah … we put… cameras in your house."

Sam eyes widened as she pounded him again and demanded, "Excuse me! You did what? What was the most important rule I told you that day you came over … WHAT?"

Trevor nodded and took a step back. "Yes … yes … but Sam …"

Sam continued to advance towards him. "But what! You decided to just ignore my rule and do whatever you wanted. How many cameras? No bullshit! Four? Six? Did you put them into the bedrooms as well? How many, damn it?!"

Trevor took another step back towards the safety of the bookshelves and pleaded, "Two… only two. Honest, it was only two."

Sam did not find this quip amusing in the slightest and laid into him with the other hand. He winced again. "Ouch!"

Susan and Jamie were listening at the door, and Susan remarked, "It's about time he got what he deserved."

Sam popped off again. "Two! … Two!? What the hell were you thinking, and how did you know Jimmy called me?! You knew, didn't you? Don't lie to me damn it…how?" Trevor was now at the bookshelf, and Sam remained directly in his face. Her inhibitions that had previously been entrenched in femininity were now null and void as she paced back and forth in front of him like a tigress guarding her young and ready to pounce in a moment's notice.

Trevor had his hands in front of him to ward off any more punches and whined, "We put a tap on your phone."

Sam was incensed. She stomped the floor and started throw another punch but decided to kick him instead. She angrily barked, "Tap ... on ... my ... phone...you put a tap on my phone! Two cameras and now a tap on my phone. Let me process this foolishness.... who in the Sam hell do you think you are ... huh?" She punched him again in the stomach and kicked him. Trevor jumped, trying to escape the punishment. Sam demanded, "So how did you know where I was... how...I know you did because Susan and Jamie showed up ... you had to have followed me or something. How did you know?" Trevor gave a weak smile. "GPS tracker.... look Sam, please, you have to understand I was scared and I ... I had to do something ... I had to ... honest." Susan and Jamie were standing outside the door laughing. They then opened the door quietly and slipped in.

Trevor was now leaning back against the bookcase and desperately attempting to defend himself when Sam hit him again. "And now I find out that you kidnapped my daughter and brought her here? What part of your twisted mind made you think you could abscond with my daughter? Who in the fuck gave you permission to kidnap her? Because it sure as hell wasn't me! What is wrong with you?!"

Trevor was again trying to protect himself and begged, "But I didn't kidnap her...honest ... she came willingly ... honest!"

Sam ignored his words. "Excuse me, but I didn't give you or her permission to come here, did .... I ...." Sam suddenly saw an 8X10 picture of a dark-haired man with long hair and a beard. He was laughing, and in his arms was a dark-haired girl. Samantha immediately recognized the woman---it was her. She also knew the man. It was Tip, and it was the same picture she had hidden in her bedside table.

Sam scowled at Trevor, and if she was angry before, now her temper was completely off the rails. She had been in his office before and had never seen that picture. Now as she scrutinized the picture, she cried out, "You stole my picture---you stole my picture from my bedroom! How dare you?! I can't believe this!"

Trevor glanced at the picture and back at Sam. "No, no, no, no … I didn't steal that picture."

Sam's mouth was agape as she teetered back and stared at Trevor. She couldn't believe this man. He placed cameras in her home, bugged her phone, put a GPS on her, kidnapped her daughter, and now he had a stolen picture from her house. She surmised that he had to have been inside of her house. Her face seethed red with fury, and her blood pressure seemed to grow exponentially.

Trevor dropped to one knee. Peering up into her face, he gently explained, "Samantha that is my picture. My full name is Trevor Irving Paterson---Tip for short. I'm Tip." Susan and Jamie were side-by-side and leaning against the wall just inside his door. They glanced at each other and nodded. This was worth the wait.

Sam felt weak. She looked at the picture then back at Trevor and inquired in a weak voice, "You're Tip?"

Trevor nodded. "Yes! I'm … Tip, and I have been looking for you for 12 years. I'm so sorry for leaving like that. I wouldn't have if I had known, but once I learned I had to find you and I … I've been looking for you ever since."

Trevor stood then and reached over to pull her close to him as he held her by the waist. Sam slowly placed her hands on his chest as the realization took hold. She looked up into Trevor's face in shock, but she was still mad as a hornet. She then slapped his face as hard as she could. Sam put her hands to her mouth and quickly said, "I'm sorry."

Sam's expression slowly changed back to pain as she pleaded, "Where did you go? I tried to find you and tell you I was pregnant, but I couldn't. No one would help me. I was lost and alone. I wanted to tell you I decided to keep the child you gave me, your daughter, but you were nowhere to be found." As she spoke, her voice rose, and she started to beat on Trevor's chest until her strength waned. Finally, she collapsed into his chest crying.

As Sam sobbed into Trevor's chest, she whimpered, "You can't believe how hard it was especially after my parents died. I didn't have any money or anyone to help me. I couldn't buy her presents for her birthday or Christmas, and I was constantly in fear that I would lose her."

Trevor pulled her into his arms so she couldn't hit him anymore then kissed her on the top of her head. "Would you like to see her?"

Sam looked up at Trevor. The thought of seeing her daughter again calmed her. It also reinforced her strength as she remembered who she was. "Oh, I need to ask your permission?"

Trevor smiled, as he shook his head no. "I only ask one thing … please hear her out first … please."

Sam was working hard to control her anger and slowly nodded yes. Trevor turned and only then noticed Susan and Jamie leaning against the wall next to the door. "I guess there is no privacy here." Susan and Jamie shook their heads no and chuckled. Susan then opened the door as they approached then followed them out the door.

Trevor took Sam by the hand and led her through the door past Susan and Jamie then down the hall. They crossed through the foyer and passed the kitchen to the next room. Sam was finding it difficult to keep up.

As they entered the control room, Trevor stepped inside and pulled Sam close to him. The room was 40 ft long and 30 ft wide. In the middle of the room was a C-shaped console with three computers. Elizabeth was sitting at the console.

Before her was a 24-inch monitor with four more 24-inch monitors on both sides of the central monitor and a 60-inch LED screen on the far wall in front of her. Liz was sitting at the keyboard keying in some commands into the computer in the center. Behind all this and halfway between Sam and her daughter was a large, half-moon shaped grey sofa. On the sofa was a man.

Trevor stepped over still holding Sam and knelt down behind the sofa. He touched the man on the shoulder. The man turned and looked back. Trevor whispered, "Samantha, this is one of the foremost hackers in the world, and his name is Gary. Sam extended a hand, and Gary took it as he scooted to sit on the back of the large, stuffed sofa.

He leaned forward and whispered to Trevor, "She is amazing! She has created a client and is now starting to engage it. I haven't seen anybody that good … since … since me."

Sam was dumbfounded. She watched as Liz suddenly moved her cursor to the far-right monitor and with a few keystrokes opened a window and started something running. Next, she moved to the monitor to her left and moved a window from there to the far-left monitor. The window was the desktop of another computer! Liz then keyed in a command and again, something started to run.

Liz went back to the main screen and keyed in a command--- another window opened. It was at this time that Liz realized Trevor and her mother were present. There was a tablet sitting on an elevated platform between the center monitor and the first one on the right. She reached over to the tablet, punched in some symbols and voila! The movie that was showing, on the 60-inch TV, changed and the window she had just opened appeared like magic.

Sam watched Liz opened another window and noticed it looked like a laboratory with people walking by, but she didn't recognize what she was seeing. "Where is that?"

Liz glanced back. "Hi Mom! Hi Dad! It's probably the police station." Liz then opened another window and initiated a copy of the "My Documents" folder. As it was copying, she monitored the activity in the room and started talking to her mother.

Without looking back, she pointed to the window on the far-left monitor. "This is Jimmy's desktop." She pointed to the window on her right. "This is the copy routine where I'm copying his hard drive." She then directed everyone's attention to the 60-inch monitor. "That is the camera on his computer so we can see what is happening and track his location. The police are probably trying to decrypt the data."

Sam looked back at Trevor with a shocked expression. Trevor held one finger to his lips and Sam gave a weak nod. Susan and Jamie leaned against the wall behind them, smiling from ear to ear. Sam looked back up at Trevor.

Liz continued, "Mom this is so cool! He has SSD drives on all three computers, and he is running synergy on them so I can operate simultaneously with one keyboard and mouse!" With that, she moved the mouse all the way to the left, opened another window, and then moved it back to the center.

Sam looked back at Trevor. "What are you smiling at? You're not out of hot water yet."

Sam looked back at the computer. "May I ask what you are doing?"

Liz was still working, and without turning around she started to explain, "Well, a week or so ago, I hacked into Jimmy's computer and copied his hard drive. I wanted to know more about him and if he was going to be a threat to you or me. When I was studying the contents of his hard drive, I didn't' understand what some of the files meant. But when I was in his office, I saw the monitors on the wall, and I figured it out." Sam turned and looked at Trevor then back at Liz as she continued to explain.

The copy had finished, and Liz said, "Okay, now I'm going to replace the file structure with the one we created, and instead of pictures and files, they will get Disney movies."

Sam looked puzzled. "If the hard drive is encrypted, how can you read it?"

Liz was still tapping away on the keyboard. "Oh, Bobby and I put together a decryption algorithm that will decrypt anything."

Suddenly, a realization hit Sam as she slowly turned to Trevor. "Hi, Dad! Hi, Mom---she knows?"

Liz was still working, and without turning around responded, "Yep!"

Sam then looked at Susan and Jamie before asking, "Did …?" Susan and Jamie both smiled and nodded yes. She looked at Gary, and before she could ask, he shrugged his shoulders and nodded yes as well.

Sam turned back to Trevor. "So…everyone here knew but me?"

Trevor stepped over to her. "I wasn't sure until that day at your office. In every picture, I saw of you, your hair was up, and you had glasses. That wasn't the Sam I remembered, but when you walked into that conference room, I knew--- I knew I had finally found you."

It all started to become clear. That was the day Sam had to step out of her comfort zone, and perform on the stage, she wasn't comfortable with---the day everything started to change. That was the day she started to lose control of her life. After that, she became mixed up with that pig, Roger Dawson, and then Jimmy Dittle forced his way into the picture. Trevor with the cameras, the phone tap, the GPS, and bringing Liz to the Plantation followed suite, and now she discovers that her daughter is a master hacker! Sam touched her forehead, and things started to spin. She felt faint, and the floor became the ceiling.

Trevor leaped forward and scooped her up before she could hit the floor. He placed her head against his right shoulder and carried her out of the room. Susan and Jamie shared a look, and Jamie held out her hand. Susan rolled her eyes, pulled a dollar out of her bra, and handed it to her.

They walked over to Liz and asked, "So what is all this?"

Chapter 44

Trevor finally confesses

Trevor carried her into the foyer. Behind the stairs was an elevator. He pressed the button for floor number 3, and the door closed. When it opened, he exited into a large living room. There were two bedrooms to the right and one larger one to the left. Straight ahead, behind a glass wall was a dining room area. Trevor turned left and walked to a wooden door after hitting the lever handle. He entered a large bedroom and kicked the door shut.

The king-size, four-post bed was in the middle of the wall on the left resting on a plush, 12X12 carpet. Matching nightstands flanked both sides of the bed along with two windows. On the far wall, the door to the large 10X10 bathroom revealed a large Jacuzzi tub and spacious shower with multiple heads. Two separate sinks lined the opposite wall with a mirror running the entire length of the wall. To the right of the bathroom door, two hidden doors led to two large, walk-in closets.

Trevor approached the right side of the bed and laid her gently upon it. He immediately removed her shoes, started to unbutton her blouse, and gently undid the scarf from around her neck. He then pulled the hairpin from her hair, walked into large bathroom, picked up a washcloth, and placed it under the faucet of cold water. After he rang it out, he folded it and returned to the bedroom to place it onto her forehead. He backed away and sat down on an overstuffed chair.

Sam's felt something on her forehead and hesitantly reached to retrieve it as she opened her eyes. The first sight greeting her was the elegant vaulted ceiling and four posts that rose up around her. She slowly realized that she was lying on a bed. She looked to her right, and there was no one---just the vast expanse of the king-size bed. She turned her head to her left, and there sat Trevor in a chair not more than six feet away. It suddenly dawned upon her where she was.

Sam bolted up and looked around; she took in the beautiful room, the open windows on the wall to either side and with a beautiful chandelier hanging in the center of the ceiling. Sam looked over at Trevor. "This must be your bedroom?" Trevor nodded yes but did not move.

After gazing around the room, Sam twisted and allowed her feet to guide her legs to the floor. She stood up on shaky legs using the bed behind her for support. She suddenly realized that her shoes, scarf, and hairpin were missing. Sam looked at Trevor and shyly asked, "So, it was your intention to bring me here to have your way with me?"

Trevor shook his head no with a smile and stood up. He walked slowly toward her not wanting to scare her. She could sense his impending approach. She suddenly realized why she was so at ease in his presence aside from her desire for him. As he came close, her left hand remained on the bed---but her right rose up to guard her heart, for it was beating so loudly she could hear it.

Sam hesitantly glanced up into his face with tears streaming down her cheeks. "No, you don't want me, not after what I have done. I have shamed myself, and that can never be forgiven."

Trevor was standing in front of her and touched his hands to her cheeks as he then gently raised her face to meet his. He brushed her hair from her shoulder and pushed it back around her ears. She feared that she had finally found the man of her dreams only to lose him because of her transgressions.

Trevor's words were reassuring. "You did what you had to do to protect our daughter. What happened was not your fault, and you have nothing to be ashamed of. It is I who has shamed myself by impregnating you and then deserting you when you needed me the most. I am not worthy of you." With that, he bent down and kissed her gently on the lips.

Sam was shocked at his response exonerating her and blaming himself. She reached up and grabbed his shirt to pull him down to her. She wanted him, and she wanted him to possess her like he had 15 years ago. She wanted to give herself to him and relish in giving him pleasure. Trevor reached down, encircled her waist with his arms, and lifted her up. Sam released her grip from the bed and held onto him. She wrapped her arms around his neck as he loosened the clasp and pulled the zipper down on her skirt, sliding it off.

Trevor then fumbled with the buttons to open her blouse until she suddenly reached down and pulled it over her head to get it out of the way. Trevor buried his face between her breasts, and Sam groaned for the first time in over a decade and a half. She was ready to have a man take her so she could return the pleasure consensually. They became one that afternoon. He was satisfying her needs, and she was willingly returning the favor.

Women don't think about sex like men. For a man, he needs the acceptance of a woman to reinforce the virility of his manhood. Man is even willing to pay a woman to pretend to accept him, and some are even willing to go along with the charade for no other reason than to feel like a man again.

But for a woman, it is different. A woman of even modest beauty can have almost any man she wants, so when she finally decides to accept him, she is giving him more than just her body---she relinquishes her heart, her soul, and her life. She places everything that she is or will ever be into the relationship---her man is her life.

Samantha Raven succumbed to Trevor Paterson have her and threw herself into this carnal liaison with the entirety of her heart and soul. It was a half an hour later before they finally lay still on the bed. The duvet was tossed to the floor, and the sheets and pillows suffered the same fate. Clothes were strewn across the room with extreme prejudice. As they lay naked and sweating on the bed, Trevor pulled her close to him and made her the little spoon. "God, I have dreamed of doing this to you for so long."

Sam pushed the hair out of her face and smiled as she drank him in. "How long?"

"15 years." Sam smiled and allowed herself to be engulfed in his arms. She was safe, warm, and protected. Trevor heard the chatter from everyone around the table on the terrace then glanced over at the clock. "Have you worked up an appetite yet?" Sam nodded.

When Sam pushed herself out of the bed, she noticed that her skirt was ripped along with her blouse and panties. Sam looked at Trevor in mock disgust. "It appears that your desire to disrobe me took precedence over the preservation of my clothes."

Trevor grinned. "Now wait, the blouse wasn't my fault---you did that."

Sam threw her blouse at him and looked around the room. "Have any of your past lady friends left anything for me to destroy?"

Trevor thrusted himself out of the bed, walked to a wall, and pushed it. The wall moved and exposed a large closet. As Sam entered the closet, she noticed that there were no women's clothing. Sam turned to look at Trevor as he smiled and said, "You are the first woman who has every graced my bedroom in this manner."

Sam blushed and started to open the doors, looking for what was available. She thumbed through his extensive Guayabera shirt collection until she found one; she liked and pulled it out. She then checked his underwear drawer removed a pair of shorts to wear. The shirt was so long that it hung down to her knees. Sam stepped out of the closet. She looked at Trevor, who was still naked. "You are going like that?"

As Trevor started to dress, he then pointed to the other hidden door. Sam pressed against the door, and as she suspected, it opened into another closet---only this time, it was empty. Sam backed out and closed the doors. She understood what he was saying but was she ready to surrender everything to him. After all this time of fending for herself, she didn't know if she could let go of the reins.

Trevor stepped over to her. "I knew one day I would find you, and I didn't want any other woman to put clothes into your closet." Sam smiled. Trevor then took her by the hand and led her out of the bedroom into the 30 x 30 ft. living room with vaulted ceiling and indirect lighting. There was a large fireplace on the opposing wall with an overstuffed couch in front of it. She spied two more doors on both sides of the fireplace. Trevor preemptively answered her question. "Two more bedrooms."

She looked left and admired the glass wall with dual French doors that opened into the dining room with a large table. As she approached the doors, she noticed a bar area. On the other side of the bar was a small kitchen along with several French doors that exited out onto a portico that overlooked the front of the house. She could see the drive as it left the forest and then circled in front of the house.

Sam walked slowly out onto the portico and touched the banister. Trevor stepped up behind her and wrapped his arms around her. "No pressure. I will support whatever decision you make, but here, the neighbors won't be able to hear you screaming."

Sam elbowed him. "What makes you think I would be screaming?"

Trevor leaned over. "I had you screaming earlier." Sam playfully nudged him again and smiled. Sam was thinking, *he did, Oh God he did.*

Sam turned to face him. "You still have some explaining to do, mister!"

"Okay! You are correct, but let's go eat first." They headed towards the elevator.

As they exited into the foyer, they heard a bunch of people laughing. Trevor took Sam's hand, turned right, and headed out onto the veranda. Sitting around a large, round table were Susan, Jamie, Gary, and Elizabeth, all laughing at some story Liz just told. When Trevor and Sam exited the house, they abruptly stopped talking.

Jamie was the first one who stood up. She started a slow clap, and the rest joined in. Even Liz stood up with her hands covering her mouth and ran to her mother. Susan smiled. "She looks better in your clothes than you do."

Trevor looked at Sam and smiled. "A valid point."

Sam hugged her daughter, and Liz looked up into her mother's face. "I told you he liked you." Sam nodded yes and hugged her daughter again. Sam then asked, "By the way young lady, what were you thinking when you left the house and came here?"

Liz looked at Trevor, and he motioned for them to sit down. Liz started to tell the story of the two detectives and Trevor running them off, revealing that he was her father. Sam looked back at Trevor and turned to face Liz. "So, you decided to run off with this strange man just because he said he was your daddy?"

Susan and Jamie were chuckling when Liz answered, "Sure! I felt safer with him than those two detectives."

Trevor shoved a fist into the air, and Sam shot him a stern look. He withdrew his fist quickly and said, "Pass the fruit, please?" In the center of the table was a lazy Susan upon with bowls of fruits, vegetables, and assorted meats. A woman came out of the kitchen with two pictures and sat them onto the table. Trevor looked up and asked in Spanish, "Consuela, how is your son?"

She smiled and replied, "Thanks, Mr. Trevor. He made the honor roll again."

Trevor looked pleased. "Tell him my promise to pay for college is still good as long as he keeps doing what he is doing." Sam sat back at him and smiled.

Trevor smiled. "I caught her son stealing my truck and ended up giving his mother a job. Now I'm helping him. No big deal."

Liz touched Sam's arm then asked her mother, "Mom, Grandma once told me that every woman deserves a good man who can be a good provider, good with his hands, and a good lover."

Sam nodded. "I remember her saying that honey---why do you ask?"

Liz looked over at Jamie. "Well, Jamie showed me the desk Trevor made in Pakistan."

Sam nodded, and Liz continued, "And from the look of this place, he is a good provider." Sam looked over at Trevor, who was smiling.

Liz finally asked, "So what about the last one?"

Sam suddenly realized where she was going. "That is none of your business."

Jamie piped up. "Yea---you can ignore the screams we were hearing earlier."

Sam's jaw dropped and looked at Trevor, who was trying to eat some fruit. He was laughing when Sam hit him in the arm. "You said they couldn't hear us!"

Susan responded with, "Normal yelps we can't hear, but that we could hear."

Jamie spoke up. "Yea, we had to convince Liz that you didn't need rescuing."

Sam's face turned red and she tried to hide behind her hands. She glanced at Liz and Trevor, who were both smiling. "I have no idea what any of you are talking about. That was Trevor screaming. He wouldn't behave, so I had to take matters into my own hands." Trevor's jaw dropped as everyone burst into a roar of laughter.

Chapter 45

Setting boundaries

They were now laughing at Trevor and Samantha's romantic exposure. They took it well, accepted the turn around with good spirits, and even laughed at Trevor's expense. Elizabeth Raven looked at her newly found father and asked, "How did you know that those detectives would come to the house?"

Trevor gazed lovingly upon his beautiful daughter. "Jimmy Dittle could not run those … establishments … without assistance from someone. He had to have some police and other officials on his payroll or had something on them to leave him alone. That would be the only way. The detectives were there to shut you up, not investigate your kidnapping. They already knew who had kidnapped you and where you were."

Samantha asked, "So what happened?"

Trevor started to speak when Liz interjected. "It was great! This one detective tried to say I had run off with Jimmy, and then he decided to take me to the station. Trevor stopped them and ran them off."

Sam then asked, "So what made you decide to come here?"

Liz smiled, "Well, he asked if I wanted to stay there and wait for them to return or come here and get even with Jimmy. I figured it would be more fun getting even with Jimmy."

Sam looked at Trevor." So…you told her before you told me."

Trevor sat back and replied, "Well I needed for her to trust me, and I knew the officers would be arriving there soon."

Sam glanced at her daughter and back at Trevor. "Did you tell her before or after you came into the house?"

Trevor shook his head. "No…No…I never went into the house… right, Liz?"

Liz was munching on an orange wedge; and smiled when she recognized she had capital to negotiate with. "I don't remember, did I let you in … I remember the detective man pounding on the door … let me think."

Trevor was smiling at Liz then at Sam. "Sam, honest … I never set foot into the house, honest."

Jamie glanced at Sam. "Never? … You never set foot in her house?"

Susan chimed in. "What about when you messed up her kitchen? How did you do that if you never went into her house?"

Liz looked at her mother quizzically and admonished her. "Mom! … You let him in … what about rule number one?"

Jamie now joined in. "Yea! Rule number one---no men, catty women maybe, but no men!"

Sam was feeling the pressure and responded, "Okay! Okay! … but I didn't really let him in … he just kind … of walked in."

Liz then asked, "But you didn't kick him out … did you?"

Sam smiled and dropped her head a little as she admitted, "No … I didn't … I wasn't in any kind of condition to kick him out, but I did later after I cleaned up the kitchen." The table erupted in laughter.

Sam looked at Liz before she could counter her. "No ... Boys are still not allowed."

Trevor looked over at Gary. "Did you get a hit on any of those pictures off of Liz's DVD?"

Jamie leaned over to Susan. "Excellent diversionary move." The both giggled.

Gary heard Jamie and smiled but and answered Trevor's question by saying, "Actually, I did. It turns out that there were a couple of police detectives as well as a Mayor and a couple of corporate heads--- yea, we got a real winner's group here."

Jaime then spoke up. "So, Sam, are you going to go through Trevor's entire Guayabera shirt collection, or are we going shopping?"

Sam looked down at the shirt she was wearing and then at Trevor. She was quiet for a moment. *God, I want to stay, but I have to set my boundaries.* She just didn't want to just jump into the life here, so she said, "Well, I have lots of clothes at my house."

Trevor got serious. "Please stay here. I can't protect you there."

Sam gave a slight smile. "Who's going to protect me here?"

Jamie spoke up. "It won't be Trevor, that's for sure."

Trevor gave Jamie an angry look, and she started to chuckle. Sam then spoke up, "She does have a point--- if I stay here, where am I going to sleep?"

Trevor replied, "I have three bedrooms in my suite."

Susan then added, "We have two bedrooms in our suite!"

Sam looked at Trevor with a raised eyebrow. "I think that is an excellent idea. Since I have a young, impressionable daughter, she will sleep in one of the bedrooms upstairs. I will sleep in your bed."

Trevor's smile grew from ear to ear as Sam suggested, "And you can sleep with Jamie and Susan in their spare bedroom."

The smile disappeared from Trevor's face. He looked at Sam to see if she was serious, and she was. He glanced at Susan and Jamie, who were chuckling. He bargained with Sam. "Okay … Okay … as for Liz … how about if she sleeps in one bedroom and you in the other. I can have my own bedroom."

Sam tilted her head and studied Trevor. She loved torturing him. "Can I trust you to remain in your room all night?"

Susan spoke up. "From what we heard earlier, hell no." The table erupted in laughter again.

Trevor nodded towards Susan. "All the doors have locks."

Jamie grinned. "And he has the keys."

Trevor looked over at Jamie. "You're not helping."

Sam then started to think about this seriously. He had been gone for so long, and she and Liz had built a life together in Winder in their little home. All of her belongings were in that little house. Her expression became serious. "I haven't agreed to move in here yet, and we have been living by ourselves for 15 years. I'm not sure if I want to give up my freedom."

Trevor's smile diminished---he knew this would be a difficult task to just uproot her and her daughter like this, but he didn't want to take the chance of losing them again. He decided to level with them. "I have been looking for you for 12 years, and I'm not letting go without a fight. If I have to pitch a tent on your front lawn and eat cold hot dogs, I will not let you stay there alone."

Liz spoke up. "She won't be alone. I will be with her."

Trevor's smiled twisted a little as he looked back at Sam. "Please stay. I don't care where you sleep, as long as you're here. Please stay?"

Liz agreed. "Oh, mom! For God's sake, sleep with the poor man. If you don't, he will be a basket case, and it's not like you haven't already."

Susan and Jamie both gave each other high fives and said, "Way to go Liz."

Sam gave her daughter a stern look. "Just because of last week doesn't mean you can talk like that, but you do have a point."

Susan and Jamie erupted in laughter. Jamie took a sip of iced tea and asked, "What I want to know is when are you two going to stop playing games, and when do we get your credit card so we can go shopping?"

Trevor looked at Jamie in shock. "Shopping for what?"

Susan chuckled. "Trevor…she wouldn't be wearing your clothes if you hadn't ripped hers off, and since she has no clothes to wear, we need to go shopping, right Liz?"

Liz giggled at the thought of shopping with someone else's money and nodded in agreement. Sam had a slight smile on her face as she looked at Trevor. He slowly nodded in his state of surrender and placed a credit card on the table. "Get whatever you and Liz want or need. I mean it---don't worry about the cost."

Susan and Jamie tossed their napkins onto the table and got up. Jamie walked around the table, picked up the credit card, and waved it in the air like a flag. She said to Liz, "Ready to go and charge it?"

Liz nodded yes quickly and got up. She pulled her mother's arm. "Come on mom, before he comes to his senses."

Susan pulled Sam's chair out. "Don't worry; there's not a chance of that happening." As she helped Liz pull Samantha to her feet, she glanced down at Trevor, who was sitting at the table with his left arm extended. He looked submissive. Susan gave him a wink as she pushed Sam and Liz towards the mansion.

The four women walked out, chatting, and laughing. Trevor leaned back in his chair and watched the four women he loved exit the building arm in arm. Gary stood up and said, "Well Trevor, I guess we need to get some work done so you can pay for all the money they are going to spend.

Chapter 46

Vice and Paris

Trevor and Gary rose and headed for the control room. Trevor walked over to the sofa and sat down as Gary took his place in front of the computer. Trevor asked, "Okay, what has the face recognition software given us?" Gary pulled up a page of all the pictures of the people on Jimmy's hard drive, and all but one had a green check.

He turned to Trevor. "Recognize any of these people?"

Trevor studied the page. "I think several, but lines four and five from the left and line seven, second from the left---who are they?"

Gray clicked on one then the other and said, "Apparently, they are two vice detectives from the Athens, Georgia Police Dept. Why?"

Trevor nodded. "They were the ones who attempted to arrest Liz. Do we have any more from Athens?"

Gary moved his cursor over several more pictures of the men. He had attached hypertext to each picture so when the cursor hovered over the picture, a quick biography would appear. He then zeroed in on one older looking gentleman. "Apparently, this man is a police captain in the Athens. He's also in vice."

"I need the dossier on them first. Then start putting together a dossier on the others and send it to my computer. "

Gary gave a thumb up. "Oh! Wait, I got something for you." He clicked on the file of videos and brought one onto the big screen. Trevor rose from the sofa and stood beside Gary to watch.

A news video appeared with a female reporter on location. Behind her was a forklift lowering down a gurney as she spoke, "Four men were found badly beaten. One appears to have died; two were taken to the hospital with severe injuries; and the fourth man was too large to bring down the stairs. They had to remove a window and use a forklift to extricate him from the premises. " They watched as the forklift elevated its forks, backed up, and lowered the gurney down. It then proceeded to the ambulance and extended its forks into the vehicle to deposit Jasper inside. As it lowered the forks inside the ambulance, the body of the ambulance also lowered, and then it backed out empty. Trevor and Gary looked at each other and started laughing. Trevor said, "Make sure you save that video."

Trevor went into his office to peruse the files Gary had sent him. His phone suddenly rang. He checked the time, and it was just after 5 pm. He picked it up, and it was his secretary at the main office. Trevor said, "Hello, Helen. Why are you still in the office?"

He listened. "Okay, put him through." Helen connected the inbound call to Trevor's phone.

It was the police captain from Athens. The captain started yelling, "Who the hell do you think you are attacking my officers and taking their guns? I can have you arrested, damn it! Now you get your ass to this police station and bring those girls in for questioning. Do you hear me?"

Trevor sat back and waited for him to finish, allowing the silence to drown out the noise before he quietly said, "Captain Fletcher of Athens Vice, I presume?" The line went silent, and Trevor could almost hear the captain's brain clicking and trying to comprehend how Trevor knew him. Trevor continued, "Since you didn't bother to introduce yourself, I guess you are surprised that I know who you are. May I ask why a captain of Athens Vice is interested in this case?"

The captain continued to be quiet for a few more seconds before responding slowly. "I don't have to explain our involvement to you, and if you don't get here in one hour, I will dispatch my men to bring you in."

Trevor was quiet for a moment then laughed and said, "To begin with, I will not bring her to you, nor will I bring her in the future unless you can explain to me why the Athens Police Dept. is involving itself in a Winder Police Dept. matter?"

The captain started to say something when Trevor interjected, "Pick your words carefully. I have friends in high places."

The captain was momentarily silent. "Okay, when can I interview them?"

Trevor was slow to responded but finally said, "You won't."

The Captain was beyond frustrated at this point. "I have been asked by the GBI Director, *Georgia Bureau of Investigation*, to look into this matter."

"So, Kevin asked you to investigate this?"

"Yes. He requested that I take lead on this."

Trevor was quiet for a moment and responded, "The director of GBI is Vernon Keenan, who is a friend of mine, and if he wanted to talk to Elizabeth, then he would have called me himself. He didn't, so you just lied to me. I will recommend that you never pull a stunt like that again. "

The captain fell silent for a second---this conversation wasn't going as he had planned. As captain of the Athens Police Force, he was used to accomplishing his goal with a boisterous persona. Trevor wasn't cowering as many before did, and he knew this captain had no authority here. He reached for his only real caveat and asked, "I need to get my officers' weapons, and I need background for an investigation I'm conducting. I would like to interview your wife and daughter."

Trevor waited quietly for a second and answered, "Call my secretary." He hung up. The captain was clearly lying. If he needed some background material for another investigation, then a polite request was all that was necessary. For some reason, he desperately needed to talk to the Raven women, and Trevor decided at that moment that it wasn't going to happen.

Trevor quickly called his secretary. "Helen, that captain is going to call again. I want you to stall him twice then agree for him to meet me here next Wednesday at 1 pm. tell him we will only allow him and the two detectives on the premises and that is the only time available to him. Now please put me through to security, thank you … Jeff, I'm going to need some men here next Wednesday … yea, 10 is good. Have them come on Tuesday morning, and they will stay here with us. Okay, thanks."

Trevor made another call. "How long will it take to have a plane here … France … Okay."

Trevor checked the clock. It was after six, so he made another call. "How much damage have you done…is that all … Okay … Look, I need to get both of them out of the country now. Don't tell her anything until it's too late. I need you back here with all your stuff in 30 minutes. Head directly to the strip … France … Okay."

Trevor then made a third call. It was 6pm on Thursday in Georgia, which made it after midnight in France. Trevor spoke in fluent French with an impeccable accent. "Hello, Maurice. Sorry to wake you . . . I need a favor … thank you. I have two ladies that need to go shopping… yes, Jamie will be there to escort them… no, she is still a lesbian, but I can tell her … Okay, but Susan will be there too . . . "Okay, won't I tell her… Yes, they will be leaving here within an hour and should arrive by 7 or 8 in the morning. Jamie will know what they need, thank you. I owe you ... yes ... I know ... thank you."

Jamie hung up the phone, looked at Susan, and whispered in her ear. Susan smiled. "I love Paris, great! What could be better?"

Jamie walked over to Sam and Liz, who were engrossed in a heated discussion about a dress, and asked, "So what's the problem?"

Sam turned. "They want 25 dollars for this dress, and I can't justify spending this much for a dress I can easily make. No, we won't get it." Liz slouched to one side with a disappointed look on her face.

Jamie chuckled. "Well, that was Trevor. He is disappointed that we haven't done more damage, so he suggested another store."

Sam looked up at Jamie. "What store is that? Most stores are closing now."

Jamie gave a big smile. "That is going to be a surprise, so let's get everything together and we will head home. Trevor will explain." Samantha gave Jamie a quizzical look and complied.

They gathered their newly purchased items together, and Jamie grabbed the dress Liz wanted. Liz had a shocked expression, and Jamie put a finger to her lips. Liz smiled, and they paid then left the store. They piled into the SUV. Susan jumped behind the wheel and headed out from Wal-Mart.

They entered through the opening of the Plantation. Sam watched as they meandered through the forest. It was already getting dark, and within the forest, the only light was from the lights along the road they followed. Sam couldn't tell, but she had a nagging feeling that it was taking longer to reach the mansion than it had in the past. They finally exited the dark confines of the forest, but instead of arriving at the mansion, they pulled out onto a landing strip where a luxurious, private plane was waiting.

Sam slowly exited the vehicle and looked at the plane. She then looked at Jamie and asked, "Excuse me, but what is this?"

Jamie smiled and stepped closer to Sam and in her normal, smart-ass manner. With a tilt of her head, she answered," It's an airplane." Sam shifted her stance. She normally enjoyed her smart-ass comebacks, but this time, she shot Jamie a look of disgust. Jamie chuckled. "Do you trust me?"

Sam looked at Jamie with misgivings, but how could she not trust her? She befriended her when she first arrived at the Plantation, and she showed up at Jimmy Dittle's to save her from being raped and free her and her daughter. Then she rescued her again at the hotel with Roger Dawson. Jamie and Susan put themselves in physical danger for her sake.

Samantha had to nod slowly---she owed Jamie too much. Jamie smiled and continued, "The store is not here, and Trevor wants you to go shopping there. So please trust me, and let's get onto the plane."

Sam looked over at Liz, who was standing looking at the airplane in shock. She walked up and put her arm around Liz's shoulders, and as they walked to the plane and boarded, Sam commented, "Having Trevor in our lives is going to take some getting used to."

As they settled onto the plane, it didn't take long before it taxied over then sped down the runway and rose into the darkening sky. Sam looked at Jamie." Can I at least ask where we are going?"

Jamie smiled and looked out the window to take in the receding landscape. She was relieved that Sam had waited until now to ask this question. Jamie looked over at Susan, who was also wearing the same broad smile, and answered, "Trevor said that if you can't find an outfit you like here … then go to Paris."

Liz was tired. It had been a long day, and the interior of this plane was far more opulent than their small house. The interior was laden with gold's, beiges, and several plush seats. The seats chosen by the four women were soft, leather, overstuffed lazy boys facing each other, and separated by a table. Liz had pulled her legs up close and cuddled down into a small ball when she heard her mother ask the question.

Liz heard the answer and sprang up wide-awake as she sat up and opened her eyes wide. "We're going where, Paris, ---as in France, Paris?"

Jamie chuckled with a nod and smiled lovingly. "Trevor is such a great boss."

Sam was sitting up straight, stunned. Her jaw dropped to her chest as she looked at everyone individually and demanded, "Excuse me, but was I asked if I wanted to go to Paris?"

Jamie smiled then glanced at Susan and chuckled before she replied, "Why ask a question we already know the answer to? Besides, Trevor wanted to prove to you that money is no object. Don't look at the price tag---he wants you to have a new wardrobe. He doesn't care about the cost, so to prove it; he is flying all of us to Paris to go shopping… and a few other things."

Sam slumped back into her seat and looked at Jamie and Susan with shock on her face. She stared down at Trevor's shirt she was wearing. "But I'm not dressed, and Liz and I don't' have a change of clothes. We don't have anything---no toothbrush or even my passport…wait I don't have… a… passport… can he really afford this?"

Jamie leaned forward. "Samantha Raven, we won't need passports. As for what he can afford, I don't think Trevor knows how much he is worth. Now try to get some sleep. We will arrive in Paris at around 7 am Paris time, and I don't intend to waste time in the city of lights sleeping."

Sam sat back and took a deep breath. "I don't think I'm ready for this?"

Liz was suddenly awake and excited as she looked at her mother. "Isn't this exciting?" Sam was flabbergasted, trying to wrap her head around what had happened to her. She was confronted at the hotel by

Susan and Jamie, then she barged in to confront Trevor Paterson only to learn that he was Tip, who had been living only an hour away from her for fifteen years. Then, after ripping her clothes off (well she did help), he made love to her as he had fifteen years ago and drove her into orgasmic oblivion. She had to put on one of his shirts in order to have dinner on the veranda, and now she was being whisked away to Paris to go shopping.

Samantha's mind was swimming. *No, this isn't happening. How could this happen? Why is it happening, and if the only reason for us to go to Paris was to shop for clothes, then why isn't he coming with us?* Jamie and Susan watched Sam as she was performing the mental gymnastics, trying to get a handle on all that had occurred.

Jamie glanced at Susan and finally asked, "Samantha, you have questions?"

Sam looked intently at Jamie and then at Susan. "Yes, I do."

Epilogue

Ever since Trevor Paterson came into her life, maintaining control was mostly a hit or miss proposition. As soon as she regained control, it slipped away until that evening when she suddenly found herself on board of one of Trevor's private jets heading to Paris, France.

Sam's involuntary relinquishment of control had been a downward spiral followed by a mix and match roller coaster of elation and sorrow. Now, she was safe…but was she? She obviously trusted Trevor, Susan, and Jamie. How could she not trust them? But her shattered ego and broken trust from past transgressions had forced her to build an impenetrable wall around Liz and herself. However, the blossoming friendship with Jamie and Susan was allowing her to open up again. And of course, finding Trevor and picking up exactly where they left off meant that she was being rewarded for her sacrifices.

Still, it is difficult for her to grasp onto any semblance of control without life's little comforts in her current situation. Samantha doesn't have a passport, clothes, or even a toothbrush. Although she knows that her life is going to change for the better, it would be nice to begin this literal and figurative journey without looking like a ragamuffin.

She feels mentally and physically naked, but at least she has Jamie and Susan. With their support and encouragement, Samantha decides to have fun. If Trevor wanted her to have a new wardrobe, then she was going to purchase one. Furthermore, the look of pure elation on Liz's face is enough for Sam to agree to take this leap of faith. Liz had been through so much pain and trauma, more than anyone should ever have to endure in a lifetime.

And they do have fun in Paris, because what is more fun than going shopping at the boutiques of best clothing designers in the fashion capital of the world---Paris?! Furthermore, someone else is picking up the bill. Most people only dream of an opportunity such as this one, and this is now hers and Liz's reality. But what of the reason for her and Elizabeth to go to Paris?

Although she tries to relax and enjoy the trip, this burning question weighs heavily on her mind. The captain of the Athens Special Victims Unit did show up at the Plantation. Also, he brought the Athens Swat Unit with him. What did this mean? Why was Athens so interested in what was going on in Winder?

As far as Samantha knew, the incident with Jimmy Dittle and Jasper had been buried when Jamie and Susan wiped up the floor with that human trash. Sam thinks back to when Jamie assured her that these men wouldn't be bothering them anymore, but she has a nagging feeling that they shouldn't have left anyone alive. Those men are hardcore criminals, and they would surely want revenge.

So, while Samantha and the girls are in Paris spending thousands of dollars in clothes and going clubbing, Trevor has to deal with an 8-man Swat team trying to invade his Plantation. Does he succeed? Does the SWAT team succeed? Will this modern family ever be allowed to have their happy ending?

This and more dilemmas are on the horizon now that Trevor Paterson has Samantha Raven by his side and Elizabeth under his protection. They will simply have to face the obstacles and prevail with the mindset that failure is not an option. Mysteries will unfold and pressing questions will be answered in the next book. Brace yourself for more thrilling and suspenseful escapades in *Samantha Raven: Volume II*.